RED MA

D0684096

Nie

DISCARD

YOUNG ADULT

Also by Terry Griggs

*Thought You Were Dead* (Biblioasis, 2009)

*Quickening* (Biblioasis, 2009; Porcupine's Quill, 1990)

*Invisible Ink* (Raincoast, 2006)

*The Silver Door* (Raincoast, 2004)

*Rogues' Wedding* (Random House Canada, 2002)

*Cat's Eye Corner* (Raincoast, 2000)

*The Lusty Man* (Porcupine's Quill, 1995)

# TERRY GRIGGS

ILLUSTRATIONS BY Alexander Griggs-Burr

BIBLIOASIS

FIRST EDITION

Library and Archives Canada Cataloguing in Publication

Griggs, Terry
       Nieve / Terry Griggs ; illustrated by Alexander Griggs-Burr.

ISBN 978-1-897231-87-6

       I. Griggs-Burr, Alexander   II. Title.

PS8563.R5365N53 2010            jC813'.54         C2010-900981-9

 **Canada Council   Conseil des Arts**
**for the Arts      du Canada**

 Canadian    Patrimoine
Heritage    canadien

 **ONTARIO ARTS COUNCIL**
**CONSEIL DES ARTS DE L'ONTARIO**

Biblioasis acknowledges the ongoing financial support of the Government
of Canada through The Canada Council for the Arts, Canadian Heritage,
the Book Publishing Industry Development Program (BPIDP); and the
Government of Ontario through the Ontario Arts Council.

Printed on Silva Enviro Edition, which contains 100% recycled post-
consumer fibre, is EcoLogo, Processed Chlorine Free and FSC Recycled
certified and manufactured using biogas energy.

PRINTED AND BOUND IN CANADA

To David

... make haste;
The vaporous night approaches.

—from Shakespeare's
*Measure for Measure*

# Contents

# One

# *Weepers & Co.*

*E*verything is different at night. Not looks different, *is* different. Nieve knew this because she'd been out late exactly when she wasn't supposed to be, seeing and feeling and breathing it in. The difference. It was because of *them* that this was so, and because of *them* that she knew it.

There had been signs, and although she hadn't taken them as such, she hadn't completely dismissed them either. Superstition was Gran's department. Nieve was more of a let's-wait-and-see person, more of a let's-not-jump-to-conclusions person. In the pond behind her house she'd seen something she couldn't identify. It was long and black and moved sinuously in the water like a long scarf swirling around and around and up and down. She got down on her hands and knees to look at it . . . it moved as one, but it was many. Hundreds of black fry all moving in concert, as if following a single thought. Little fishes, she said to herself, standing up and brushing the mud off her knees. Practicing their synchronized swimming. Not so strange, really. Although she had to admit that she'd never seen them in the pond before.

What else? Spiders. Nieve had nothing against spiders. She liked them very much in fact. A spider here, a spider there, interesting. But lately there had been spiders here there everywhere . . . dangling from Nieve's toothbrush when she raised it up to brush her teeth before bed, scrambling out of her pockets when she slid in her hand to retrieve a piece of string or a marble, dropping on her head from the beams in the ceiling when she zoomed by underneath. Spiders, spiders, spiders, all sizes, all kinds. Gran said that it was bad luck to kill a spider, and Nieve would never have done that anyway, bad luck or no. So she was being extra careful not to squash any by mistake. This required some cautious walking, and running (her favorite form of locomotion), and much paying attention to tiny things that skittered by.

She saw a tiny thing skitter by that was NOT a spider. It looked more like an elongated spider's *shadow*. But as shadows don't run free on their own, she didn't want to think that it was. That would be jumping to conclusions.

Three other happenings.

One: Nieve's big, orange cat, Mr. Mustard Seed, shot through the door one morning with his fur sticking out all over as though he'd been electrified. He didn't stop for his

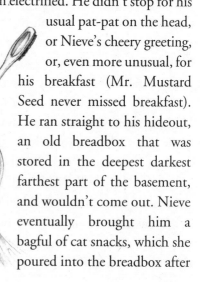

usual pat-pat on the head, or Nieve's cheery greeting, or, even more unusual, for his breakfast (Mr. Mustard Seed never missed breakfast). He ran straight to his hideout, an old breadbox that was stored in the deepest darkest farthest part of the basement, and wouldn't come out. Nieve eventually brought him a bagful of cat snacks, which she poured into the breadbox after shooing away a couple of spiders. They scurried away over the lid. (In the deepest darkest farthest part of the basement one *expects* to encounter a few spiders.) Mr. Mustard Seed thanked her by mewing once, quietly and tremulously.

Two: Her parents' business had suddenly picked up. Not a bad thing in itself, as it brought some decent desserts into the house. *And* a new, nifty, lime green shirt for Nieve. Not that she overvalued trendy clothes and name-brand runners and all that, but the odd cool item was useful, even necessary. She could hold her head up in school and not be marked for ridicule as some unfortunate kids were. When Alicia Overbury cooed, *Oooooooh, I liiiiikkkke your shiiiiiirt*, Nieve responded by nodding curtly and saying, *Yeah, thanks, I like it, too.*

So the problem with her parents' new popularity had more to do with the nature of their employment itself. They were professional sympathizers. Their business ad went like this:

> Feeling troubled, feeling low,
> Lost your dog, lost your job,
> Don't know which way to go?
> Need a hand to hold, or a
> Tissue for your nose?
> A pat on the back, a hug, a rose?
> Call Weepers & Co.
> Friends-in-Need Support Services.

They had a sliding pay scale with hugs ranging from 50 cents to a dollar and up, depending on how long they lasted, and with pats on the back and shoulder squeezes costing 20 cents each. Sympathetic murmurs were a bargain, although copious tears and custom-designed indignation on the client's behalf were pricey.

Nieve and Gran – who were a lot alike in many ways, except for the superstitions – both thought that this was a really dumb line of work. Although there was clearly a call for it, and lately there seemed to be an overwhelming call for it. That was the troubling thing. *I wonder why more and more people are unhappy?* Nieve thought, tucking into the fancy chocolate torte that her dad, Sutton, had brought back from the city. She felt pretty good herself . . . except for a little niggling uneasiness crawling around in the pit of her stomach. And it wasn't from eating too much rich dessert, even though she had.

"Dad," she said. "I'm an eensy bit worried."

"Hey, nothing to worry about, En." Sutton poured himself a coffee, while wiping the tears from his face with his shirt sleeve. (He'd been rehearsing for an important sympathy gig.) "Like the torte?"

"Yeah!"

"Great," he said, and left the kitchen.

Given their profession, Nieve's parents were remarkably unsympathetic on the homefront, but being understanding and lovey-dovey could get tiresome, she reasoned, especially if one had to dish it out all day long.

Three: This was the worst of all. The very worst. It had happened to Doctor Morys, who was the funniest, smartest, nicest man in town, and who had delivered all the babies for the past fifty years, including Nieve and her parents, and all of Nieve's friends and their parents. She got fidgety and upset just thinking about it, but she had to think about it because it wasn't right. It was fishy. Not that she'd connected it up with

12

all the other not-right things that seemed to be happening. Not exactly.

"He was *old*," said Alicia Overbury cooly. "I wonder what the new doctor will be like? Dreeeeamy, I bet."

"Dreamy?" Who'd want that, Nieve thought? You might go to him with a stomach ache (like the kind she had right now) and he'd give you the wrong medicine. "We might not even get another doctor. Besides, Dr. Morys isn't *that* old."

"Collapsed?" said Gran, when Nieve ran up the hill to tell her. "James?"

"Right in the middle of telling a joke," Nieve nodded. "The one about why ducks fly south to Florida every year. Rob Cooper had already started groaning because that one's so corny, and then all at once Dr. Morys got this puzzled look on his face and reached out with one hand like he was grabbing at something and then he fell down. That's what Rob said."

"He's . . . ?"

"Alive, but in a coma. Mayor Mary rushed him to the city in the ambulance." The town ambulance was actually an old station wagon.

"Jim." Gran sat down very slowly at the kitchen table. "Jimmy." Every time she said Dr. Morys' name it got younger and fonder. He and Gran were great friends and had been for years. Although neither of them were old, Nieve thought, not *dying* old.

Gran was wearing her dress inside-out. This wasn't because she was dotty, or 'daft,' as she might say. She was as sharp as anything, and even laughed about the superstitions, of which the inside-out dress was one. It was meant to ward off harm, as was the blue woolen thread she wore tied around her wrist, and the acorn she carried in her pocket. "It's more fun to believe in these foolish freets than not," she'd often said to Nieve. "Habits leftover from the Old Country, pet." She always smiled when she said it, amused at herself but content nonetheless with her contrary cast of mind. "They're part of our family history, you mustn't forget."

When Nieve had arrived at Gran's to tell her what had happened, she paused before leaping over the broom that lay across the threshold of the cottage. She liked leaping over it when she came to visit, but had to wonder if Gran's precautions would stop bad luck from entering. The broom didn't stop bad news. News that she herself was bringing.

Gran wiped her eyes with her sleeve, as Sutton had done, but her tears weren't a rehearsal. Nieve felt her own eyes well up. She said, "Artichoke's gone, too. He ran off."

Artichoke was Dr. Morys' dog, a black lab who seemed to wag his whole body when he wagged his tail, so happy he was to see you.

"Oh, *Nieve.*"

A fat black spider with red spots on its abdomen dashed across Gran's oak table and wedged itself into the crack where the leaf fit when she needed a bigger table for company. They both watched it go, watched it *squeeze* itself into the crack and disappear.

Gran then raised her eyes to meet Nieve's, eyes of the very same seer-blue shade, and said, "They're coming, you know."

And they did.

# —Two—

# *The Weed Inspector*

*I*n the beginning there weren't so many. Nieve encountered the first one while she was wandering along the road outside of town. Not that she knew it for sure right then. Gran had warned her about the wandering. Normally this was not a problem for she was accustomed to going off by herself to climb trees in the woods, or run through the fields, or simply hang out. She liked the outdoors. All of it. She liked the cushiony feel of moss, the yellowy yellow of buttercups, the medicinal smell of cedar, the sweetness of wild strawberries, the sound of wind in the poplar leaves *tappity tapping*. Not to mention the squirrels, red-winged blackbirds, foxes, grasshoppers, bluebirds, ants, snakes – every living thing, including the rocks. She especially liked the land that bordered her town, as familiar to her as her own arms and legs, and yet inexhaustible as far as curiosity went. And hers went pretty far.

Anyway, she was out because she couldn't be in. It was too weird. Her parents were having a bout of dysfunction. Usually their partnership, business and otherwise, worked like a well-oiled machine. But not this day. Nieve had been sitting in the kitchen, drinking a glass of ginger ale (treat! it was for her upset stomach), and flipping through the newspaper. Partly because she was considering a career in journalism and was testing the depth of her interest, and partly because she was searching for news of *them*. Who were they, *what* were they? She knew she needed to prepare, but didn't know how. Maybe, just maybe I'll find a clue in the paper, she had thought, something strange might have happened in another town. She hadn't found any stories of unusual or inexplicable occurrences (only the regular bad and sad news), but every time she had turned a page she got the impression of *something* slipping away out of sight, a something that slithered behind the lettering of the newsprint before she could see what it was. It sort of shimmered, and then was gone. She had begun to turn the pages faster and faster, trying to catch sight of it, and couldn't. It was immensely frustrating, and she was concentrating hard, and rattling the paper like mad, when she'd heard her mother's voice raised to an unnaturally high pitch.

"Sut-*ton*! A baby can cry better than *that*."

To Nieve's ear it sounded like a slap, only made of words. Her parents were in the living room, rehearsing for the big sympathy gig. She figured the job must have been commissioned by some wealthy hotshot who needed a flood of heartfelt tears to make himself feel better, but she'd been too preoccupied herself to ask about it.

Her dad said, "C'mon, Sophie, I'm doing my best."

"No you're *not*, you're *not* even trying. You're *wasting* my time."

Slap, slap, slap. That was the sound of Nieve's mother storming out of the room, her flip-flops whapping against her heels.

Nieve had put down the paper and walked softly down the hall, stopping at the entrance of the living room. Sutton was sitting on the couch, staring at nothing – or at nothing she

16

could see. He looked as though he might cry for real. She knew this had to be humiliating for a professional weeper, and instantly stepped back out of view. Then she had very quietly, and gratefully, slipped out the front door.

She was kicking a stone along the road that leads out of town and raising some dust, the kind that felt as silky-soft as talcum powder. Earlier, she'd been crouched down drawing her initial – a loopy, fancy N – in this dust when she spotted the stone on the side of the road and took up stone-kicking instead. The stone was white and egg-shaped, richly speckled with flecks of black granite. Nicely rounded, it was practically made for kicking along the road – so that's what she did. She was kicking, walking, kicking, thinking, while the stone bounced and rolled ahead.

She didn't like it, this thing with her parents. Dealing with unhappiness was their job not their problem. Unhappiness didn't belong in their house, but somehow it had crept in, unnoticed. It was like a virus, not something you could see, but something that made you sick. Nieve wondered what an unhappiness germ would look like if you could capture it and observe it under a high-powered microscope. Ugly, splotchy, and *thrawn*, as Gran would say. Twisted.

A bee zimmed past her ear. Then another zimmed past, and another. Beeline, she thought. She heard an odd sound above her head and looked up. Three ducks were flying southward, their wings making a whistling noise as they rowed rapidly through the air. Ducks always made flying look like such hard work, which it probably was, although other birds seemed to pull it off more effortlessly. Just their style, she supposed. *Why do ducks fly south?* Dr. Morys had asked before he collapsed.

Nieve studied the fields on either side of the road. It was awfully quiet. No other insect activity, no birds, no breezes shushing through the tall grasses and wildflowers. Well, *she* could make some noise . . . and she gave the stone an extra hard kick. It shot away, then skipped once *pok*, twice *pak*, and tumbled into the ditch. She ran ahead to find it. Easy enough, since the spot where it had vanished was marked by a patch of dried teasels, spiky and brown.

When she got to the spot, though, she found more than she had bargained for. If Alicia Overbury saw what met Nieve's eye, she would have run screaming back to town. But Nieve was not a screamer, nor a coward. (And being endlessly curious, she wasn't easily routed, either.) She *did* catch her breath. A man was lying in the ditch . . . asleep? She wasn't sure, as he didn't look too healthy, too alive. His skin was a greeny-white shade, and he didn't appear to be breathing. He was dressed in a rumpled black suit and was wearing dusty old shoes with triple-knotted black laces. His clothes were stippled with burs and beggar's ticks, and he had a sprig of poison ivy in his buttonhole, which was not *too* surprising. What *was* surprising, and Nieve squirmed inwardly to see it, was that the stone she had been kicking was resting on the man's forehead – exactly in the middle. She knew she hadn't harmed him in any way, but still.

She stood staring at it and at him, wondering what to do. Go for help obviously. Fetch Mayor Mary, who was temporarily filling in for Dr. Morys and who always knew what to do in a sticky situation.

The man's eyes popped open. He said, "Your name?" He didn't just say it, either; he grumped it, the way some crabby official might.

But he was alive at least. She stared at him and he stared back. His eyes were the strangest she'd ever seen, like something dug up out of the ground. Deep green and hard, like emeralds, but not as nice.

"Nieve," she answered, and instantly regretted it. Somehow she felt as if her name had been snatched out of her mouth. She felt as if she'd given something away that she should not have.

He smiled faintly, then reached for the stone and plucked it off his forehead. For a moment she thought he was going to say *Is this yours?* the way a teacher does when you're caught in class with school contraband – gum, or comics, or a note from a friend on the other side of the room. He didn't say anything however. Instead, he closed his long-fingered hand over the stone (seriously dirty fingernails), enclosing it in his fist. When he opened it again, he was holding, not the stone, but a mass of tiny, black, wriggling *things*.

Nieve gasped. They weren't insects. No heads, no legs. Maybe larvae of some sort. They were tear-shaped and oily-looking, squirming in his palm. She took a cautious step backward (an Alicia Overbury response might have been more sensible after all). He nodded at that, approvingly, and then flung his hand outward scattering the twitching *whatevers*. Most flew into the ditch or the field, but one landed at Nieve's feet on the road's verge. She watched it slip like water into the dry, gravelly ground. She continued to watch, amazed, as something then began to poke through. It was a black shoot that grew twisting into a black stem and upon which immediately sprouted leathery leaves, then thorns, then a glossy, blackish-red flower that smelled like rotten meat.

"You're a magician?" She was determined to keep any giveaway quivers or catches out of her voice.

"Negative. Weed Inspector." He gazed at her as though *she* were a weed.

"What do you inspect them for?" She'd never heard of such a job.

"Viciousness," he said, rising up. "Noxiousness," he got to his feet. "Rudeness." He climbed out of the ditch and stepped onto the road, placing himself too near for her liking. "All of the required qualities."

"Weeds can't be rude," she said. "Or vicious."

The Weed Inspector raised an eyebrow. The black plant belched (*ew*) then leaned toward her, hissing like snake. Nieve didn't move, even though the thing frightened her. She stood her ground and glared at it, giving it the baleful stare she reserved for people who really annoy her, and it backed off, righted itself and fell silent. He *was* a magician, she decided, but what kind of magician she couldn't guess. She looked around and saw that more of the nasty plants had sprung up in the field, corkscrewing and writhing into the air, and flowering (darkly) with astonishing speed. Other plants near them, normal plants – grasses and flowers – withered and dropped out of sight as if they'd been yanked into the earth. The black weeds *were* noxious, but as far as she knew this was not a quality required for anything.

"Are you from the city?" Nieve asked. Whenever people in town complained about lousy roads, or a lack of services, or new laws that made no sense, the city was usually invoked.

"The City," he agreed. "The Black City. You're not as stupid as you look."

"I'm not stupid!" Talk about *rude*.

He gazed down at her, green eyes burrowing into her head as if he were X-raying her brain. "You will be. Soon. *Very* stupid." Dribbles of mist had begun to leak out of the seams of his coat.

Nieve turned on her heel and walked away, briskly, not so fast as to lose face, but fast enough to save her life. The man was mad and dangerous. She glanced back quickly over her shoulder.

He was gone.

# Three

# Night Run

Nieve brushed some clingy cobwebs away from her wardrobe mirror and studied her reflection. *Do* I look stupid? she asked herself. No way. She looked the same as ever: alert and intent, friendly, but no fool. During dinner she had not mentioned the Weed Inspector to her parents and now wondered if she should have. Was *that* being stupid? Would stupidity sneak up on her the way unhappiness had snuck up on them? The next time she gazed in the mirror, which didn't happen very often – she wasn't stuck on herself – it might be with dimmed blue eyes and a dummy's vacant stare.

Dinner had been awkward. Even handling her knife and fork had make her feel self-conscious, as if it weren't something she'd done every evening for most of her life. There had been no conversation and no dessert, both of which were the whole point of dinner as far as she was concerned. Usually her parents chatted and talked about their day; no incident was too minor to be of interest. She was always included. But tonight . . . nothing.

Sutton *had* cleared his throat at one point and asked, "So, how was school today, En?"

This just about floored her. It was the kind of desperate question you got from an adult who has no idea what to say to a kid.

"Dad," she'd grimaced, feeling sorry for him. "It's Saturday."

Sophie gave a little scornful snort at this, but beyond that did not break her silence.

How could she have told them about the Weed Inspector? The silence had seemed to suck up all the sounds in the room. What would they have said about him anyway? Would they have believed her, told her she was being silly, her imagination running wild? Some poor homeless person they'd say, at the same time forbidding her to wander outside of town. Then again, maybe she should have tried. It might have given them something more important than their disagreement to fret about, which *was* stupid as far as she could see.

After dinner, Nieve had taken some leftovers (there were lots) downstairs to Mr. Mustard Seed and set the dish flush against the breadbox so that he could reach out and nab the scraps with his paw. Then she'd cleaned his litter box so he wouldn't be too grossed-out to use it. Before she left, he poked his head out and she gently scrubbed the fur around his ears and under his chin. She told him that she knew something bad was happening, but not to worry, she'd take care of it. He purred briefly in response, offering encouragement. He believed in her, she liked to think, although she hoped he didn't consider her to be all-powerful. No, he knew the score. Mr. Mustard Seed was no fool, either.

Nieve made a face in the mirror. She stuck out her tongue, bugged-out her eyes, placed a finger on the tip of her nose and pushed up until her nostrils flared. All-powerful? Yeah, right.

She walked over to her bedroom window and placed her palms flat against the glass as she stared out. Night had already fallen, which was a funny way of putting it, she thought. She had tried to watch night falling many times and that wasn't what happened. Night crept upward, out of potholes and cracks, out of bushes and shadowy corners, out of the places that were dark even in daylight. Night happened almost too slowly to observe and then it was everywhere.

If it weren't so late, she might run over to Gran's place to tell her about the Weed Inspector. Gran wouldn't doubt her. Her parents would never let her go now, though. She couldn't call Gran, either. Despite her parents' badgering – probably because of her parents' badgering – Gran didn't have a phone.

"I don't trust phones," she'd said. "They spread lies. The ringing is annoying. I prefer visits."

What she hadn't said, Nieve knew, was *Don't boss me around. Mind your own business. I don't want a phone!* "Whisht," Gran sometimes said, which meant, basically, "Shut up, will you."

Nieve heard someone thumping around upstairs in her parents' room, likely her mum. Unless this Saturday night was different than any other (it sure felt different to her), then Sutton would be in the family room watching baseball – in winter, hockey – entranced, so involved in the game that he'd be talking to the TV, cheering or moaning or angrily giving his favourite team coaching advice. This meant that she could sneak out easily, make a quick visit to Gran's and be back before either of them had a chance to clue-in. If she said her goodnights early, pleading exhaustion from a full day of running everywhere, they'd never suspect.

Since she was too restless to read, and too troubled to do anything else, this is what Nieve decided to do. She mounted the stairs slowly, dragging her feet and honing her yawning skills on the way up. She needn't have bothered. Her mother was too busy pacing around the bedroom to notice whether she was faking or not. (Nor was going to bed early anything that parents got too worked-up about.) Sophie didn't even ask Nieve if she was feeling all right. She was preoccupied, mulling something over as she paced, stopping briefly by her nightstand, then her dresser, distractedly picking things up and putting them down – a comb, her jewelry box, a bottle of perfume. After a couple of rounds of this, she walked over, gave Nieve a hug, and told her to "sleep tight."

Likewise, back downstairs, Sutton gave her hand a squeeze and, without averting his face from the screen, sickly pale in the TV light, said, "Sweet dreams, En."

*Fat chance*, she thought, returning to her room by way of the kitchen, where she had retrieved a flashlight from the odds-and-ends drawer. Then, window or back door? She pulled on her navy blue sweater and turned off the bedside light. Window, she decided. Best not to wander through the house again, and at night the doors were kept locked, front and back. The doors were squeaky and the locks, stiff from disuse, might be tricky to open. Locking-up was not something her parents had bothered to do until recently. About a month ago there had been a break-in at the pharmacy. Bored teenagers from the city, Theo Bax, the sole member of the town's police force, had concluded. Nothing much had been stolen: some petty cash and a bottle of headache pills. People shrugged it off and forgot about it . . . but not entirely. At night, keys turned in locks.

Nieve unlatched her bedroom window and raised it slowly, smoothly. Before climbing up onto the ledge, she checked for dangling spiders by swishing her hand back and forth in the open space. The air felt cool, not much summer left in it. All clear, she climbed up and out, letting herself down carefully, landing in the flowerbed under her window, her shoes sinking into the soft earth.

She'd hardly had time to fill her lungs with the delicious night air when something *hissed* at her. Startled, she jumped aside, crashing into a prickly rose bush.

A cat out prowling? Or a skunk – not good! Nieve edged carefully out of the bush and retreated to the edge of the flowerbed before turning on her flashlight. It wasn't an animal at all, but one of those repulsive leathery weeds growing right under her very own window! The thing hissed again and leaned toward her. She trained the beam on it, the way you do when you shine a flashlight in someone's eyes (and they get pretty annoyed). It jerked backward, avoiding the beam, and she noted, *Doesn't like intense light.* Fine, she'd give it intense light. Tomorrow she'd dig it up and burn it.

But at the moment she was on a mission. An even more urgent one, seeing as those abhorrent plants were spreading. Not that she saw any others when she strafed the garden with her flashlight, playing the beam over Chinese lanterns and chrysanthemums and clumps of dead nettle. All ordinary, unthreatening plants that she'd never before been so glad to see. She flicked off the flashlight and moved toward the front yard, waiting there briefly for her eyes to adjust fully to the dark. She figured that she could find her way to Gran's blindfolded, but was glad all the same that the sky was clear with a nearly new moon rising and a brilliant array of stars on display. The Big Dipper was serving up a vast helping of night and Orion was striding along, unhobbled, despite having the star Rigel stuck in his left leg.

Nieve suddenly felt the thrill of being out late, unknown to anyone, the shrouded night-world so different from that of the day (although not as different as it was soon to become). She told herself that she should come out more often after dark, but then could almost hear Gran's voice in her head saying, *Do what you enjoy, Nievy, and do what you must. But don't weigh yourself down with 'shoulds' and 'oughts'. That's like filling your pocket with rocks.* "Right on, Gran," she whispered, and darted off, no rocks in her pocket tonight.

Swiftly she crossed the yard, ducked through the hedge, and headed down the lane into town. Swiftly, almost flying, she pelted past the Post Office, the Library, the Town Hall, Warlock's Books, Redfern's Five & Dime – named at a time when you actually could buy something decent for 5 or 10 cents. Was it her imagination, she wondered, or did she run faster at night? Both feet seemed to lift right off the ground as she sped along. And then . . . *was* it her imagination, or was there some sort of pattering sound behind her? She stopped to listen. No sound. She started to run . . . and there it was again. A soft *pat pat pat*, as if someone were lightly tapping on a drum. Her excitement about being out and tearing down the deserted street turned into apprehension. A cold drop of fear trickled down her back. A *spider* of fear crawled back up. She ran harder, the street narrowing as it led out of the main part of town, past some houses, and then up the hill toward Gran's cottage. The pattering sound was getting closer, but she knew better than to break her stride, or her nerve, by glancing back. She ran faster than she had ever done before in her life. She ran so fast that she felt as though she might fly apart. The only thing that seemed to be holding her together was a painful stitch in her side.

She was almost there, the cottage ahead began to loom larger and larger. But strangely it was wrapped in darkness. Not a single light was lit. Gran in bed already? She *always*

27

stayed up late. Nieve tore up the path and lunged at the cottage door, rapping frantically, gasping for breath. No answer. "Gran!" she shouted. *"Gran, it's me!!"* Still no answer. She rattled the handle. Locked! Locked?

Desperately, Nieve reached down and grabbed the broom that lay across the threshold and turned to face her pursuer. A crouched, black shape veered silently off the path and melted into wood that flanked the cottage.

*Artichoke,* she thought. Was it? Was it him? She called the dog's name, but neither Artichoke nor any other being reappeared.

# —Four—

## Rain

"Why didn't you tell me?" Nieve knew that she sounded more exasperated than she had a right to be. Besides, her dad didn't need another member of the family to be peeved with him.

"Forgot," he said. "Does it matter?" He addressed this question to the inside of the fridge where he was rummaging around for a midnight snack.

*Yes* it mattered, but she could hardly say so. Nieve was heating up a saucepan of milk on the stove and gave it a stir with a wooden spoon so it wouldn't burn. She'd been so worried about Gran – and so worried period – that she couldn't sleep. She had returned home – *fast* – without incident, and had clambered back in through her window without discovery, but still shivered to think of her close call. If that's what it had been, she didn't know. Nor had she known that Gran had gone to the city hospital for a few days to be with Dr. Morys, who was still in a coma.

Sutton's hand appeared above the fridge door holding a carton of gooseberry yogurt. "Want this?"

*"No thanks."* She poured the hot milk into her old, chipped Bunnykins mug.

"Gran came by earlier to let us know. I meant to tell you."

He pried the lid off the carton and plucked a spoon out of the dish rack. "I would have tomorrow."

Nieve nodded, but she doubted it. Her father wasn't exactly with it these days. He hadn't even mentioned the scratches on her hand that she'd gotten from crashing into the rosebush. Usually he was much more observant. Although now she knew that Gran was safe and accounted for and that was the main thing. Gran wouldn't be sitting idly by Dr. Morys, either. She'd be talking to him, calling him back, working hard to help him.

"Dad." She took a sip of her milk. "Where's the Black City? Is it near here?"

"Black City?" He set the yogurt on the counter and stared through the kitchen window, perplexed, as though a city might have sprung up outside without him having noticed. "Nowhere. Never heard of it."

"Ick." The skin that had formed on the surface of the hot milk had come off and stuck to Nieve's lips like a popped bubblegum bubble, only it was white and rubbery. She felt so goofy with it stuck on her mouth that she started to laugh.

Sutton didn't join in, only stared at her absentmindedly for a moment before wandering out of the kitchen without a word, his uneaten snack abandoned on the counter.

Nieve picked the milky seal off her lips and, filling in for her dad, said, "Try to get some sleep, En."

"I will," she promised.

*

She did, too. She slept as if *she* were in a coma, or as if she'd spent the night underground, dreamless in a deep cavern. When she woke, she even had strands of cobweb trailing across her chin as if she had emerged from some hidden, spidery place. Nieve brushed the cobwebs away with her pyjama sleeve, not much liking the idea of spiders taking shortcuts across her face during the night. She rubbed the sleep out of her eyes and blinked a couple of times. It was still fairly dark in her room, yet she had a feeling that it was late morning. For a minute or two she lay listening to a soft tapping sound on her window. That creepy plant outside came to mind . . . and then . . . *rain*, she realized, her heart sinking. Then *school*, and her heart sank farther. Not that she minded school, but a dreary Monday, and the smell of damp clothes in the classroom, and math, and the hands on the classroom clock moving so slowly that they seemed to be injured . . . then *no*, it was Sunday!

Nieve sat up. Sunday, no problem. A rainy Sunday indoors was bearable. She was never at a loss for things to do, drawing, reading. Her friend Malcolm might be over his measles by now and they could get together at his place or hers, play some cards or crokinole. She was a wizard at crokinole. Or, even better, they could start a newspaper. This would give Nieve some journalism experience, see if she was suited for it.

Getting dressed, she considered what to call the paper. Not *The Star* or *The Sun*, both of which were taken already. *The Moonbeam*? Too cute. *The Beacon*? Too boring. The Comet maybe . . . or how about *The Laser*? Yeah, that was more like it: incisive, probing, up-to-the-minute news.

The house was hushed and dim, no sign of the parents. Nieve made her way to the kitchen and fixed herself an ample breakfast: cereal, toast with loads of butter and jam, juice. She was careful not to make too much noise. Her parents might feel better if they got to sleep in. *She* certainly felt better, although there was something at the back of her mind

31

struggling to get to the front. Something she was supposed to do? Didn't matter, if it was important, she'd remember eventually. If it was about burning that freaky plant out front, the day was too wet. She might try cutting it down, but pictured it fighting back, or springing back up, twice the size. She pictured it *bleeding* all over her . . . and then she told herself to wise up. That wasn't possible.

When Nieve finished breakfast, she carried the dishes to the sink and called Malcolm's place. No answer. She hung up and tried again, in case she'd punched in the wrong number. There was still no answer. Her luck, he and his mother were away somewhere. Malcolm must be better, which was great. Maybe they'd gone out for a morning hike . . . in the rain . . . .

Nieve wandered into the living room and looked around. It was awfully quiet, not to mention gloomy. She turned on the lamp beside the couch and the light that poured out made the whole room cozier and more inviting. What would it be like to produce light simply by snapping your fingers, she wondered? She tried this, although finger-snapping wasn't one of her finer talents, and nothing happened of course, but there was no harm in pretending that it had. FINGER-SNAPPING GIRL GENERATES LIGHT read a headline in her (so far) imaginary paper.

Rain was pounding down on the roof and she could hear thunder in the distance. When she walked over to the window and gazed out, she saw that the front yard had huge puddles in it, and the spruce trees that lined the walk were twitching and shaking their branches as if they were mightily angry. A vein of lightning streaked across the sky and the boom of thunder that followed was a whopper, a house-shaking *crash* that made her jump. Somebody was getting pummeled.

Nieve had always found storms exciting, and when younger had begged to go out in her swimsuit and jump around in the rain. Silly, since she could have gotten fried by lightning, and she'd never been allowed to anyway. Storms terrified her mother. During a storm, Sophie usually hid in the downstairs closet with a shopping bag on her head. Nieve smiled at that, and it occurred to her to check the closet in case her mum *was* in there. The moment she turned away from the window to do this, though, the front door sprang open.

"Dad!" She whirled around. He'd given her a start. "I didn't know you were up."

"Yep." His hair was plastered to his head and his sneakers made a slurping noise as he pried them off.

"What were you doing outside?"

He unzipped his sodden windbreaker, which was sticking to him like an extra skin, and peeled it off. "Walking."

Weren't single-word answers the kind only kids delivered when they were trying to be evasive? Apparently not.

"In *this* weather?"

"Great for ducks," he said.

"I suppose." She also supposed that corny humour was better than none. "Is Mum up? I was going to check the closet."

Sutton gave her a blank look. A blank, wet look, as there were drips of water hanging off his nose and chin.

"You *know*, in case she's hiding from the storm."

"I already checked there," he said, heading toward the bathroom.

She watched him go, watched as his socks left big wet splats on the floor. *Ducks*, she thought.

\*

Nieve spent the rest of the day working on her newspaper, although she found it hard to concentrate. *Where was her mother?* She drew a picture of Artichoke for the front cover and wrote a story about him, about how Dr. Morys had found him, a puppy abandoned on the side of the road (people from the city often dumped their unwanted pets in the countryside, which infuriated her, but she tried to give her story a neutral tone). She wrote about what a smart and loyal dog he was, and how he had gone missing. Missing . . . where *was* her mother? Every time she asked herself this question, a knot in her stomach tightened. By dinnertime her stomach was practically all knot and she couldn't have forced a single thing down. Not that any cooking smells were wafting out of the kitchen.

But then . . . Sophie reappeared. She walked through the front door at six-thirty carrying a pizza! And not only was she back, but she was back to her old self. Except that she was chattier than usual; she hurried through the house, talking a mile a minute. Nieve didn't care. She didn't even care that the pizza had spinach on it. Relief swept through her, unpicking the knot on its way, easily undone as a slipknot. She scrambled to get some plates on the table. This was more like it! She was ravenous.

As she ate slice after slice of pizza, she watched her mother's animated expression with pleasure, and listened to her talking about the storm with mounting interest. This was definitely going into her paper, front page news.

"So many trees down, it was incredible." Sophie was waving her hands around, too worked up to eat. "Power out all over the city, I *did* tell you I was going to the city, didn't I? Nora Mullein called last night, you remember her, don't you? Friend from way back, maybe you don't. She was all in a stew about . . . nothing really, some personal problems, but

34

I had to go, she was flipping out. I'm *positive* I left a note beside the phone. No? Gosh, sorry you two, hope you didn't worry . . . ."

Sutton was also watching Sophie and smiling. Smiling *and* frowning. "Where did you get that ring?" he asked.

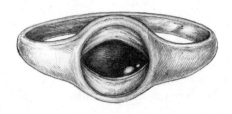

"This?" Sophie looked at her hand in surprise. "Oh *this.*" Nieve had noticed it, too, a gold pinky ring set with a jet black stone. "Piece of junk. Nora insisted I take it, guilty for dragging me all the way in to the city, I guess." She pulled it quickly off her finger and slipped it into her pocket.

Sutton shifted uneasily in his chair and continued to frown.

Nieve didn't want to think about what the frown meant, didn't want another dinner ruined, but when she climbed into bed that night, she did have to admit to herself that things weren't quite right with her mother. But they were more right than they *had* been. Whatever the not-right thing was, it didn't get in the way of sleep. The storm had spent itself and she drifted off listening to the rain *plicking* softly against her window. It sounded like a clock that kept wonky, imperfect time, but had a hypnotic effect just the same.

It was only the next day that the forgotten matter that had been idling at the back of her mind finally worked its way to the front.

# Five

# Jenny Green-Teeth

Homework! Nieve was confounded. She had completely forgotten. What was even more confounding was that the *whole* class had forgotten . . . except Alicia Overbury. Alicia marched up to Mrs. Crawford's desk with her finished assignment, delivered it with a flourish, then returned to her own desk and sat down, primly, but not without first giving the whole class a satisfied smirk.

The weird thing was that the assignment had promised to be fun, everyone had been keen on it. It involved a report, with drawings, on some aspect of folklore and old-time beliefs. So you could write about night-hags or changelings, magic talismans or hell hounds, whatever you wanted. Nieve had chosen a creature that Gran had told her about called Jenny Green-Teeth. Jenny was a water-demon who lurked at the bottom of deep wells and ponds. If children got too close, she stretched out her long arms and grabbed them, pulling them under and drowning them. Sometimes she was called Nelly Long-Arms and lived in trees. At night you could hear her moaning and sighing like wind in the branches. Scaring the wits out of kids to make them behave, or to keep them safe, was Nieve's take on this. Still, since hearing about Jenny Green-Teeth she herself had been more wary of the pond out back of her place. Pure make-believe, but once you knew about her, she somehow became more real. Nieve could easily picture her in all her grim, stretchy-armed scariness – a warty, tack-toothed Jenny, horrible enough to make your hair stand on end (like Mr. Mustard Seed's fur the morning he ran terrified through the door), and she relished the idea of drawing a picture of her. How could she have forgotten?

Mrs. Crawford, normally mild-mannered, was a bit horrible herself about the homework. She was convinced that the mass-forgetfulness had been some sort of conspiracy the class had cooked up to balk her and wouldn't listen to their protests of innocence. She gave them a severe talking-to, plus extra math homework, plus a detention after class. Everyone, that is, except Alicia, who managed to smirk throughout the whole day, which must have been hard on her face, but obviously worth it to her. The most confounding thing, though, was that by the end of the day, Mrs. Crawford *had forgotten*. Had this ever happened before? Never.

"Tomorrow, class, your folklore assignments are due," she said, directly after the three-thirty bell rang. "I must say that I'm looking forward to them very much."

"But . . . but, the detention!" said Alicia. "Don't you *remember?*"

"Detention? If you'd like to stay after class Alicia, I'm sure I can find something for you to do."

"What!"

"Don't say what, dear. Now everyone scoot. You, too, Alicia, or you *will* have to stay. Goodness!"

"What are *you* grinning at," Alicia snarled as she shoved past Nieve on her way out the door. "Snotface."

Alicia was the snot, but Nieve let it go and didn't respond. She had more important matters on her mind.

Like remembering, for one thing. Mrs. Crawford's surprise memory lapse had been easy to take, but it had also made Nieve feel uneasy. It wasn't normal. Nor was her own forgetfulness, or her father's . . . or her mother's. So she was determined to keep sharp. I'm going to remember everything, she thought. Even the bad stuff . . . especially the bad stuff, or there'll be no getting rid of it. For instance, where was Malcolm? He hadn't shown up at school, so he wasn't over his measles after all. Nieve decided to take a detour on the way home, drop by his place to see what was up.

Before turning off Main Street, she passed by Warlock's Books, which appeared to be closed. Tatty green shades were pulled down over the door and windows. Not much business Monday afternoon, she supposed. She didn't like going into this store because Dunstan Warlock made her feel uncomfortable, and she got the impression that he didn't even like books – or children. He wasn't anything like the kindly booksellers that you sometimes encountered in books themselves, who were always old and wise and somewhat mysterious. Dunstan Warlock was mysterious all right, but in a nasty way. He rarely spoke, scowled a lot, and always wore grubby black jeans and a black T-shirt with an "Eat the Rich" slogan on it that barely stretched over his fat stomach. On his head he wore a black Stetson with a snakeskin hatband. His store didn't contain anything intriguing, either, mostly bashed-up, second-hand paperbacks and books about war and weapons. It was certainly a mystery how he made a living. Nieve could understand why he might want to eat the rich, and given the size of the stomach maybe he had.

That his store was closed wasn't a big deal, but Exley's pharmacy next door was closed, too. Not only that, but when she peered through the darkened storefront window, she saw that all the stock was gone, the shelves had been wiped clean. Even some of the shelves were gone. When she'd passed by the store on Friday, *three* days ago, those same shelves had been crammed with boxes and bottles of this and that, toothpaste and witch hazel and soap and everything you needed in a pharmacy. Now you'd be out of luck. Weird!

Nieve turned away and was about to pelt down the street, when she bumped into Mayor Mary, who'd approached from behind.

"Gosh, sorry," she said, stepping back quickly.

"That's all right, Nieve." Mary smiled as she rubbed her arm. "Don't think its broken. Serves me right for sneaking up on you." She nodded at the empty pharmacy window, her smile losing its shine. "I don't get it."

"You didn't know?"

Being the mayor, and an excellent one in Nieve's opinion, Mary usually knew every single thing that was happening in town. Besides which, she was enthusiastic and smart and full of ideas. Although at the moment, she looked stumped.

"No. I was in here on Saturday buying supplies for the clinic. Good thing I did, too. Mr. Exley didn't say a word about closing-up."

"Maybe he sold it," offered Nieve. "And the new owners want to take over really soon, and he . . . *forgot*. Forgot to tell you."

"Maybe." Mary gazed into the dark interior of the store. "Whatever's going on, I don't like it and I'm going to find out."

"Um–" Nieve couldn't help but notice that Mary's hair was a mess. It looked like she'd forgotten to comb it that morning . . . and the morning before. She even had a long, dusty strand of cobweb entangled in it, a strand that was floating in the breeze and twisting around her head, as if it had come to life. Nieve didn't want to be rude, but thought she'd better mention it. "You have–"

"Gotta run, Nieve. Thousand things to do. Say hi to your folks for me. Maybe *I'll* need their services soon."

She was joking, right?

Nieve watched her stride away, cobweb and all – a stride that was as close to a run as walking can get – and then she herself took off in the opposite direction. She *did* run, and it was the best feeling she'd had all day, her legs practically a blur as she whipped along at champion speed. She peeled around the corner of Redfern's Five & Dime – *it* was still open – and shot down Duck Street to Malcolm's place. (Duke Street really, but everyone called it Duck.)

Malcolm lived with his mother, Frances, in a broken-down old house at the end of the street. Nieve liked the house because it had lots of little rooms in it, some that didn't seem to have any reason to be there at all. Frances did her best to fill them up with furniture and purpose, but she didn't have much money, so said things like, "This one is the Thinking Room, Nieve. That's why there's only one chair in it. You don't need anyone yakking at you while you're trying to think, do you?"

True, although Nieve wished there were someone at Malcolm's place right now to yak at her, if only a little, and tell her what was going on. She knew it was no use. The house looked abandoned, and sad on account of it, but she climbed up the front steps anyway – steps that she and Malcolm had painted a peacock blue only a few months ago. The doorbell was an old-fashioned mechanical one with a key-shaped ringer. When she gave the ringer a firm twist, the bell made a rattly-clattery-jangly sound that brought no response whatsoever (although it usually did, so it wasn't the bell's fault). Since it was against her nature to give up easily, and because she dearly wanted someone to answer, she knocked several times as well. More pounding than knocking, which made the house sound strangely hollow. She moved over to the front window and peered in, holding her breath in case it *was* hollow, as empty as the pharmacy had been. But the saggy old couch was still there with a plaid blanket tossed across it, and books and newspapers were piled everywhere as usual, and there were dirty dishes on the floor . . . only no Malcolm. And no Frances.

They've gone somewhere, that's all, Nieve told herself as she walked slowly back up the street, hands shoved in her pockets. A visit to some relatives, a short holiday to cheer Malcolm up. Frances wasn't the sort to take school very seriously, or rules about regular attendance. They're bound to be back soon, she concluded. Although she wasn't much consoled by this. Her heart felt heavy, as if it were a clump of earth stuck in her chest. It didn't help, either, that the day, overcast and grey, seemed as desolate as she felt. Yesterday's storm hadn't cleared the air at all.

When she got home she made a pot of tea and poured herself a cup. She added lots of milk to it, plus an extra spoonful of sugar, which *was* consoling in a small sort of way. When she went off in search of her parents to see if they'd like a cup, she found only her dad home and he was locked in the study, crying. Rehearsing, had to be. The important sympathy job was tomorrow night and he was brushing up on his skills, she thought, trying his best to please Sophie. Nieve decided not to interrupt and went back to the kitchen to work on her folklore report.

It was brilliant. Totally. Not that she'd say this to anyone except herself, and maybe Mr. Mustard Seed. The drawing was especially good, especially scary. She gave Jenny two rows of teeth that were sharpened to fine points, like pike's teeth, and she coloured them a violent green. She showed her rising up out of a river and reaching out, her scaly arms three times the length of any human's, her wrinkly, gnarled hands like claws, black talons dripping with slime. A terrified child was standing on the bank of the river, about to be snatched up and plunged under the water. Nieve allowed a remote possibility of escape – she didn't want to seal the kid's fate entirely. But it wasn't likely.

All in all, she was highly pleased with her report and felt much better for having done it. It wasn't until the next day in class that she realized her mistake. When the substitute teacher, Ms. Genevieve Crawley, snatched up her drawing and smiled delightedly at her, Nieve saw that real monstrosity could be far more subtle. Ms. Crawley's hands were almost normal, and her arms weren't overlong, and her large square teeth were only *very* faintly green.

# —Six—

# *Eye Candy*

Ms. Crawley wore gooey black lipstick that was as thickly applied as icing on a cake. How she managed not to get it on her teeth was a puzzle because her mouth was extremely active. She smiled constantly, even when she was speaking, which was also most of the time. As she strolled up and down the aisles exclaiming over their folklore reports, she marvelled at how clever the class was, how talented, how *extraordinarily* well-behaved . . . the compliments were laid on as thick as the lipstick.

Nieve for one didn't like being called clever. Word-wise, clever was too close to cunning. Slyboots were clever, crooks and cheats were clever (sometimes), and Ms. Crawley herself might be clever. That remained to be seen. Alicia Overbury wasn't much appreciating the compliments, either, given her sour expression, but that's because they weren't exclusive to her. The rest of the class seemed merely bewildered. The substitute teachers who were sent from the city were usually shy and inexperienced, easy to manipulate. Ms. Crawley, on the other hand, had spent most of the morning manipulating them.

("I must inform you that dear Mrs. Crawford has had a most unfortunate accident," she'd announced right off the bat, smiling hugely. "I may be here for quite some time.")

"Simply *lovely*," she said when she arrived at Nieve's desk and snatched up her drawing of Jenny Green-Teeth for a closer inspection. A musty damp-basement smell wafted off her, and Nieve saw that her earrings, moistly black as tadpoles, *were* tadpoles, alive and wriggling, pinned on the fleshy lobes of her ears. "*Very* imaginative." Ms. Crawley gave Nieve a shrewd look as she set the drawing down.

"I believe this calls for a special *treat*," she enthused, swishing back up the aisle, her floor-length skirt rustling like dried reeds. On the teacher's desk sat a purse big as a bowling bag and made of brown fur. Muskrat, Nieve guessed. Ms. Crawley made straight for this, unfastened its claw clasp, then plunged her hand in and began to dig around. This produced some squelching noises and even an alarmed *squeak*. Shortly, she pulled out a long black tin which she held up triumphantly, while repeating, "Special treats!" She gave the tin a little shake, and by the sounds of it the contents might easily have been marbles or stones. They turned out to be jawbreakers.

After prying off the lid, Ms. Crawley walked up and down the aisle again, letting everyone choose a candy. Nobody hesitated, nor was there any hemming-and-hawing about which one to take since the jawbreakers were all identical: each one was white with a large black dot in the centre. When Nieve reluctantly chose hers, she inspected it briefly – it reminded her of an eyeball – then set it down on her desk as far away as possible. Her fingers had felt funny holding it, sort of tingly, and there was no way she was going to put it in her mouth.

The other kids in the class weren't as fussy, though, and having been told they didn't have to wait until recess to enjoy their candies, were chewing and slurping noisily on them. In fact, Ms. Crawley insisted that they eat them immediately by urging, smoothly and smilingly, "No point in saving yours, Ben. Your friend has his eye on it. That's it, Susan, aren't they scrumptious? James, don't be a slowpoke, I might want to sample it myself. They're *so* irresistible."

Nieve knew that Ms. Crawley was watching everyone carefully, so she made a show of scooping hers up and popping it in her mouth. What she actually did was let it roll down the sleeve of her hoodie. When Ms. Crawley finally turned toward the blackboard, she slipped it into her front pocket.

At recess, Nieve did something that she had occasionally been tempted to do, but never before had the nerve – or a good enough reason. This time she had both. She sauntered around to the side of the school where no one bothered to go and waited there for the recess bell to ring. When it did and everyone else was pouring back in and shouting their last shouts before being confined once again, she dashed out of the schoolyard and kept on running and running . . . until she was home. She didn't care what her parents said, she *was not* going back while Ms. Crawley was there.

Nieve planned to tell them that she felt sick, which wasn't entirely a fib. If need be, she'd bring up the subject of measles and Malcolm and how her symptoms *might* be similar. But as it turned out, there was no need, which was even more troubling. They didn't seem to notice that she'd come home in the middle of the morning. Her mother gave her a quick wave as she rushed out the door, and her father wrapped his hands around his coffee cup, and smiled faintly at her, as if she were an acquaintance he'd encountered on the street. He said, "Hey, hi there En. What's new?"

New? He didn't want to know.

"I left school early."

"Yeah?"

"Because our substitute teacher is one of *them*."

"Fantastic. Glad to hear it." He nodded approvingly. "Well, can't stand here all day twiddling my thumbs. Got work to do."

"Right."

"You know, I envy you En. It's great being a kid. No troubles, no responsibilities. Enjoy it while you can."

"Sure."

Nieve was so annoyed and baffled and upset that she spent the rest of the morning on her bed with a pillow pressed against her stomach.

On top of that, she was worried about her teacher and Malcolm and his mother and her parents and . . . she didn't know what to do. Outside of Mr. Mustard Seed and Mayor Mary, she was the only one who seemed to be alarmed by what was happening. (Whatever *it* was.) She felt she had to do *something*, but what could one kid do? If only she could talk to Gran. Maybe she'd be back soon, maybe even tomorrow. Dad had said she'd only be gone for a few days. Nieve's spirits lifted a little at the thought. Gran always listened to her and believed what she heard. They'd come up with a plan. In the meantime, there was her newspaper; she could put in all the suspicious happenings, keep a record of what was going on. It might even be an idea to print up copies and deliver them around town.

Nieve stretched out on her bed and gazed up at the ceiling. *Holy smokes*, she thought. Those crazy spiders! Above, stretching from one wall to the other, there were enough cobwebs to make a canopy for her bed. Was she going to have to do the housework now too, since her parents seemed to have forgotten about that as well? What she really felt like doing was hiding under her bed until everything became normal again. Only it wasn't going to, she knew that. So there was no use being scared and going all wimpy. She'd have to settle for being scared and resourceful. She was determined not to give up, no matter what happened. Whatever it took she'd . . . she'd . . . what? What had she been about to . . . she couldn't seem to remember. Her resolution had drifted right out of her head. Whatever it was . . . was . . . oh, who cares. She yawned and stretched comfortably. She was so sleepy. Her limbs felt heavy, her legs, her arms . . . how relaxed she was as wave after wave of warmth washed over her . . . and then . . . .

She sat up! As soon as she did, the sleepy sensation fell away like a fuzzy blanket sliding to the floor.

Nieve squinted warily around, searching the room. She had an eerie feeling that someone was watching her. Then she saw it. Directly across from her on her dresser sat the jawbreaker, which must have rolled out of the pocket when she tossed her hoodie there. The candy more resembled an eyeball now, complete with red veins branching through the white. With the curtains drawn and the room darkened, it appeared to glow – *and* glower – radiating a faintly greenish light. Nieve had suspected from the first that the thing was poisonous, but she'd underestimated just how poisonous.

She hopped off the bed, and, grabbing a ruler from her desk, used it to whisk the candy, so-called, into her garbage can – *clunk*. This she carried to the kitchen and tipped into the garbage under the sink. The jawbreaker tumbled to the bottom beneath a pile of wadded paper and pizza crusts and coffee grounds. Good riddance! (She'd have to remind her parents about composting, but not with that thing in there.) Even though she hadn't touched it, Nieve washed her hands. Then, since she'd taken the trouble to wash, she thought she might as well make a peanut butter and honey sandwich for lunch. When she'd done this, she poured herself a glass of milk and took her lunch outside, where she ambled toward the picnic table that was still left out from the summer.

The table was on the edge of their property, situated on a hill that overlooked the town and the road leading into it. Nieve climbed onto the seat and sat down on the tabletop itself (without spilling a drop of milk), so that she could take in the panoramic view. She often sat here; it was one of her favourite places. Today she came for the comfort of the familiar, but also to keep an eye on things, to see if anything looked *un*familiar.

Sure enough, she saw that out in the fields those noxious weeds were spreading. Near the road where she'd encountered the Weed Inspector, there appeared to be a lake of black ooze. From where she was sitting, the plants more resembled an oil spill than a mass of growing, living vegetation. Before school, she had checked on the one that had appeared under her window and was surprised to see that it had vanished, which was odd, but a relief all the same. So they *could* be gotten rid of. To her even greater relief, the Weed Inspector was nowhere to be seen. But she did spot something else. Someone else . . . two someones advancing over the top of a rise in the road.

She was sorry she hadn't brought binoculars out with her, but her eyes were sharp and what she saw clearly enough was a tall, skinny man on a creaky old claptrap bicycle, to which was attached a kind of sidecar and in which rode a small, plump man – a man with a face as round and white as the moon. The bike was creaking noisily as the tall one laboured along, pedalling hard, his long spindly legs pumping vigorously. The noise his bike made sounded to Nieve like a super-creaky hinge on the door of a haunted house. A haunted house came to mind because a cloud of bats were swirling around the heads of the men.

Bats? At midday?

Yes bats, and that wasn't the only unnatural thing. Unnatural and *terrible*. Nieve stared in disbelief. The men appeared to be dragging a *darkness* with them. Darkness billowed out behind them like a vast black cloak that smothered the daylight as they advanced steadily, creakily toward the town.

Nieve knocked over her glass of milk as she scrambled off the picnic table. She hurled her half-eaten sandwich onto the ground and sprinted toward the house. In the kitchen, she made straight for the phone. She called Theo Bax at the police station; she called Mayor Mary at the clinic; she called Mr. Shearing, the principal of their school. But try as she might, calling number after number, no one picked up the phone at their end of the line.

# –Seven–

# *Wormius & Ashe*

"*A* total eclipse," Sutton said.

Sophie, when she got home from wherever, said, "What a marvellous eclipse! Everyone's out watching it."

Nieve knew better. It was *not* an eclipse, or not what normally constituted one. For one thing, it lasted for hours, then never really ended. The sky remained overcast and dark at the edges as though bordered in black. It was unnatural and frightening, although her mother didn't seem troubled at all, and her father only frowned and shook his head as he stood blank-faced at the window staring out.

That night in bed Nieve kept mulling it over. What had happened was impossible, but it *had* happened. She'd seen it; she'd seen *them*. Two more of them. But who were they? Why were they here in her town? What did they *want*? Too many questions, all barring the way to sleep. Her thick white cotton sheets rustled like sails as she turned on her side, and then as she turned onto her other side, and then when she kicked her feet – she was so restless! – and *then* when she flipped onto her back. She knew she should get up and make some warm milk, or read the dictionary, or do *something* . . . when she heard an unfamiliar noise. She lay very still, no more fidgeting and rustling the sheets. She listened intently. It wasn't a middle-of-the-night house sound, one of those abrupt creaks or cracks she sometimes heard, and it wasn't a Mr. Mustard Seed sound, the kind he would make if he were to creep up from the basement to check things out. It sounded more like a marble rolling across the hardwood floor. It was faint at first, but as it got closer to her room, it grew louder, and seemed to be rolling faster, gaining momentum. She lay rigid listening to its approach. *It can't be*, she thought . . . and then it shot under her door, and across her floor, and before she even had a chance to react, it was on her bed, and *on her!* She jumped in fright and smacked at it but couldn't stop it as it rolled up her arm, over her shoulder, her chin, and plunged into her gaping mouth. That blasted candy! She gagged and spat it out and scrambled out of bed, coughing violently.

Still coughing, she bolted over to her closet – the thing was following her! She grabbed the baseball bat that she'd shoved in there after her last game of the summer. Before the jawbreaker could roll onto her foot, she took aim and whacked it hard . . . once . . . twice . . . and the third time she whacked it even harder. It exploded with a *BOOM!* like a fat firecracker going off. What was left of it sizzled and burned and finally expired in a cloud of fluorescent green smoke, leaving behind nothing but a scorch mark on the floor and a putrid smell in the air.

Nieve stood trembling, staring at the spot where it had been, and expecting her parents to show up any minute, angry, rubbing the sleep out of their eyes, and demanding an explanation for what they might think was a stupid prank.

They didn't come, which was worse than being unfairly scolded. What if she'd been seriously hurt? Her only consolation was that she didn't have to try to explain what had happened.

Once her heartbeat had slowed to normal, Nieve leaned the baseball bat up against her nightstand, close by just in case, and opened her window. The stench in her room was unbearable, a rotten swampy sulphuric smell. She climbed back into bed, a little nervous about the window being open, but she couldn't stand the stink. The cool, fragrant air that wafted in did help dissipate the fumes, although before they were completely gone, and probably because of them, she grew drowsy and soon drifted off. And because she was so soundly asleep, she didn't hear the silky voice that was also carried into her room, a thin thread of sound woven into the night breeze. *Nieve*, it said softly. *Nieve, Nieve* . . . .

*

The next morning, Sutton asked her if she'd run to the pharmacy to buy some tissues. That very night was to be the sympathy gig for which he and Sophie had been rehearsing so strenuously – *he* had anyway. He figured that five or six boxes might be needed.

"But Dad," she said, "don't you know it's closed?"

"Not any more, En. New owners. That's what your mother said."

"Oh. I wondered about that. And they're open *already*?"

"Apparently so." He pulled his wallet out of his back pocket. "Here's a ten, that should do the trick." Normally, he'd also tell her to buy a treat for herself, a chocolate bar or a bag of chips, but this time he didn't.

Forgot, Nieve sighed, as she started toward the door. She knew there was no point in telling him what had happened last night, but just because her parents had lost interest in her didn't mean that she felt the same way about them. She turned to look at her father, saying, "What *is* this job you're doing, I keep meaning to ask?"

"It's for Mortimer Twisden."

"That rich guy from the city?"

Mortimer Twisden, owner of several huge pesticide factories, had recently bought the oldest and most beautiful and most secluded house in town (there was only one, actually) and used it as his weekend place. The house, which had belonged forever to the Manning family, used to be call "Woodlands," but for some reason no one could figure out, he changed it to "Ferrets."

"The very same. His wife died unexpectedly, about a week ago. He's holding a wake for her at his place here and Sophie and I have been hired to provide the . . . you know, the grief. It's a pretty big deal."

"I'll say. He must be really sad."

Sutton nodded, and said, without much conviction, "Yeah. Inconsolable."

When she stepped outside into the dim, overcast morning, Nieve tried not to let it get to her, the unnatural light, dusky-dark with a faint yellowish tinge. It seemed to be neither day nor night, but some lost place in between. How *long* was it going to last? She did have a sense that the sun was trying to break through, which might only be wishful thinking. But then, if the sun weren't trying there might be no light at all, only deep unrelieved darkness.

Nieve ran down the lane to town, enjoying the running at least, the thrill of surging free through the morning (no school!), and the familiar feel of her hair whapping against her back. Her enjoyment didn't last long. She came to an abrupt stop at the foot of Main Street, where someone had erected a new street sign, if you could call a sign new that was so weathered and bent. A prickly, purple-leaved vine twisted around its cast-iron shaft, and the sign affixed to the top of it read, *Bonefyre Streete*.

What? Main Street wasn't the most original name around, but it had always been called that. Looked like somebody was trying to turn the place into a tourist town with fake, old-fashioned "streetes" and "shoppes." Odd that Mayor Mary had allowed it. But then, maybe she didn't know. The sign can't have been up for very long, Nieve thought, despite looking as though it had been rooted on the spot for centuries. If so, she'd make sure Mary knew. Once she was finished at Exley's, she'd find the mayor and tell her.

Arriving at the pharmacy, Nieve saw another new-old sign. This one, a wooden signboard hanging above the door, was carved in the shape of a mortar and pestle. Except that the mortar was a skull with the top sheared off and the pestle a bone sticking out of it. The sign's white paint was cracked and dirty and the black letters painted on it were faded to grey. Barely legible, Nieve read the names *Wormius & Ashe* that arched across the skull's forehead. Below, the word *Apothecaries* formed a kind of grim smile that served for the skull's mouth. The sign swung back and forth on its rusted bracket, squeaking and creaking, despite the stillness of the morning. This didn't appear to disturb the chubby bat that was suspended upside-down from the tip of the pestle, wrapped up

54

in itself like a round brown parcel. Greedy thing must have eaten a bagful of moths last night, Nieve thought. She even thought she could hear it snoring contentedly. But surely not.

She wasn't at all sure that she wanted to go in. Shielding her eyes, she tried peering through the door, but it was too dark within to make anything out except for some bulky, indefinable shapes. Dad was wrong, she decided, it's not open . . . that is, she *hoped* it wasn't, but when she tried the handle it turned easily and the door gave way.

Nieve stepped cautiously over the threshold and into the store. Despite the weak light coming through the front window, it was very dark inside. No overhead lights were on, and yet as far as she knew there hadn't been a power outage in town. Towards the far end, where the dispensary was, she did see a small light shining and she headed toward that, navigating between the counters more by touch than sight. Her fingers trailed over bottles and jars, and moving along, she touched something soft and thick that felt horribly like human hair. She pulled back her hand in alarm, but then remembered that Mr. Exley used to sell wigs for people who got sick and lost all their hair, so this was probably one left-over from when he must have so hastily cleaned off the shelves.

Still, she felt uneasy. She told herself to turn around, to leave. It was dumb to be fumbling around in the dark, dangerous even. The new owners couldn't be wanting business too badly. But she couldn't stop moving toward that light – it seemed to draw her on. It flickered and wavered, beckoning. Candlelight, she realized, and the closer she came to it the more agitated the candle's flame grew, as if she were a

55

gust of wind that had stirred up the air in the dusty old store.

As she arrived at the dispensary, a figure rose up suddenly from behind the counter, clearly calculated to startle her. She *did* give a start, but more so because she recognized him. It was the same tall gangly man she'd seen bicycling into town dragging the darkness with him. He stood directly behind the candle and the light it cast gave his already narrow and ghastly face an even more ghastly aspect.

He smiled down at her with an equally ghastly grin, and said, "May I be of some service, young lady?"

Nieve, determined to keep her cool, said evenly, "Yes, I would like to buy some tissues. Six boxes, please."

"Tissues?" he said. "*Tissues.* What an interesting request."

She didn't like the way he said "tissues." And she couldn't think of anything less interesting.

Nevertheless, he said it again. "Tissues. Hmmm, let me see." He placed a long, stick- thin finger on his bony chin and tapped it a couple of times. "Mr. Wormius, tell me, would we happen to have any *tissue* on hand?"

Confused, Nieve looked around to see who he was talking to, and it was only then that she noticed the top of someone's head – wide and moon-white – behind the counter, barely cresting it.

"Tissue, Mr. Ashe?" The round head now rose above the counter and came into full view. (He's climbed onto a stool, Nieve thought.) He appeared with a considering expression on his large, smooth, dish-like face. His eyes were as grey as gravel and unadorned with either lashes or eyebrows. "Why, I believe we do, Mr. Ashe," he said in a raspy voice. "I believe we have several boxes of . . . *tissue.*"

Nieve squirmed a little and bit her lip. They were trying to creep her out and coming very close to succeeding. "Tissues," she said firmly. Not *skin*. Jeepers! "Made of paper, to blow your nose on, dry your eyes, stuff like that."

"Ah, I see," said Ashe. "Bodily excrescences. Tears! Mr. Wormius, I think this young lady needs a little something to cheer her up."

"Oh indeed she does, Mr. Ashe," said Wormius. "She's terribly pale. Trouble at home, a best friend missing . . . why, it's enough to make anyone weep."

Nieve narrowed her eyes.

"Have a medicinal candy, my dear," offered Ashe. He extended a skeletal hand into the gloom and pulled a glass apothecary jar toward him. "A sweet to soothe the aching heart."

Nieve couldn't help it. When she saw what was in the jar she gasped. It was *those* jawbreakers again! They rattled and clinked and shuffled in the jar until the black eyespots were all turned toward her. She made a face, thinking of the bitter taste left in her mouth from the one last night . . . how *alive* it had been, the explosion, the stink in her room.

Ashe, eyeing her closely, said, "You appear to be ill, my dear. How worrying, especially with no one to look after you. No one at all. But we can help, can't we Mr. Wormius?"

"We *can*, most certainly, Mr. Ashe."

"Why don't you stick out your tongue for me and say, *Ahhhhhhhhhhhhh*."

Ashe made this sound like he'd fallen down a mine shaft.

Nieve *was* seriously tempted to stick out her tongue, but not in the manner he intended.

Instead, she said, as haughtily as she could manage, "I don't require any help thank you." She then turned and walked back down the aisle, quickly, in case they followed after and tried to grab her. She didn't glance back to see if they *were* pursuing her – or to see if they'd completely vanished as the Weed Inspector had done – but kept walking swiftly toward the door, focused solely on getting through it.

"You've forgotten your *tissue* . . . *Nieve*," she heard Wormius chuckle.

"Yes, *Nieve*," Ashe called after her. "*Nieve,* dear, whatever will you do without it?"

# Eight

# Dark Matters

*I*n her rush to get through the door of the pharmacy, Nieve didn't observe as closely as she might have done the woman who passed her going in. She *did* note that the woman radiated a frostiness because she felt it in passing, as if she'd pushed through a cold current. This caused her to glance up briefly, taking in the woman's pale, perfect features, the elegant, upswept hairdo, the ritzy clothes, the confident stride. Altogether the woman looked as if she knew exactly where she was going, and why. Nieve didn't try to warn her off.

Instead, she hurried down the street, trying not to think about how those two creeps in the pharmacy had known her name . . . and that wasn't all they seemed to know about her. As she passed the bookstore, she saw that Dunstan Warlock was arranging a new window display. This was something he did so infrequently that there were thick shoals of dust in the window and long-dead flies belly-up on the foxed and yellowed books.

Glancing out at her, the bookseller straightened, tipped his hat, and smirked. He'd never acknowledged Nieve before and she couldn't see why he did so now. She ignored him and kept on. But her stomach tightened in distress only a few steps ahead when she realized why he'd tipped his hat at her. On his little finger he was wearing a gold ring with a black stone, the very same kind of ring that her mother had been wearing the night of the storm. He had wanted her to see it.

Nieve picked up speed. The street was oddly empty: no one was out shopping or running errands, visiting the library or dropping into the post office for a chat with Mrs. Welty, the postmistress. When she'd passed by Redfern's Five & Dime, she saw that it was closed now, too. The storefront win-

dows were covered with black paper. Wishart's Bakery was open, but when she stopped to see what kind of cookies and squares they had on offer, she saw instead a single cake displayed in the window on a peculiar pedestal cake stand. The stand was made of grey marble, stained and chipped. Around its base were detailed carvings of strange men. They were like bald, ugly children, pug-nosed, with crafty eyes, pointy ears, and sharp teeth filling their leering mouths. These carved men were holding up a marble plate upon which sat what Nieve thought must be a chocolate cake, although it was so dark it could have easily been licorice. The cake's icing had been whipped into fierce peaks as sharp as claws. In colour and consistency the icing reminded her of Genevieve Crawley's lipstick.

Nieve gazed at the cake, unable somehow not to. She had no desire to sample it. Her stomach tightened even more the longer she looked at it, and yet it was . . . .

"Divine," someone beside her said.

Nieve had been so absorbed that she hadn't noticed Alicia Overbury sidle up beside her.

"It's icky, if you ask me." Nieve pulled her gaze with difficulty from the window. "Why aren't you in school?"

"Why aren't *you?*"

"I'm sick." This wasn't a lie, she'd witnessed enough this morning to make anyone sick. Although Alicia *did* look sick. Not only did she appear wan and listless, but she was a mess. Her clothes were rumpled and torn, and her face was dirty, flecks of mud on her cheeks and the corners of her mouth smudged with jam. Not at all her usual prim and prissy self.

"You're missing out. We play games all the time and get loads of treats." While Alicia spoke, she continued to stare intently, hungrily at the cake.

"Why aren't you there then, if it's so much fun?"

"Night school," she said tonelessly. "We're starting night school."

"Night school?"

Alicia nodded and licked her lips, her full attention devoted to the grim pastry in the bakery window. That's when Nieve saw that her tongue was black. It wasn't simply stained from eating black candy, but had turned black. She tried not to stare, but it was so freakish and ugly. Not that Alicia noticed.

"I don't want to go to school at night," Nieve said quietly. Amazing, but she was beginning to feel sorry for Alicia. "Going during the day is bad enough. Why do you?"

"No choice. You'll have to go, too. The truant officer will come and get you. He's horrible. I've seen him. He'll come at night and drag you out of your bed."

"I'd like to see him try," Nieve said stoutly.

"Don't worry, you will." Alicia finally turned to look at her.

Nieve saw then how zoned-out she was, her eyes drained of their usual spark and glint. This wasn't the exasperating Alicia she knew. Exasperating, but still lively and full of herself and with-it. Those treats aren't jawbreakers, Nieve thought, they're *mindbreakers*.

"Alicia, listen, don't eat any more of those candies or anything else like them. They're *really* not good for you. They're harming you."

"That's a laugh," Alicia said, not laughing at all, but turning once again toward the window to stare and stare at the black cake.

Nieve knew she had even more reason now to see Mayor Mary. She backed away from Alicia and ran headlong to the clinic, troubled, but not without hope that Mary would understand what was happening and know how to stop it. When she arrived, however, and pushed eagerly through the door, she found the clinic abandoned. No one was minding the front desk and no one was seated on the chairs lined up against the wall reading tattered old magazines and waiting their turn for whatever medical advice the mayor had to offer.

Unsure of what to do next, Nieve walked over to the receptionist's desk. She'd noticed that a pile of papers had fallen onto the floor beside it, along with a couple of pens and a tongue depressor. A coffee mug with a jokey **I'd Rather Be Dancing** inscription lay toppled over on the desk, as if the mug itself had given dancing a shot and it hadn't worked out. Drips of coffee were splattered on the pages of the appointment book and a large, sloppy stain had spread over the ink blotter. She touched it – still damp. Several empty medicine bottles sat on the blotter, lids tossed aside. She picked one up and read the label: **SCATTERBRAIN'S SUPER-DUPER EXTRA-STRENGTH HEADACHE PILLS.** Mary must have come down with a terrible headache, Nieve concluded. No surprise there. The headache must have been so sudden and sharp that she'd knocked over her coffee and the papers and . . . and . . . had gone home.

At a loss, Nieve supposed she'd have to go home, too. Spotting a box of tissues on the filing cabinet next to the desk, she wondered if it would be okay to take it if she left a note promising to replace it later. Hesitating – it didn't seem right – she heard a faint muffled sound coming from somewhere in the back. She crept over to the door of the consulting room and put her ear against it. Nothing. As quietly as possible, she turned the knob and opened the door a crack. She peeked in, but saw no one. Nor was there anywhere for a person to hide – or be stashed – since the room contained only a couple of chairs, an examining table, Dr. Morys' desk, a small cabinet, a garbage can, and a sink. This was a room she was familiar with, having seen Dr. Morys here for some bad colds and sore throats, and once a sprained ankle. ("Ahh, Nieve no more running for you, I'm afraid," Dr. Morys had said. Fortunately, he'd winked at her when he said it.)

She heard the voice again, still muffled but louder, so slipped into the consulting room and crept over to the window that overlooked the lane behind the clinic. Outside were three child-sized figures dressed in black leggings and short cloaks, baggy hoods over their heads, obscuring their faces. They were struggling to load a body into the back of the idling ambulance, a body that was wrapped from head to foot like a mummy in gauzy swaths of spider silk. Their captive was fighting hard, squirming and wriggling in an effort to wrench free. Muzzled, the captive's angry protests were smothered, the voice squashed and unrecognizable. *Almost* unrecognizable.

Nieve tugged desperately at the window, trying to yank it open. It was jammed shut. The only way out was through the front door. She tore out of the consulting room, ran past the reception desk, and out the door. Without slowing, she turned sharply at the corner of the building and sped down the alley beside the clinic . . . but she was too late! By the time she got to the back lane, the ambulance was pulling away. Frantically, she searched the ground, seizing a rock to throw at it, a last ditch effort to stop them, but already the ambulance was speeding down the lane toward the road that led out of town.

She hurled the rock furiously in its wake.

Mayor Mary! Nieve had failed her, but what could she have done? Not only had she been outnumbered, but the figures themselves, although small, were *not* children. When the ambulance had peeled away, spinning its tires and spitting gravel, one of the abductors had turned to stare at her. His hood had fallen onto his shoulders revealing a bald head and a clenched, rag-grey face. His yellow eyes, taking her in, were as sharp as pins.

## −Nine−

# *Truant*

"The nights are getting longer," Sutton said, staring out at the starless sky.

*That's for sure*, Nieve thought. Longer, denser, and more *sudden*. At exactly five o'clock the dark had come racing in from all sides and swallowed up what little light was left in the day.

"Dad?" She tried to get his attention, not easy these days. She'd never known her father to stand around so much like a gowk – Gran's word – aimless and jingling the loose change in his pockets. "*Is* Gran home yet?"

"Nope. She'd drop by if she were, wouldn't she?"

"Guess so." She listened to him jingling his change, which reminded her. Reaching into her pocket, she said, "Here's that ten dollars."

He smiled down at her, accepting the bill. "Hey, thanks En. I'll pay you back."

"No Dad, it's your–"

"This'll top up what I need for the sitter."

"But–"

"Nieve is old enough to stay on her own." Sophie had swept into the room, dressed to the hilt in a black evening gown and satin heels, tear-shaped onyx earrings and matching necklace. Splashy compared with her usual working clothes, but Nieve knew this job involved high-class sympathy. Probably lots of weeping of a snobbier sort, snivelling discreetly into lacy hankies between sips of champagne.

"I don't want her to be alone," Sutton shrugged. "I called Becky to come over."

"Unnecessary." Sophie pulled on a pair of long black gloves. "You're not a baby, are you, dear?"

Nieve shook her head, watching her mother tug on the gloves, flexing her fingers and smoothing the wrinkles out of the silky material. The gloves disguised but didn't completely hide the ring she was wearing, which rode like a bony bump on her little finger. But then, Nieve had caught sight of it before the gloves went on . . . and the ring had caught sight of her! That's what it seemed to do anyway. The ring's stone was as soft and black as a pupil, and she could have sworn that she saw a thin golden membrane falling quickly over it, blinking as it vanished into her mother's glove. It *was* the same kind of ring she'd seen earlier on Dunstan Warlock's fat finger, too.

"Did you get the tissues?" Sophie asked briskly.

"Darn," Sutton said. "Forgot."

Sophie sighed and snatched up her evening bag from a side table. "You'd forget your head if it wasn't attached." This was the sort of thing she usually said with a fond laugh, but Nieve didn't hear any fondness in it, only impatience. Plus something else, something harder. "Come on, let's go." Her mother marched down the front hall, spikey heels drilling into the hardwood floor. "Don't be late for school," she called back to Nieve.

\*

Becky didn't show, which probably meant that Sutton hadn't gotten around to calling her. Nieve *hoped* that's what it meant. She liked Becky, they had a riot when she came over. She was game for anything, and didn't head straight for the TV, with the inevitable detour to the kitchen, the moment she walked in the door. Yet tonight she would have happily put up with someone who devoured all the treats in the house while settled like a zombie in front of the tube. Her mother was right, she didn't need a babysitter, and she liked being on her own, but it was so unnaturally dark outside, and she felt so . . . uneasy.

Nieve curled up on the living room couch and began thinking things over, while staying alert to any unusual noises. The problem was that there was *too* much to think over. She picked up a book off the coffee table, new, but probably one of those tear-jerkers her parents liked to read. She opened it, stared unseeing for a moment at a page of print, then snapped the book shut. Ignorance is bliss, isn't that what her dad said? *I wish*, she thought. Then, *no, I don't*. Somebody had to do *something*, and more and more she felt it was going to have to be her and her alone.

She kept replaying over and over in her head what she'd witnessed behind the clinic. What should she have done? After seeing Mayor Mary so horribly dragged off, she ran to the police station for help, and had found Theo Bax gone, too. His wooden swivel chair lay tipped over on the floor and nothing remained of him at his desk except two small piles of fingernail clippings neatly mounded on either side of a half-eaten doughnut. Next, she'd tried the Town Hall, but the clerk there had only laughed at her and told her to run along. She knew that Mrs. Welty would listen to her, and she did, but then – speechless and dazed – the postmistress had walked promptly into the Post Office supply room and locked herself in.

Goblins, Nieve thought. Not that Mary's abductors exactly fit the description. And not that she believed in such things. More likely they were criminals dressed-up in costumes and masks. Short criminals. Circus performers down on their luck. Actors.

She didn't believe that, either.

A bell began to toll, slowly, mournfully.

The only bell in town, in the cupola of the Town Hall, had been silent for years. Silent since Dr. Morys, as a young man, had climbed onto the roof and stolen the clapper. He claimed that the bell, like a harbinger of dread news, cast a pall of gloom over the town, and he couldn't stand listening to it anymore. Nieve had to agree, hearing it now. The sound was distant, but still seemed to vibrate in her bones and shake her spirits into her socks. Listening to it, she pulled her knees up to her chest and hugged them. It tolled nine times then stopped.

Nieve wondered if Mortimer Twisden had it fixed for his wife's wake. Or maybe it was the bell for night school. *Don't be late . . .* how did her mother know about night school? Well, *too bad*, she wasn't going. Child dropout. So what if she had to dig ditches for the rest of her life? She clenched her hand into a fist and punched the arm of the couch, sending a cloud of dust spiraling up, motes illuminated in the lamplight. One thing, she'd keep the ditches free of Weed Inspectors!

On her way home that afternoon, she'd encountered more of his vile weeds, and other icky kinds as well, some with red spots that oozed like sores, others metallic-grey with knife-sharp leaves that clattered and clinked together. Clumps of them were spreading out of control and wiping out whatever got in their way, and not only greenery, she suspected. Nieve had skirted around them as best as she could, and yet one low, toady plant shot a coiling tendril along the ground as she passed and almost snagged her around the ankle. She stomped on it and took off, giving the rest of them a wider berth.

Before going in the house, she'd checked under her bedroom window to see if the one that had mysteriously vanished had sprung up again. What she found was even more upsetting. Footprints. They were too large to have been made by Mary's abductors, who had small thick feet shod in leather boots. And even though the prints were about her size, they weren't hers. Whoever made them hadn't been wearing shoes. She'd squatted down, studying the prints with mounting alarm. Bare feet and only *four* toes on each foot! No mistake, someone, or some*thing,* had been spying on her, watching her through her bedroom window while she'd been asleep and defenseless.

Nieve was so annoyed, recalling this discovery, that she was about to give the arm of the couch another good wallop . . . then stopped, her fist suspended above it. Footsteps, outside. Someone was coming up the front walk. Not Becky, with her light, skipping tread. These footsteps fell heavily on the flagstones, heavily enough to crack them. She caught her breath, listening, trying to figure out who it might be. Soon, too soon, her visitor was at the front door, pounding on it, hard. The door rattled and reverberated, sounding as thin as plywood under the fist assaulting it. She slid onto the floor and crouched behind the coffee table.

"Truant Officer. OPEN UP!"

She crouched lower, waiting. When he finds no one home, he'll leave, she thought. Won't he? Sensibly, she had locked all the doors and windows after her parents left, although he sounded fierce enough, strong enough, to rip the door off its hinges.

The truant officer bellowed, "YOU CAN'T HIDE FROM ME!! I KNOW YOU'RE IN THERE AND I'LL GET YOU NO MATTER WHAT!! OPEN UP NOW OR ELSE!!" He started pounding again.

The only thing pounding harder was Nieve's heart. She'd have to make a break for it, get out. Keeping low, she scurried into the kitchen, grabbed the flashlight off the counter, and unlocked the back door. Before slipping out, she reset it so that it would lock behind her. That way he wouldn't guess her escape route. Better yet, he might get the message that no one was home. The second she heard the door click shut behind her, though, she remembered that someone *was* home. *Mr. Mustard Seed.* But surely a truant officer wouldn't drag a cat off to school? Not even a truant officer who sounded like a monster? Nieve hesitated. How *could* she abandon him? She stared hard at the locked door. With the racket and bellowing out front growing even louder, all she could do was think hard, really hard, trying to send her thoughts straight to Mr. Mustard Seed. She implored him to be very quiet and keep hidden.

The flashlight's narrow beam sliced through the thick darkness as she darted across the backyard and swerved around the pond, which gurgled like a drain when she passed it. Another time she might have stopped to check it out, but not now. She struck out for the wild area behind the house. Unfortunately, there was no choice about the flashlight, a dead giveaway if the truant officer spotted it, the only light for miles bounding away. Her only hope was that by the time he crashed into the house, she'd be out of sight.

While long grass whispered against her legs, and dry weeds rasped and snapped under foot, none snatched at her or tried to trip her up. Knowing the terrain, she dodged swiftly around rocks and bushes, yet watched her step, not wanting to stumble into any groundhog burrows, which is how she'd gotten the sprained ankle that had sent her to Dr. Morys.

She ran headlong, breathing hard, until she arrived at her secret place, a tree house that no one knew anything about, not even Malcolm. She'd built it slowly over one whole summer, buying nails with her allowance and borrowing tools from the basement workshop, always careful to return them. Loose planks she'd dragged from a derelict shed not far away and hauled them far up among the maple's leafy branches. It was the perfect hideout, a place to go when she needed to be alone, safe *and* secret.

She clicked off the flashlight and leaned against the tree's trunk, its rough, grooved bark a reassuring sensation against her back, and stared at her home, by now a fair distance away. Earlier, because she'd felt so uneasy, she had turned on all of the lights in the house, and now watched as they went out one by one. She winced as each light was extinguished, as if she were seeing her home vanish bit by bit, consumed by the darkness.

Nieve was so absorbed in watching this spectacle that she was completely unaware of the arms that were reaching down out of the tree. They reached slowly and silently, stretching toward her, long arms as rough and lichenous as the branches above that in the past had always offered her protection.

# –Ten–

## Ferrets

$\mathcal{N}$ieve heard a faint creak in the branch above her, a sound easily enough dismissed. Wind in the branches . . . although there was no wind. The night was as calm as it was black. She heard a soft cooing sound, the sort of sound a mourning dove might make . . . but not at night . . . .

Instantly, she sprang away from the tree, barely evading the hands that plunged down and snatched at the spot where she'd been resting. She whirled around and switched on the flashlight, gasping to see a pair of mottled, mud-green hands clutch at the air, clawlike hands with thick, pointed black nails that clacked together in frustration – or eagerness. For a heartbeat, she froze. She stared at the hands as they now began to motion her forward. The creature, still hidden in the tree, extended its arms toward her – extremely long arms, scabbed and scaley. Again, she heard that cooing sound, soft and strangely appealing.

But not appealing enough. Nieve began to back away slowly, keeping an eye on the motioning hands in case the creature made a lunge for her. Then abruptly she wheeled around . . . and stopped cold. Directly in front of her, blocking her way, was a figure that must have risen silently out of the long grass while she'd been turned toward the tree. She didn't think, didn't have time to. The flashlight, pointed at the ground, illuminated the figure's bare feet – four toes on each foot! – and that's all she needed to see. She swept her arm upward and struck it with the flashlight. The figure moaned and doubled-over, hands flying up to its face. She must have hit it square on the jaw – if it had one – but didn't wait around to find out. She sprinted off, tearing back through the field, but veering away from her house. She ran and ran, putting as much distance as possible between herself and *them*, one of which was now chuckling softly to itself as it slithered down from the tree.

By the time Nieve got to the edge of town, she slowed to a walk and turned off the flashlight, which had begun to dim and flicker. Casting an anxious glance back, she was keenly aware that the dark was populated with unseen dangers – including the fact that she might blunder into a wall, or fall into a hole – but there was nothing for it, she'd simply have to keep her senses on high alert. She began to edge along Main Street (she *refused* to think of it as Bonefyre), sliding along the storefronts and slipping into doorways. Here, a few antique street lamps – another recent addition to town – cast a weak, brownish light that helped her to see where she was going.

Passing by Warlock's store, she glanced in, recalling the display he'd been setting-up in the front window earlier that day. What she saw were books with lurid, blood-splattered covers that depicted ghouls and ghosts, vampires and werewolves. She found the images too cartoonish to be scary, too familiar to take seriously, and, oddly, she even felt some relief in looking at them. What alarmed her more was what she couldn't see, what unsuspected horror might be lying in wait for her. She turned away from the window and surveyed the street. It *seemed* empty – not a single moth swirled around the street lamps. And yet . . . and yet . . . .

Nieve hurried by the pharmacy, the Wormius & Ashe signboard creaking noisily as she passed beneath it. She noted that the bat was no longer hanging from it (which might explain the dearth of moths). Taking a deep breath to calm her nerves, she detected an unusual fragrance in the air, sickly sweet, that went straight to her sinuses and made her eyes water. The remaining summer flowers in the streets' planters were slumped and blackened, and the Morning Glories that had twined vigorously up the parking signs now hung as limp as boiled spinach. Not them, then. She thought of the classy woman she'd passed earlier going in the pharmacy. Perhaps a perfume she'd been wearing had lingered. More likely, the woman herself was lingering in the pharmacy doorwell, about to nab her. But, no, that wasn't likely, either. The woman was attending the wake at Mortimer Twisden's. Why else was she in town?

Right or wrong, Nieve expected to find out because that was where she was going. Her parents might have gone kind of funny, but they *were* her parents and they would protect her from weirdo truant officers and . . . other *things*.

Stepping off Main Street and onto the road that led out of town toward Ferrets, Twisden's grand house, she felt the darkness close around her like liquid. The few houses that were arrayed along the road had lights dimly aglow in their windows, which did help some. Nieve figured she knew this road pretty well, knew its dips and twists, its rocky spots and potholes. Yet, the farther along she got, the less familiar it appeared. Where the road should have curved, it went straight, and where she expected to tromp through a dusty patch, she splashed through a puddle and soaked her feet. Burly, man-shaped bushes fronting the houses, seemed to shake themselves awake and lurch toward her as she passed by. *It's only the dark*, she told herself, *the dark changes things.* She *knew* they were only bushes. Although knowing it didn't stop her from keeping a wary eye on them and picking up her pace to get beyond their reach.

Once she'd left the last house behind, she began to hear an eerie rustling noise, as if someone were passing through dried grasses along the side of the road, someone walking exactly parallel with her and keeping pace step for step. Nieve stopped and the sound stopped; she started walking again and the rustling sound started up. She stopped and turned on the flashlight, playing the weakening beam over the place where the grasses *had* been – someone had scythed them down. Her light began to flicker again, about to die entirely, but still she could see that nothing was disturbed, nothing was moving . . . no one was there.

She turned off the flashlight, conserving whatever power remained, and kept on. The rustling resumed, only now she began to hear a voice as well. An extremely soft voice, so faint as to be almost inaudible. *Nieve*, the voice sighed, *Nieve, Nieve* . . .

This was *too much*. Unnerved, she took off, determined to outrun it whatever it was!

But she didn't outrun it, nor did the pounding of her feet on the road drown out the whispering in her ear . . . *Nieve, Nieve.*

She stopped again, fists clenched. She didn't turn on the light this time, no point. That *voice* . . . it reminded her all too well of how she'd been taunted by Alicia and her pals when she'd first started school. *Nievy, Nievy, nick-nack,* they'd chanted over and over as they formed a tightening circle around her. Closing in, they'd started to shove her from one to the other, *Nievy, Nievy, nick-nack, Nievy Nievy, nick-nack!*

Nieve didn't cave, didn't give them what they wanted: outrage, or tears. She didn't even fight back. Or not in the way they might have been expecting. She simply stared them down, calmly, if intently, one after the other. The taunts died in their mouths, their arms dropped limp as ropes to their sides, and they turned away, startled and speechless. She'd given them a good blue-eyed "blasting" as Gran called it, and they'd never bothered her since.

But on this road, in the dark, there was no one she could see to blast.

Instead, frustrated, she said, "Whisht!" She didn't know why she said it, why it came to mind, but it felt good. So she said it again, louder, "WHISHT!!"

And weirdly . . . it worked. The voice ceased; the rustling sound, too. "Whisht," she repeated, softly, to herself. Silence. Complete silence, except for the distant sound of a dog barking, but once only, a short, clipped report.

Cautiously, Nieve started to move forward. Thinking about that word, Gran's word, it struck her: Gran *is* home. She was sure of it, positive. Gran *had* come by the house that morning when Nieve was out, but her dad had forgotten as usual, or what had become usual. Why hadn't it occurred to her before? The book Nieve had picked up and flipped through while sitting on the couch hadn't been there yesterday and must have been a present from Gran. She paused, undecided about what to do. Retrace her steps and try to find her way up the lane to Gran's? Her preference, definitely, but she had to be nearing Twisden's place by now, and the less time spent wandering around in the dark the better.

Switching on the flashlight briefly to get her bearings, Nieve saw Ferrets' massive fieldstone gateposts only a short distance ahead. She decided to keep on, get a ride home with her parents, and visit Gran first thing in the morning. There was a ton of news to tell her. Most of it disturbing, but the thought of sharing it with someone sympathetic and smart lifted her spirits. A "cunning woman" Dr. Morys had once called her, which didn't seem an altogether nice thing to say, although Gran had been pleased.

Urn-shaped lamps sat atop the gateposts but hadn't been turned on, or weren't working. Nieve wondered how many guests had missed the turnoff and had gone wandering into the night. Cheery, welcoming lights might not be appropriate for such a sad occasion, though they sure would have been useful. The wrought iron gates stood open in any event, and, starting down the drive that led to the house, she did see a light glimmering in the distance.

When she was about halfway down, she heard a car turn in off the main road. She heard it, but couldn't see it, because *its* lights were turned off. She scrambled to get out of the way and groped around on the side of the lane for something to hide behind. Mainly, she didn't want to get run over, but she also didn't want to be seen. Not by anyone who drove a car without lights, yet had no problem navigating in the dark. The strangeness of this vehicle was only heightened as it neared. It seemed to be muttering to itself as

78

it cruised along . . . *closer, closer*. Nieve ran her hand over the rough grainy surface of a large rock and slipped behind it as the car glided smoothly past, *someone, someone* . . . Okay, maybe it wasn't all that strange. She'd heard of cars that told you to fasten your seat belt and that sort of thing, although no one she knew in town owned one.

The car pulled into the circular drive that fronted the house and stopped before the wide steps that led up to the front door. Above the door a single lamp shone dully, yet was bright enough for Nieve to see that it *was* a singular sort of car. Long and sleek, a soft silvery colour, it reminded her more of an animal than a machine. The driver jumped out and hurried around to open the back door for a solitary passenger. A woman emerged, dressed in a long black gown, a lacy shawl, and a large hat covered in a swirl of black feathers. The hat's thick smokey veil concealed her face. It might have been this, or something else about the woman, as magisterially tall as the chauffeur was short, *goblin-short*, that made Nieve change her mind about going up to the front door herself right away and asking for her parents.

As soon as the woman reached the top step the door swung open and she swept in, wisps of her shawl fluttering and snapping around her. The driver then moved the car ahead, parking it some distance from a cluster of others in a graveled area off to the left.

Nieve moved ahead soundlessly, stepping off the drive and onto the lawn, keeping to the right and well away from the silver car, which, while no longer running, still seemed to be muttering to itself (*boring, boring*). She stole around the side of the house, hoping that there weren't any security lights or alarms to set off. Or guard dogs!

So far so good. Somewhere deep in the woods behind the house a fox barked, but no other sound other than chirring crickets disturbed the night as she crept along.

All of the windows were dark with the exception of a large, central one, and even that was illuminated with the meanest of lights, as if nothing were happening here at all. According to Gran, wakes in the Old Country were lively affairs, with lots of talking and singing and drinking. But this wasn't the Old Country, and Nieve suspected that everyone was sitting around the coffin – would there be a coffin? – hushed and respectful, while her parents cried their eyes out. They must be doing a terrific job, she thought, and was glad she hadn't interrupted them. Best to wait until the soppy stuff was over.

Since the window was too far overhead for Nieve to reach, she scouted around for something to stand on. After checking out a fallen birdbath and a broken chair – a surprising amount of litter was scattered around – she settled on a small wooden crate, first testing it for sturdiness. Overturning it beneath the window – it was a bit wobbly – she climbed up and grabbed the sill, stretching herself to her full height. Standing on tiptoe, Nieve peered into a huge gloomy drawing-room, the only light source being a couple of fat candles flickering in tall ebony stands beside the . . . the . . . there *was* a coffin! But to her horror, she saw that it contained not one body, but . . . six or seven, it was hard to tell how many. They were carelessly heaped one on top of the other, this way and that, like a haul of fish in a basket. The topmost body she even recognized . . . Theo Bax!

Several people were casually milling around, drinks in hand, chatting and laughing, as if there was nothing out of the ordinary about partying near a pile of corpses. Dunstan War-lock, grubby fingers clasping a sweaty glass and cowboy hat pushed back on his head, was sniggering at something he must have said to a young woman who was standing beside him. Even in the dimly lit room, with juddering shadows cast on the walls from the flickering candles, Nieve recognized her as the woman she'd seen going into the pharmacy. So she *was* here . . . and *there* was Sophie, not working at all, but standing near a cold marble fireplace talking with a man who was dressed in a white tuxedo with black fur trim on the cuffs and lapels. Mortimer Twisden. Nieve recognized him from newspaper photos. He sort of resembled a ferret, she realized now, with his pointy face and small eyes. He and her mother appeared to be deep in conversation, while her father . . . where was he? She cast around and finally located him seated off to one side of the coffin, almost lost in its shadow. He *looked* lost, dry-eyed and stunned.

Nieve felt stunned herself, horrified by what she was seeing. She had no idea what it all meant, or how she was going to get her parents out of there. She was still staring at her father, when the tall, veiled woman stepped out of a darkened entranceway. As she glided regally toward the centre of the room, all talking, all laughing, all motion stopped; even the shadows froze on the walls. The woman inclined her head minimally, this way and that, acknowledging those assembled. Most bowed or smiled nervously back, except for Dunstan Warlock, who beamed goofily at her as if they were the best of friends. She turned toward the coffin briefly and gave a faint nod. Then she turned toward the window. She stood very still, lifting her chin slightly, and Nieve caught a silvery flash beneath the veil.

Quickly, she ducked below the sill. Which is when something – *something* with sharp teeth – seized her by the leg and yanked her off the crate.

# Eleven

# Skin & Bone

Nieve tumbled backward and landed hard on the ground. Before she had a chance to jump to her feet, to kick or strike out at her attacker, she heard a subdued whimper and felt something chamois-soft and wet land on her chin. A dark shape was leaning over her, some sort of beast silhouetted against the weak light from the window, and it was *licking her face*. She couldn't see clearly what it was, but she could smell its breath – an unmistakable and not entirely fabulous smell.

"Artichoke?" she whispered.

Maybe not. It might be a guard dog after all, although not a particularly effective one.

But then, the dog gave a clipped bark, an identifying and anxious *yip*, that told Nieve it was indeed Artichoke. And now he was dancing around her urgently, tugging at her sweater, nudging and pulling at her. There was no time for hugs and a happy reunion. She could hear voices, low and chill, coming around the side of the house – one voice in particular, ice-cold and imperious, slid like a knife into her heart. Which didn't stop it from beating faster, faster.

*"I want her."*

Nieve didn't need to hear more. She leapt up, and with Artichoke streaking ahead, fled toward the back of the house.

Here she encountered even more jumble, an obstacle course of objects that had evidently been chucked out the back door. The light that dribbled through a muzzy porch window fell on an upended deep-freeze, an electric fan, and an old cabinet Hi-Fi, a jagged crack streaking through its walnut veneer. She had no time to wonder at the weirdness of this, but ducked down behind the deep-freeze before her pursuers could spot her. As they approached, she heard a low laugh, followed by an amused command.

"Go fetch Gowl. He's my most efficient rat-catcher."

Someone grunted in response and shortly the back door opened and slammed shut.

Nieve wasn't tempted to peek around the side of the deep-freeze to see who remained, awaiting the arrival of the "rat-catcher." She knew well enough who it was, if not why the woman was after her. She felt Artichoke nudge her. Hunkered down, he'd crept up from behind, and now gave her sleeve a quick tug with his teeth, trying to pull her deeper into the concealing dark. Nieve pivoted slowly on her heel, and, still crouched, followed as quietly as she could.

"The night will deliver you into my hands," the woman called out, her voice seeming to come from all directions at once. "There is no escape, *none whatsoever.* Everywhere you turn, I'll be there."

While she was broadcasting her sinister threat and clearly relishing every word of it, Nieve and Artichoke snuck into the overgrown garden that stretched out behind the house. *Keep on talking,* Nieve thought, *and we will escape.* She was determined to put up a good fight no matter what, although her hand trembled as she reached out for Artichoke, her guide dog in this blind flight. In the depths of the yard, beyond the scant smattering of light from the porch, visibility was nil. She had a

83

vague idea of where things were, having snuck into the grounds once with Malcolm before the house had been sold. She recalled the stilled fountain, the ancient gingko trees and twisted rhododendron bushes, the high hedges and tangled flowerbeds, the abandoned apiary boxes piled in a back corner by the crumbling stone wall . . . but she didn't know what else she might encounter. A minefield of junk to trip her up? Or weeds with grasping, long-fingered leaves and hydra-headed flowers with sharp, snapping jaws?

Artichoke's fur felt dull and powdered with grit. In trying to get a secure handhold on his coat – his collar hung loose as a necklace – she realized how skinny he'd grown while running wild, searching for Dr. Morys. Yet, even in this absolute dark, he seemed to know exactly where he was going. He led her deftly through the garden without once faltering, the ground spongy underfoot, the smell of decayed leaves rising up as they dodged through.

Then abruptly Artichoke came to a standstill, the hackles on the back of his neck rising.

Nieve heard the woman say something, but not in English, not in any language Nieve had ever heard before. A harsh, guttural tongue. The only word she recognized was "Gowl."

No sooner had she spoken its name than the creature was hurtling through the darkness making a clattering noise like bones hitting rock. All Nieve could see of it were its luminous, ghost-white eyes getting closer and closer. Not blind, it charged straight at them.

"Go! Don't stop," she implored Artichoke. "The wall, we can–"

Artichoke wasn't having it. With a low, rumbling growl, he turned toward Gowl and lunged forward, slipping out of

84

her grasp. A vicious snarling erupted, followed by a savage, ravening noise as the two met head on.

Terrified, Nieve began to scrabble around in the dark searching for a weapon to club the beast with – her flashlight was gone, lost when Artichoke had pulled her off the crate. Her hands flew through the dark in search of a rock, a fallen branch, *anything*, before Gowl ripped Artichoke apart. In her desperate scrambling search, she knocked over a pile of wooden boxes, sending them cascading to the ground. She lunged at one of these, running her hands over the rough surface to quickly assess its size, then grabbed it in both hands. It was one of the apiary boxes, a bee box, empty, but heavy enough to do some damage. She ran at Gowl with it, taking aim at his cold, blank eyes.

But something happened that caught her off-guard, and she hesitated. The box had begun to glow. Tiny beads of light appeared within and were swirling around and around, expanding rapidly, soon filling the box entirely with light. It glowed like a lamp in her hands, casting a revealing light on Gowl. He flinched and recoiled from the sudden brightness, and Nieve flinched, too, crying out, shocked at the sight of him.

She hadn't known what to expect – an ugly and vicious dog bred to kill rodents? – but she would never have expected *this*. Gowl was a living nightmare, a creature with a human head on mastiff's body. His hideous face was squashed and broken, his dog's body raw and burnt. The flesh on his legs and feet was completely gone, bare bone only remained.

Nieve stared at him in horror as he advanced toward her, snarling and baring wolf's teeth.

Artichoke leapt up and knocked the bee box from her hands. As it crashed to the ground, the light inside spilled out

– or rather, what spilled out was a shifting, incandescent cloud, buzzing and crackling. What had emerged appeared to be a mass of swarming, angry insects, but ones that were as fiery as sparks, flaming, white-hot sparks that surrounded Gowl and began settling on him like a searing, radiant cloak. He let out an unearthly, heart-rending moan, then turned and tore back toward the house, shrieking, filling the night with a wail of torment that was half-human, half-animal.

His mistress, livid at being so unexpectedly balked, shrieked even louder. Words, however unrecognizable, that needed no translation.

Nieve and Artichoke didn't waste a moment. They clambered swiftly over the rubble tumbled from the garden's broken wall, and, squeezing through a gap in it, disappeared into the blackness of the forest behind.

# –Twelve–

## *Lias*

It was hard to say who was more surprised when they stumbled through the door of Gran's cottage. Everyone spoke at once.

"Nievy!" Gran jumped up, knocking over her chair. "Artichoke, too? Bless me!" She'd been sitting by the hearth, jabbing at a smouldering log with a poker. As she rose the poker slipped from her hand and fell to the floor with a ringing clatter.

"You!" chimed in a stranger, also seated by the fire. The speaker, glaring at her, was a boy about Nieve's age with a mass of auburn hair that sprang up from his head in flame-shaped tufts. He also had a badly bruised and swollen jaw.

"Gran!" said Nieve, confused by the boy's presence, but deciding to ignore him. She rushed into her grandmother's arms and received the warmest and most welcome embrace she'd had in weeks. She longed to stay glued to Gran forever, safe as a nub of wool on her comfy old cardigan, but broke away almost instantly. "Artichoke's *hurt.*"

"No wonder, if he was with *you.*" The boy stood and strode over to the dog, who was still standing by the open door, grinning uncertainly and barely able to wag his tail. "A *gyre carline,* eh, auld Shock?"

Artichoke neither agreed nor disagreed, but sank down gratefully at the boy's feet.

The boy crouched beside him and placed a hand gently on his head as he assessed the sores on the dog's body, his emaciated state, his lamed paw, the cuts and slashes freshly inflicted, and the one eye, closed and rimmed with congealing blood. "You've had a rare tangle, my friend." He looked up sharply at Nieve. "What with?" A fair enough question, and yet he managed to imply that whatever had happened had been her fault.

Nieve returned his accusing look, but gave no answer. She was alarmed herself to see how badly hurt Artichoke was, wounds that had not been visible during their flight through the forest. Incredible, how brilliantly he'd navigated in the complete dark, and she had relied on him totally, clutching his collar the whole way. How she regretted now not making him slow down, not taking better care of him. This stranger on the other hand, this intruder . . . she didn't regret in the least that he was the one she'd clobbered.

Gran meanwhile had already secured a handful of healing ointments and scrolls of bandage from her medicine cupboard. "Nieve, bring the quilt from my bed, will you, dear?" Before kneeling down beside the boy to minister to Artichoke, she closed the front door firmly and looped the blue thread from her wrist around the latch. "And let's keep the night and its wandering spirits out."

Once Artichoke's wounds had been cleaned and bandaged, they wrapped him in the quilt and moved him carefully onto the hearth rug. A chill had taken hold of him that wouldn't let go and he'd begun to shiver uncontrollably. While the boy piled more logs onto the lacklustre fire, Gran spoon-fed Artichoke one of her potions that smelled of cinnamon and bilberries and wild roses. "Good for heart and soul," she said. Which it did seem to be, for after she got some of it into him, he stopped shivering and fell into a sound sleep. Nieve stroked one of his ears, wishing him a sleep so sound that no dream terrors would be able to find him. The night had been full of terrors enough, and real enough, too. Without him, she would never have made it to Gran's, let alone Twisden's back garden.

When Gran went off to fix tea in the kitchen, declining both offers of help, Nieve and the boy took seats by the fireplace, as far away from one another as possible. Alternately they stared at Artichoke, who was lying on the rug between them, and at the pile of still-smouldering logs.

After a long moment, Nieve addressed a weak flame that had spurted up. "I didn't *know*," she said. "I thought you meant to hurt me."

"Should have." This comment was also directed at the flame, which began to flutter erratically.

"You've been spying on me," Nieve said, recalling those footprints under her window. She glanced slyly at his bare feet, which were dirty and disfigured, the little toes on each foot missing.

"Trying to protect you."

"I don't *need* protection."

"You can say that again." One of the logs belched a plume of smoke, which began to drift toward them instead of disappearing up the flue.

As he reached out to wave it away, Nieve glanced at him again. He was decent-looking, she had to admit, but odd, and it wasn't only his feet. His clothes were odd, too, more like something you'd wear to a costume party if you were going as

90

a peasant from the Middle Ages. A peasant who'd been in a fight. His woolen pants and tunic were muddied and ripped, and one sleeve had been torn entirely off his filthy linen shirt, exposing a trail of claw marks on his arm, as if he'd been swiped by a bear.

*Yikes*, she thought. She hadn't been the only one to do him harm. "Did that thing . . . what *was* it anyway?"

"The Nelly? She got me, but not for long."

Nelly Long-Arms! She *knew* it (school projects weren't entirely useless), but shuddered to hear her suspicions confirmed. "Look, I'm sorry," she blurted. Nieve had a personal rule about not needlessly apologizing, but still, she'd acted too impulsively. *As anyone would*, she added to herself.

Directing his attention away from the foundering fire, he studied her for some time before saying, "You can run."

"I'm not a coward."

"Didn't say that, did I?" He smiled faintly, then winced. His jaw was a mess. "Where's your torch?"

"My what?"

"Flashlight," said Gran, setting a tray of tea and goodies on the table beside her chair. "Lias, if you won't use an ice pack for that jaw, why don't you let me fix a poultice? Goodness, I haven't even introduced you properly to my granddaughter."

"Oh, we've been properly introduced," Lias said, smiling again.

"Nieve, don't tell me that you . . . ?" Gran gave her a shocked look.

"No, Grandmother," he said, "she wasn't the one who tried to rip my arm off. Though she did try to improve my looks."

"I didn't–" Nieve began. Who *was* this person? And whoever he was, he had no business calling *her* Gran "grandmother."

Lias raised a hand, stopping her protest short. Having arrived at the cottage not long before she had, only long enough to receive sympathy and some salve on his arm, he now filled Gran in on how he'd come by his injuries.

Gran shook her head. "Nieve, you were lucky to escape."

"How *did* you?" Nieve asked him.

"Like this." He snapped his fingers and a small bright coin appeared in his palm. He then flipped this into the fireplace where it landed on one of the sputtering and smoking logs, which instantly burst into flame. Soon the rest of the logs caught fire with a roar and an engulfing wave of light. "I warmed her up, cold-blooded creature."

"Tsk," said Gran.

Seeing as Gran was not much impressed with this performance, Nieve was trying hard not to be, too, but without much success. "How did you do that?"

"You mean you can't?" His eyes widened with mock-surprise.

"Come, you two. Get your mouths busy with these before they go stale." Gran handed around the plate of jam tarts and fat raisin-studded scones and buttery oatmeal cookies pressed together with a date filling. They both tucked in gratefully and hungrily, while Gran poured the tea.

"We have to work fast," she said. "And I don't mean with the food, either. I was expecting you to come hours ago, pet." She handed a cup to Nieve. "So tell us what happened tonight and all that's been going on since I've been away. Lias knows some of it, because I asked him to keep an eye on you, but he has to be careful that no one sees him.

Before you do, you'd better get those shoes and socks off, your feet are soaked."

"Mm," Nieve bit into a scone. "Walked through a puddle." After she'd polished off the scone and had a sip of tea, she took off her shoes and socks and set them near the fire to dry. Then she began to tell them about the Weed Inspector, and Genevieve Crawley's jawbreakers, and Wormius and Ashe, and her parents' dysfunction and forgetfulness, and the pinky rings, and all the changes in town, and Malcolm's disappearance, and Alicia Overbury's black tongue, and Mayor Mary's abduction, and the truant officer, and the dead bodies piled at Twisden's wake, and Artichoke's fight with Gowl, and the bee box, and how they escaped through the woods . . . and *everything*. By the time she'd finished she was hoarse and had to gulp down her entire cold cup of tea to find her voice again. Everything that had happened in a few short days was truly frightening, and much of it unbelievable, but she was so relieved at finally being able to unburden the weight and worry of it that she unexpectedly felt a surge of happiness.

Not that she was jumping for joy. No one was. Lias gazed at her in a steady, thoughtful way, eyes as cool as Mr. Mustard Seed's, and nodded, as if nothing she'd revealed had surprised him. Gran was regarding her with a mixture of pride, concern, and resolve.

"Nieve," she said quietly, "do you remember what I once told you your name means?"

"Yes. You said it means 'fist.'" Nieve now made a firm fist with her right hand and held it up.

Gran smiled, "That's right, pet. Don't forget it."

"You *are* a gyre carline," added Lias.

"I'm not a . . . what did you call me?"

93

"A carline."

"And what's that supposed to be?"

"A hag."

"I am not a *hag*." Her fist was still clenched.

"Och, Nievy." Gran said, pouring more tea. "But you are."

# –Thirteen–

# Two Pairs of Shoes

Admittedly, Nieve was taken aback, but then she had to laugh. Gran and Lias were watching her with such solemn expressions, as if they weren't joking.

"Gran," she said, snatching up a strawberry tart. "That's not very nice! I thought you didn't go in for name-calling."

"I don't, hen. Hag has more meanings than you realize. "*Megrim*" might be a better word."

"Meaning?"

"Let's just say that I think you have a drop of something unusual in your blood, something . . . out of the ordinary."

Nieve sighed. Here we go, she thought. "Gran, really. Things are weird enough without this, aren't they?"

"And will get weirder," said Lias.

"Why do you think you've gone unharmed so far, dear?"

"Because of Artichoke, and because I can run, like Lias said." This was the first time she'd referred to him by name, and in doing so she noticed that he was watching her very closely.

"Aye, pet, you *can* run, and it's a good thing. But you have other . . . abilities, as they well know. Whatever followed you the night you came to see me, the night I was away, I doubt it was Artichoke."

"Okay, what abilities?"

"That remains to be seen. Outside of your fierce-eye, that is."

"Right." The last thing Nieve wanted to do was hurt Gran's feelings, but she was starting to get annoyed.

"Grandmother, does she not know that you're a Cunning Woman?"

Enough of this! "She's not cunning and she's *not* your grandmother."

"Nieve, anyone may call me 'grandmother,' it's a custom in the Old Country." She sipped her tea. "Cunning Folk are simply healers. Like Dr. Morys, only dabbling in different cures and wares."

"They do more than that," said Lias.

"True, but I'm not much of one. Your great-grandmother Nievy, was a great one though, and your mother *could* be if she weren't so busy getting herself into trouble, serious trouble by the sounds of it." Gran set her teacup in its saucer with deliberate care. She and Sophie had never gotten along particularly well. "Nieve, you have to help her. Your father, too, and Mayor Mary–" she stopped and reached over to take Nieve's hand. "I know it's too much, too much to take in altogether, but we need to decide what to do."

Nieve responded by nodding dumbly. Of course she'd help, she'd do everything she could, but she still didn't understand what Gran was getting at.

"Are you telling me that I've inherited some kind of, I don't know . . . witch gene?"

Gran smiled, and squeezed her hand before letting go. "This isn't a fairy story, hen. It's real."

"But no less dark," added Lias.

Nieve certainly felt as though she were fumbling around

in the dark. "Dunstan Warlock, it has something to do with him, right?"

"Fat nuisance." Gran snorted. "Which doesn't make him any less dangerous. Meddling where he shouldn't be. "

"That woman who tried to catch me?" If anyone was a witch, it was her.

"A nightborn thing," said Lias, scowling.

"It's true," said Gran. "These creatures, they arrive with the darkness of night and soon there's nothing but darkness *and* night."

"Cold, too." Lias shifted closer to the fire.

"Aye, no sun, no life."

"But where do they come *from*?" said Nieve.

"Some might say the Old Country. That Gowl you saw tonight sounds very like a Bloody Bones to me. Very like, but they can take different forms and are just as much a part of this world. The order of nature is upset and they creep in through the cracks."

"How? I don't see how that can happen."

"Greed, cruelty, stupidity . . ."

Nieve tried not to look as skeptical as she felt. Those were bad things, sure, but unfortunately always present. She *did* read the newspaper, she knew what went on in the world. Given the amount of stupidity she'd witnessed in the school-yard alone, the town should have been crawling with supernatural vermin long before now.

"Singular acts spring open dark doors. Like Mortimer Twisden doing away with his wife so that he could marry that young woman from the city."

Nieve caught her breath.

"It's an ongoing struggle, pet. James and I have worked together for years, as have others, to keep them in check."

"And now Dr. Morys is–?"

"Gone."

"No!"

"Not dead, thank the heavens. Not that I know of, and I'm certain I would know if he were. He's missing. Stolen out of his hospital bed right under everyone's noses, including mine. I spent two days at his bedside working every charm in the book, but Jim was too far away, too far under. In spirit at least, and now they have his body as well. I stepped out to buy a sandwich – ten minutes gone, *ten!* – and when I got back the nurses were running from room to room in search of him."

"But that doesn't make sense. He's in a coma, he can't tell them anything, or do anything. He's–"

"Useless? Harmless? I'm not so sure. They wouldn't have taken him otherwise. The only thing I know is that we have to find him. For both his sake and ours." Gran regarded her calmly, but pointedly, blinking a couple of times before letting her gaze drift over to Artichoke. "Forfared, poor pup. He won't be able to go with you, I'm afraid."

"Gran?"

"Lias will, though."

"Not if she wallops me again, I won't."

Nieve groaned inwardly. So much for them deciding what to do. Gran had already decided. How was she – a kid – supposed to find Dr. Morys? It was so dark out, pitch black in case no one had noticed, that she'd be lucky to find her own feet once she stepped out the door. Besides, Dr. Morys had gone missing in the city, not in town. She'd been to the city lots of times with her parents – to the museum and the mall and the dentist (fun) – but she'd always found it overwhelming. The buildings towered; the streets were clogged with traffic; people hustled past you on the street, their faces tight with worry. If that wasn't bad enough, Gran was now telling them that parts of the city were still without electricity following that fierce storm.

"The hospital is using generators, but much of the city remains in darkness. You two will have to be extremely careful."

"This is nuts," Nieve said.

"Oh, it is! Frightening besides, and desperate, and I'm asking my own beloved granddaughter to be involved."

"Are you asking?"

"I am, hen. Because you're more capable than you know."

"And because there's no choice," Lias said.

"That too," admitted Gran.

No one said anything for a few moments, until Nieve, brushing the crumbs off her shirt, asked, "Will you look after Mr. Mustard Seed for me?" She felt a stab of worry for having left him in the house with that truant officer crashing around.

"I will. Mr. Mustard Seed and Artichoke both. Don't think I'm going to send you two off empty-handed, either."

"We could use another bee box, a really big one." Nieve wasn't serious, although she did suspect that whatever Gran had in mind – blue string or a gold thimble or a stone with a hole in its centre – would be well-meant, but not helpful at all.

Gran stood and began to rummage in the pocket of her baggy old cardigan. "Now that's a mystery. What that box was, what those beasties were. Firebees? Is there such a thing? Professor Manning, remember, the one who owned the place before Twisden, he's a biologist, retired. I suspect he may have been doing some experiments, crossbreeding, not the sort of thing I approve of but . . . where is that–?" She had plunged her hand into the very depths of her pocket. "Ah, found it."

She retrieved a tiny silver canister, which she offered to Lias. "Fern seeds."

*Great*, Nieve sighed, *fern seeds.*

Lias, however, accepted the seeds with a surprised smile and slid the canister into a pouch that was attached to his rope-belt.

"You have your amulet, Lias?"

He nodded toward a cloak that was tossed over a kitchen chair. Nieve noted a small pewter brooch pinned on the wool, and thought, *I guess we can take on anything now.*

"I'll see if I can find you a clean shirt," said Gran. "But first, I want you to try something." She hurried into her bedroom and came back carrying a box, which she handed to Lias. "A present. Brought these back from the city."

Lias seemed more alarmed than delighted. "Never had a present." He lifted the lid cautiously, as though this *were* another bee box, and stared hard at the contents. He opened his mouth to speak, but couldn't manage anything more than a soft intake of breath.

Nieve leaned over and peeked in.

"Running shoes," she said. "Pretty flashy." Gran had gone all out – cushioned mesh, gel soles, lightning-bolt appliqués. "Why don't you try them on?" She didn't add, that way I won't have to look at your gross feet.

"How?"

Never had a present? Never had shoes? "Who *are* you?" she said.

"Later for that, Nievy." Gran was already crouched in front of Lias like a saleswoman, helping him to pull on a pair of socks that were also in the box, and then the runners. "There! Perfect fit. They'll take some getting used to, dear. But you'll want to keep up with Nieve, won't you?"

"That I will." Lias jumped to his feet and began bouncing a bit, gazing down at his new shoes, entranced. "It's like wearing fancy cakes." He trotted to one end of the room and back, raising his legs high, like a pony. "They're . . . magic!"

"No, no," Gran laughed. "They're only shoes, Lias. Although I do have a special pair for Nieve. Her present."

"I already have runners." Nieve indicated the ones by the fire that were getting crustier by the minute as they dried.

"They won't do."

Gran moved over to the fireplace and reached up, pushing aside an old clock that had sat on the mantel for as long as Nieve could remember, its hands stopped at midnight. Nieve saw that the clock had been hiding a narrow cavity in the wall which appeared to be stuffed with brown paper, probably to keep out drafts. Or, knowing Gran, to keep out evil spirits. Gran tugged at the paper, winkling out first one piece, then another. These two tattered segments she held up, one in each hand. Nieve realized then that they were supposed to be shoes, or slippers maybe, thin and flat. Nor were they made of paper, but dried leaves. They might easily have been two ancient squashed cigars, so old and delicate that if anyone sneezed on them they'd blow them to bits. Yet Gran was smiling broadly as she held them up, as if she were holding the greatest treasure on earth.

"Nievy," she said, "now *these* are magic."

# –Fourteen–

## *Night Sight*

*N*ieve refused to wear the shoes, shaking her head adamantly as she tied the laces on her runners. Knowing that Gran wouldn't let her through the door without them, though, she did agree to take them along.

"You'll be glad of them when the time comes," Gran finally said, knowing herself that Nieve could only be pushed so far.

They'd been standing in stubborn silence listening to the mantel clock, which had unaccountably begun ticking – loudly, adding its two cents worth – the moment she was handed the shoes.

Nieve gave her grandmother what she hoped was a grateful smile as she folded the shoes carefully and slid one into each of her back pockets. If the time should come when she needed them (it was hard to imagine), and if she recognized it when it did, she was certain that the shoes by then would be nothing but broken leaf bits and dust.

Lias emerged from Gran's bedroom wearing one of her old blouses under his tunic and not embarrassed at all about it. Again, Nieve had to wonder who he was – certainly no boy she knew would have been caught dead in a woman's blouse, except maybe on Halloween. Which this night was beginning to resemble more and more. Only a Halloween with real terrors and no treats.

"Your arm?" Gran asked him.

"Better thanks, Grandmother." Touching his swollen jaw lightly, as if adding, *and no thanks to her,* he said, "I suppose I'll have to lead her by the hand?"

"What do you mean?" Nieve started to ball up her fist.

"You'll be blind as a grub out there."

"And you won't be?"

"Course not." He grinned at her, then gave a little hoot, like an owl.

"Don't tease, Lias," said Gran. "Remember, you two are going to have to get along. He can see in the dark, Nieve. Some call it night eye. He can mine the dark for the tiniest speck of light and use it to see with."

Not likely, she wanted to say, but had in fact read about this. It was an ability that nocturnal animals had. She'd been interested in how it worked for Mr. Mustard Seed, how an extra layer of cells behind the retinas made his eyes glow with reflected light, and had spent some time trying to examine them. This prompted her to step closer to Lias for a better look at his eyes. Did they have vertical slits?

He danced away from her. "Don't you give me a blasting."

"Or a bashing?" Her turn to grin. "Better watch it then. Gran, do you have a flashlight I can borrow? Lost mine at Ferrets."

"No, sorry hen."

"But how–?"

"I've something better."

Nieve grimaced. *Please*, no more amulets and charms.

Gran dug into her cardigan pocket again, even deeper this time, and pulled out an azure glass bottle capped with a dropper. She held the bottle up and tilted it back and forth to check how much remained of the silvery liquid within. "Only a smidge left, but enough to do the trick."

Nieve grimaced even more. "That stuff isn't going into *my* eyes."

"Ah, but Nievy, one drop in each eye and you'll be able to see in the dark, too. It won't be bright, not like daylight, but it works well. Will seem as if everything is bathed in moonlight."

Nieve hesitated.

"Or I *could* hold your hand the whole way," Lias offered.

"Put them in, Gran."

Would the drops work? She very much doubted it, but she'd never convince them if she didn't try. Nieve tilted her head back and gazed at the ceiling (not a cobweb to be seen), while Gran administered the drops – one, two, easy as pie. Easy except for feeling as though someone *had* dropped a pie into her face, blinding her with crumbs and sugary grit and globs of lard. Her eyes stung and watered and she couldn't see a thing.

"Don't rub them." Gran patted her arm. "They'll be fine in a tick."

True enough, Nieve blinked and blinked until her eyelids began to feel oddly slippery, and then her vision became blurry, and then, as if she'd suddenly emerged from under-water, she could see clearly again. Everything in the room looked exactly the same. The drops hadn't done a thing.

She marched over to the window, and leaning close to the glass, nose almost touching it, looked out into the black night. "Oh!" She craned her neck, gazing upward to see if the moon *had* come out. "Holy smokes." No moon, but the moon's silvery light seemed to be everywhere she cast an eye, illuminating the path that led up to the cottage, the stand of birches off to the right, the sundial on the left.

"This is *so* cool." She didn't even try to suppress the excitement in her voice.

"It is, Nievy. But it will only last so long. You and Lias will need to act as quickly as possible."

As if backing her up, the clock on the mantel struck a few insistent notes on the quarter hour.

"But how?" Nieve returned from the window. "How are we supposed to get to the city? *How* are we supposed to find Dr. Morys even if we do get there? And why *us?* I don't get it, I don't get *any* of it."

"It's not easy to get, Nievy. My thinking that you're the ones for this, it's only a hunch, but a strong one. I could be wrong, mind, although I pray that I'm not. As for how you'll get on when you arrive, well, you'll have to follow your nose, I'm afraid."

"Noses," said Lias.

"Noses, right you are. I know that doesn't sound very . . ."

"Helpful?" said Nieve.

"Aye, not helpful at all. But I have faith in you, faith in you both. If things start to go amiss, get word to me. Lias knows how. As for getting there, I've arranged a ride. A ride to the hospital, that's the place to start."

"Who with?" Not her dad, she didn't think. Nieve bit her lip, wondering where her parents were right now, wondering what had happened to them at the wake after she'd fled.

"Frances Murray."

"Malcolm's mum? But they're . . . are they back? You've seen her?"

"At the hospital. I hate to tell you this Nieve, but Malcolm's very ill. They don't know what it is, he's delirious half the time, he's . . . not well at all." Gran gave her an apologetic look. "Frances has been with him constantly, but she's had to make a few quick trips home and she's back tonight. She said she'd wait until half past the hour for you."

With that, they all looked up at the mantel clock. It was banging away as though soldering minutes and tossing them out willy-nilly, rather than simply recording them. Twenty-five past twelve.

"Tsk," said Gran, seeing how late it was. "I've kept you too long."

"That's not even the real time," Nieve objected.

"It is now," Gran said. "It's *their* time, and it'll only take us deeper into a night without end."

"Let's go, then." If Nieve managed nothing else, nothing in this crazy exploit, she was determined to see Malcolm and do whatever she could to help him. "Are you ready?" she asked Lias.

"I am," he answered, already fastening his cloak.

# –Fifteen–

# Luck

After a few hastily applied pats to Artichoke's dreaming head, and two equally hasty hugs for each of them from Gran, they were out and running toward town. Despite their hurry, Nieve ran a tad slower than she might have because she couldn't help but look at everything in passing. Whatever caught her eye became illuminated with a pale, ghostly light: the path beneath her feet, the grasses alongside, a rabbit tearing away at the sound of their approach (and no wonder, with Lias thudding along behind in his new shoes). She found it eerie and fascinating. A boulder loomed out of the dark like the frosty white tip of an iceberg. An old, wizened crabapple tree that she'd passed a thousand times before was transformed into another kind of tree altogether, its fruit dark, glistening jewels.

But there were things, too, that she would rather not have seen. Things that made her pick up the pace. Cobwebs had appeared everywhere, covering bushes like giant hairnets, most weighted with drooping egg-sacs. In one chokecherry bush an orb-weaver as big as her hand was delicately enfolding some unfortunate struggling creature in a silky tomb. Gazing up, she saw a swirling mass of bats, their shadowy forms boiling above her head. Glancing aside, she spotted a wisp of

trailing, diaphanous material that snatched itself quickly away. What was *that?*

"Faster!"she called out to Lias, and then heard him go down. A scuffling sound was followed by a *thump* and a muffled curse.

When she ran back to see if he was all right, he was already clambering to his feet and brushing himself off. His face might have been red – hers would have been – but, moonwashed, it was hard to tell.

"Something tripped me."

"Yeah, your shoelaces."

Nieve wondered if his snazzy runners were such a good idea if they were only going to slow them down like this. (And they looked ludicrous with the rest of his medieval getup.) The laces on one shoe were undone, overlong and trailing. "Want me to–?"

"I can fasten latchets," he said testily. "I'm not a *bawheid.*"

"You better do it then. We've got about a minute left to get there."

"Got to walk nine paces with them unfastened first."

"What?"

"Bad luck otherwise."

"Good grief," Nieve muttered, turning away. Just *her* luck to get stuck with someone as superstitious as Gran. No surprise, really, given the amulet and all the rest. If "bawheid" meant some sort of dunderhead, he was right about that.

But then, if they were late, and if they missed catching a ride with Malcolm's mum, that might not be so terrible. She could go home, have a snack, dive into bed . . . no, no she couldn't. What would Gran say if she chickened out? What would she say to herself? No, if Frances had already left, she'd find some other way to get to the city, with or without her clumsy companion.

She started to run again, but not at a wicked speed, giving him time to perform his ritual and catch up. It *was* going to be a long night if they had to do this every time his shoelaces came undone, or a black cat crossed his path, or any of a million other "unlucky" things happened.

"Magical thinking," Sophie would say dismissively whenever Gran tossed salt over her shoulder or knocked on wood to dispel bad luck. Nieve liked the sound of that, though, because there was something magical about thinking, how you could make interesting things happen in your head even if they weren't happening in your life.

When she arrived at the edge of town, with only a few blocks to go before reaching Duck Street and Malcolm's house, she paused again, listening for Lias. No sound at all this time. He wasn't lost, surely? He'd been shadowing her for days, so she figured he had to know his way around. It struck her that the haunting voice she'd heard while walking to Ferrets, the voice that had dogged her, whispering her name, might have been his. Maybe he was one of *them,* and Gran's trust in him was dangerously misplaced. But whatever had followed her had been invisible and she doubted he was up to that, given the difficulty he had in simply staying upright in a pair of shoes. He'd need a brainstorm of magical thinking to pull that one off.

Nieve tugged her sweater closer to her. The air was cool and the night streaked with drifting patches of fog. She had passed one particularly dense patch that had gathered in front of Warlock's Books, not giving it a second thought until she turned around to look for Lias and was surprised to see it

110

trailing behind her. It was moving swiftly, like a ragged sheet caught in a wind, and moving with intention.

Hastily, she scurried away from it, but before she could pour on more speed, it hit her with a wave of clammy cold. Suddenly she was immersed. On all sides nothing but a chill fog – the street had vanished. She struggled to fight her way out of it, flailing her arms and kicking at it, but it made no difference. It was like fighting the air itself. But it was more than that. She watched astonished, as it thickened, gaining in density and weight as it swirled around her legs, her arms. She felt it wrap itself heavily around her shoulders and neck. A frigid, smothering breath pressed against her face. She opened her mouth to shout for help and the cold slid in, freezing her tongue, numbing her throat. Terror passed like a dead hand through her. And then she heard it, again, that insinuating voice sinking like needles into her head, *Nieve, oh Nieve . . .*

Then, faintly, as if from miles away, she heard another voice, someone reciting two unintelligible words over and over. Over and over, like an insistent, pesky insect whine. *Mizzle* was what it sounded like, *mizzle rouk . . .* The longer this went on, the louder the voice grew and the more familiar it became. The clinging, heart-chilling vapour weakened its hold. It gradually began to melt and loosen and come apart, until finally it broke up entirely and began to dissipate, drifting away in shreds.

Lias was circling her, no longer speaking, but waving his hands vigorously, chasing away the last of it.

"What *was* that?" she gasped, shivering.

"I wouldn't care to name it."

Nieve stamped her feet and tried to rub some warmth into her arms. She even had to warm her words with her breath before they sounded right. "Good thing you were held up."

He smiled. "Lucky."

"More than that I think." She hated to concede the point. "But, Lias . . . thanks." Not such a bawheid after all.

He nodded. "Better go."

"Yeah, we're late!"

Running flat out for the rest of the way helped Nieve warm up. A nagging, leftover feeling of dread and helplessness melted away as well. What had that thing been, after all, she asked herself, but mist? Fog. It was what the weather forecasters called "an isolated atmospheric incident." So nothing but weather. *Bad* weather, though.

Tearing up Duck Street, Nieve heard Frances Murray's car idling in her driveway. She'd waited for them! It was an old car that rattled like crazy, sounding like it might fall apart at any moment. Once when Nieve had wondered out loud about this, Frances had explained that thanks to the excellent binding properties of hockey tape and chewing gum, her car was as reliable as any on the road. Sometimes it was hard to tell when Frances was joking.

As they approached, Frances waved and leaned over to unlock the door on the passenger side. Odd, Nieve thought. Frances wasn't the nervous type and never locked the car, especially not when she was *in* it. This was likely a precaution to keep the doors from falling off.

"You can ride in the front," Nieve said to Lias. A generous offer, since she sometimes got carsick if she rode in the back. But considering the way Lias was gaping at the car – it wasn't *that* big a wreck – she thought he might suffer from a worse case of it.

She ran around to the other side, where Frances, leaning over the seat, unlocked the back door.

"What a relief!" Frances said, as Nieve climbed in. "I

was starting to worry, big time. What's wrong with your friend?"

Lias was hovering outside the door, staring in.

*Lots,* Nieve wanted to say, but instead, remembering his response to the shoes, said, "Don't know. Maybe he's never been in a car before."

"Seriously?" said Frances. "What, you steal him from some Luddite cult?" She smiled encouragingly at Lias, while pointing at her wrist, which is where she'd be wearing her watch if she hadn't pawned it to buy skates for Malcolm.

"Yep," Nieve laughed. Frances always cheered her up.

Mystified, Lias nonetheless nodded and opened the door, but gingerly, as if the handle were burning hot. He settled cautiously on the passenger seat, and sat stiffly, gripping his knees and giving the interior a wary once-over.

Nieve tried to imagine what it would be like to ride in a car for the very first time. For her, probably like riding in a spaceship. And the way Frances drove, the comparison wasn't far off.

"This is Lias," she said, remembering her manners.

"Pleased to meet you, Lias. I like your cloak. Not too sure it goes with that blouse, though."

Lias gave her a sick smile.

"Thanks for waiting, Frances," Nieve added. "We got, um . . . held up."

"I won't ask." Frances was squinting into the rearview mirror, watching her. "But I will ask if you honestly want to go with me. I suppose your Gran knows what she's doing sending you two off in the dead of night to do who-knows-what in a city that's turned into Weirdsville." The hazel eyes Nieve saw reflected in the mirror were full of concern. Those eyes, so often crinkled with amusement, were bloodshot now from too little sleep and too much anguish. Frances gripped the steering wheel, and said quietly, "Malcolm will be so happy to see you."

"Me too! How . . . is he?"

She shook her head. "Worse."

Nieve didn't know what to say. "No one told me."

"Really? I thought your mother would have. I ran into her in the hospital about a week ago."

"The *hospital?* What was she doing there?"

"Got me, Nieve. She seemed, I don't know, agitated, not herself. I hope nothing's wrong."

There was plenty wrong, but all Nieve said was, "Hope not."

"Anyway, we'd better jet." Frances slammed the car into reverse and backed out of the driveway. "I hate leaving Malcolm, but he begged me to bring him that arrowhead you two found near your Gran's place."

"Arrowhead?" said Lias. He'd been tentatively examining the dial on the radio, but now paused, giving Frances a sharp look.

"Uh-huh. I know it sounds loony, but Malcolm thinks it will help him. And if he *thinks* it will, then who knows. At this stage, I'm telling you, I'll try anything. Okay kids, enough flapping our jaws. Hang onto your hair, it's time for *blast off.*"

As the car lurched forward then shot off down the street, Lias did exactly that, quickly sinking both hands into his tufty auburn hair and hanging on tight.

# Sixteen

# Car Trouble

At the speed they were going, Nieve figured they'd get to the city in no time. The scenery zipped by like an old black and white film on fast-forward. The car was rattling and banging like mad, and something had already fallen off, the muffler by the sounds of it. If Lias was terrified, he had every right to be. She saw that he was scrunched down, no longer holding onto his hair, but gripping the sides of the seat for dear life. *Dear life* . . . she wondered what she would say if that were the salutation of a letter. How very much she'd like to stick with it?

The ride was thrilling just the same. Her parents rarely drove over the speed limit, while Frances never drove anywhere near it. Every so often she slowed down, no doubt reminding herself that it was reckless and that she had kids in the car *and* there were no seat belts . . . then before you knew it, the speed crept up again until she was rocketing along.

When the car decelerated sharply, Nieve thought Frances must be having one of her conscience-stricken moments, but then noticed her peering into the rearview mirror, frowning and puzzled.

"Some joker's tailing us," she said. "Driving without lights, the *idiot*."

No lights? Nieve's heart gave a fisted thump against her chest.

"I've given him plenty of room to pass, but seems he wants to play a little game. Fabulous. Like we really need this? I can't even *see* the driver. What is he? A hobbit? Listen you two, make yourselves scarce. Your Gran said that the fewer people who notice you the better. Get down, Nieve. There's a blanket in the back, throw it over you if you have to, and Lias . . . Lias?"

He had disappeared. *Gone. No Lias in sight!*

"Holy! By scarce I didn't mean . . . Nieve did you see . . . oh cripes, hang on!"

The car behind, the quirky silver car Nieve had seen at Ferrets, had glided up smoothly and given their car a sharp bump. She ducked down – where *was* Lias!? – as it gave their car another harder bump. Even with one ear pressed into the seat, she could hear the thing muttering *garbage, garbage.* It hit them again, and again, causing the car to shunt forward in abrupt jerks, losing parts as it went – a fender, a hubcap, the side mirror.

Frances spoke through gritted teeth, "No way, José!" She slammed her foot down on the gas pedal and they shot ahead, but the car behind was back on their tail in seconds.

Nieve heard it making a deranged roaring sound, a robotic yet eerily human noise that she realized was laughter. She thought, *Okay, I'm supposed to have "abilities" . . . so I'll make them go away, make their car break down, make–*

It rammed them again, so hard this time that it knocked her onto the floor.

"Ow!" said Lias from the front, even though there *was* no Lias to say it.

"Drat," growled Frances. "The lid on the trunk's flipped up. Can't see if . . . *double* drat! There goes my parachute!"

"Parachute?" Nieve was still on the floor, wedged between the seats.

"Garage sale." Frances swerved, barely missing the ditch. "Forgot it was in the trunk. You never know when you'll need a . . . a . . . ha! *Got 'em.*"

Nieve clambered onto the seat to look out the back window. The windshield of the attacking car was completely covered in a billowing parachute. She heard a shriek, *blind, blind,* followed by the sound of brakes squealing. The car skidded, spun out of control, then plunged off the road. The last Nieve saw of it before they zoomed ahead was a flash of silver swallowed up by the dark.

After a few moments, Frances said, "Well, that was fun."

Fun maybe, but she still had a white-knuckle grip on the steering wheel.

"Yeah, I thought so," Lias said. He had reappeared head first, Cheshire Cat style, but minus the grin and rubbing his brow.

Frances gaped at him, then had to brake and swerve again so they wouldn't end up in the ditch, too. "Welcome back," she said, once the car was righted. "And again . . . I won't ask. Good car," she added, giving the dashboard a pat.

"I *will*," said Nieve. "How did you do it?"

"Trade secret."

"Come on, tell me."

Lias turned to face her, and now did have a cat-like grin on his face. His initiation into Frances' demolition derby style of driving seemed to have cured him of his passenger's anxiety. "No way, José," he smirked.

Frances laughed, but Nieve was *not* amused. She supposed this was what it must be like to have a brother. Annoying. Visiting friends, she'd witnessed lots of sibling teasing and fights and hadn't liked it one bit. Which didn't stop her from saying, "I didn't know they talked that way in the Dark Ages. That's where you're from, isn't it?" She stared pointedly at the goose egg shaping-up on his forehead.

"The Dark Ages is where we're going," was his response, turning away and no longer much amused himself.

*

When they entered the city, Nieve had to wonder. It wasn't as if they'd entered a time warp or anything, but the city did seem older, worn, less glitzy, and it was certainly darker. Darker because of the power outage, yet there was something else, she could feel it. Some sort of heaviness . . . and menace. A deeper darkness.

The excitement that usually gripped her when she came to the city shifted into apprehension. Except for the sound of a siren in the distance, it was strangely quiet. And unpopulated. Not much of anything going on. A few candles flickered in the windows of the tall buildings, but most were as black as graves. No one was out window-shopping or walking their dog. There were no honking taxis or sleek limos or fancy European cars racing down the street. Even Frances slowed the car to a crawl as she passed through an intersection with a bank of blacked-out traffic lights.

"Don't want to hit anything," she said. "Emphasis on *thing*."

Nieve didn't like the sound of that, but was too absorbed in scanning the streets and sidewalks to ask what she meant. She recognized an art gallery her parents had visited once. The work it carried had been too upbeat for their tastes and they hadn't bought anything.

Upbeat was no longer a problem. The gallery, now called Hangman's, had on display in its window what she supposed was an action painting. The massive surface of the still-wet, blood-red canvas was writhing with maggots. If revulsion was the artist's desired response, it worked.

Farther along she saw a confectionery called Grimm's. You'd think you could rely on a candy store for some enticement, Nieve thought, but flies dusted with icing sugar? And dead rats dipped in chocolate? And marzipan hands raggedly lopped-off at the wrist (she *hoped* it was marzipan), and cotton candy as grey and appetizing as old man's hair?

If this wasn't the Dark Ages, it might as well be.

"You okay?" Frances asked.

Had she groaned aloud? "Be glad to get there." Nieve watched a shadowy form slither across a movie marquee and disappear around the side. It reminded her of that spider's shadow, unattached and running free, that she'd seen in town early on. Only this one was much larger.

Frances glanced up at the movie advertised on the marquee. "Nosferatu? Sheesh, what an oldie. Silent flick but totally high on the creep meter. Blast!" She hit the brakes.

"Did you see *that*? My gosh, a streaker! I nearly flattened him!"

A naked man, arms flailing, had run in front of the car, then scurried away into an alley on the other side of the street.

"A brag," Lias said grimly.

"Yeah? He didn't have much to brag about," Frances said.

And not much to brag *with*, Nieve said to herself, but could not – *would* not – say aloud. Because *he had no head!* She slumped down in the seat. She'd seen enough, she'd had enough. She wanted to go home.

But they weren't going anywhere because the car obviously wanted to pack it in, too, and did. When Frances tried to move ahead, it sputtered and stalled. "C'mon, baby," she urged, turning the key in the ignition. The engine made a game *rnnn rnnn* noise, as if it were trying its best, but didn't catch. She tried six, seven more times before giving up. "It's kaputski. Flooded, needs some down time. Guess we hoof it from here, it's not far anyway."

"You can't leave it, though, can you?" said Nieve. "Here, I mean, in the middle of the road?"

"No one in their right mind would steal it (sorry, old thing!), but you're right, we'll have to push it over to the side. Hope you kids had your Wheaties this morning."

The trouble was no one wanted to get out of the car, not even Lias, who originally hadn't wanted to get in. They sat listening to the engine *tick tick,* and staring out the windows, wondering *what else* might be running loose on the dark city streets.

An ambulance roared by, careering around them, horn blaring, followed by another shortly after.

"You know, I can't figure it," Frances said. "The hospital is freakin' busy. More and more people admitted all the time, and yet there still seems to be plenty of room. No idea where they're putting them all." She pounded the steering wheel and the knob on the radio tumbled to the floor. "Okay, let's go. I've left Malcolm alone long enough."

# Seventeen

# The Inhospitable Hospital

The hospital wasn't the hushed and orderly place that Nieve had been expecting. It was a madhouse. The walk there had been brisk and tense – they had even held hands like little kids – but she'd assumed that once they pushed through the hospital doors they'd be safe. In fact, they might have been safer staying outside.

The Emergency Department was closed, perhaps because a sense of emergency had spread throughout the whole building. Ambulances arrived at the main door every few minutes and paramedics rushed in bearing stretcher after stretcher, while nurses and medical technicians, exhausted and harassed, hurried every which way. The foyer was packed, almost impossible to push through. People jostled each other with impatience, or stood irresolute, wringing their hands, looking anxious and lost.

"Use your elbows," Frances advised. The elbow technique got them to the hallway, but then Nieve was almost run over by a surly, acned, dire-haired teenager in a wheelchair. Lias pulled her out of the way just in time, only to be dressed down by a passing doctor for fighting.

"*Look* at that jaw of yours!" The doctor glared at Lias. "See where brawling with your sister gets you. Don't expect us to fix you up, we have enough to do! " Her mouth was stretched into a taut line, yet she managed to snap at Frances, "Can't you control your children?"

"They're monsters," Frances agreed happily.

If Nieve had known that was going to be the last funny thing Frances said, she would have laughed harder.

The elevators were crammed, but none were going up anyway, so they took the stairs, two and three at a time. It was work trying to keep up with Frances. Nieve couldn't tell if the source of her urgency was eagerness or fear, but she herself felt a queasy mix of both as they arrived at the fourth floor and hurried to Malcolm's room. On the way an orderly swished by, rapidly wheeling a gurney down the hall, its passenger stretched out and covered head to toe with a white sheet. Lias paled when they passed and touched the pewter amulet on his cloak.

If his gesture was meant to bring them luck, it didn't.

Arriving at the opened door of his room, they heard two people arguing. The voices had a snarling intensity, but were too low for them to catch the gist. Frances didn't pause to eavesdrop in any event. She stepped smartly into the room, Nieve and Lias directly behind, and the two people stopped arguing at once. One was a young, red-faced nurse and the other a tall man in a black suit, black shirt, black tie. His face was gaunt and bony. He had thin purplish lips, a beaky nose, deep-set dark eyes, and a jutting brow that was decorated with outlandishly bushy eyebrows combed up into barbs ("the devil's own eyebrows," Frances observed later). Both stared at the intruders, the man with keen irritation.

"But it's *criminal* to–" The nurse's words still hung in the air, as if etched there by the sharpness of her voice.

"Criminal to what?" Frances might have asked if in a different mood. Or she might have teasingly dressed *them* down for fighting – *tsk, tsk*. Instead, she said, "Where's Malcolm?" When neither responded, she repeated her question, upping the volume, "Where is my son?"

Malcolm's bed was empty, the rumpled sheets pulled back, his frayed plaid bathrobe tossed over a chair. The three other beds in the room were also empty, although tidily and tightly made up.

"If you'll excuse me." The man haughtily waved them aside as he strode out.

Nieve was only too glad to get out of his way. He smelled peculiar, like the jars in science class that contained frogs preserved in formaldehyde.

"Creep." Frances said under her breath. Then, "Julie, what's going on? Where *is* Malcolm?"

The nurse sank down onto the end of the bed, her anger subsiding into frustration. "I don't know, Frances. I don't even know who that guy is, some sort of administrator, supposedly. Told me he was a specialist from Down Under when I challenged him, but he sure didn't sound like an Aussie to me." She ran a hand distractedly over the blanket that was heaped-up beside her. "I was called to another room to help with a patient, and when I got back . . . Malcolm was gone. I went to the nurse's station to find out what was going on and the head nurse told me that we needed the bed and he was moved to another ward."

Nieve glanced at the three other empty beds and exchanged a look with Lias.

"Okay, what ward? Where?" Frances said.

124

Julie shook her head. "There's no record of it, which . . . I thought had to be an oversight, somebody forgot, we've been so busy. Anyway, I went to look for him. Frances, I searched everywhere. I promised you I'd keep an eye on him, and I . . . I'm so sorry. I kept searching, poking around, asking questions. You wouldn't believe how many sick people have been 'moved to another ward.' That's why they sent that guy to threaten me."

"Threaten you how?"

"Said if I didn't watch it, I'd be moved, too. Moved right out the door. Then he said something really weird and sexist. He said that was fine by him because nurses make such good doormats."

"A creep *galore*. Julie, you did everything you could." Frances touched the young woman's shoulder. "I appreciate it. Honestly I do." Her grip tightened. "And now I'm going to find Malcolm. I'm going to find him if it's the *last* thing I do."

*

Frances was true to her word. The "last thing" part anyway, because they searched the hospital room after room, floor after floor, and she was still going strong, although growing more frantic and wild-eyed. Nieve was afraid that she was going to flip out. She felt like flipping out herself, but was determined to keep her head (unlike that brag guy). If she was to find her friend, and she *was*, she knew she'd need every nanogram of cool and logic she could muster.

After looking everywhere, including storage cabinets and supply rooms, Frances had become convinced that Malcolm was in the operating theatre, hauled off there by mistake. It was a plausible theory, since they'd seen an inordinate number of gurneys rattle through the double doors to the OR, one after another after another. More patients than the largest team of surgeons could handle. They'd been sitting in the OR waiting room for about ten minutes, in which time Frances had bugged the medical staff non-stop, peppering them with endless questions about Malcolm's whereabouts. While promising to investigate, it seemed more likely that the increasingly unsympathetic nurses at the desk might send Frances through those double doors to have her mouth sutured shut.

No danger of that at present, though, for she'd taken a pestering-break and was sitting with her lips clamped tight, a pervasive condition here, Nieve had noticed. Frances was obviously scheming, figuring out her next move.

"Are you two hungry?" she finally blurted. "Bet you are and you're too polite to say anything." She was making an effort to sound casual, despite the quaver in her voice. "Cafeteria's closed, but there are those machines on the first floor. Drinks, snacks. Why don't you go get something?"

Before they could respond, she began to dig in the pockets of her jacket (Frances was the only non-purse carrying mother Nieve knew) and pulling out loose change and crumpled bills. Along with this, she also pulled out the arrowhead that she'd brought for Malcolm . . . the *very* thing that had caused her to be absent when he had needed her the most. She stared at it with distaste, then flung it onto the floor. The arrowhead landed on the tile with a flinty *clack* amid a shower of bills and coins.

Lias pounced on it. On second thought, he scooped up the money, too, including a couple of quarters that were still rolling away. When he had it all collected, he offered it back to Frances, who said, "Shame on me, I'm acting like a spoiled adult, aren't I? A coffee will set me straight, even ghastly

126

machine coffee. Geez, I *really* could use one, now that I think of it. Be sure to get yourselves whatever you want. Go wild." She paused to consider something. "Look Lias, why don't you hang onto Malcolm's good luck charm for me? Until I start behaving myself, eh. I wouldn't want anything to happen to it."

He nodded, handed the money to Nieve, and slipped the arrowhead into the pouch that was tied to his belt.

Nieve didn't like the idea of leaving Frances alone, but she thought a coffee might do her some good, calm her down. Admittedly, the idea of the snacks also appealed – lots of snacks! – too many for her to carry on her own.

When she and Lias set off on their errand, she whispered to him, "Let's hurry, before she starts bugging the nurses again."

The elevators were all stalled at the lowest level, so they decided to take the stairs.

"Why do these elevators only go *down*?" she said.

"Everything does," he responded, which she didn't consider much of an answer.

Before they got to the door of the stairwell, they both stopped and looked at one another. The machines on the first floor weren't working. They knew that, and Frances knew it, too. They had all glanced at the "out-of-order" signs in passing when scouring that part of the hospital for Malcolm.

"Does she mean the ones on a different floor?" Lias said.

"No!"

They raced back to the waiting room, just in time to see Frances sneaking past the nurses. They didn't notice because they were preoccupied with a new arrival. A distraught man, who was being wheeled toward the OR on a gurney, had jumped off. The nurses, along with the orderly who brought him, were struggling to force him back onto it, but he was scrappy and fought hard, swinging at them left and right. He *did not* want to go in there, nor, given his robust state of health, did he appear to have any need.

Frances, however, did. She pushed eagerly through the double doors and was gone. Seems she wasn't behaving herself quite yet.

# Eighteen

# Strange Operations

Nieve fully expected Frances to be expelled from the OR, but that hadn't happened. Neither she nor Lias knew what to do. They had considered sneaking in themselves to look for her, except that an orderly who more resembled a bouncer – all muscle and tattoos – had arrived to stand guard at the double doors. Nieve hoped he wasn't there because Frances had been caught. More likely he was the heavy sent to prevent other patients from escaping. Secretly, she had cheered on the man who had jumped off the gurney, keeping her fingers crossed while he struggled with the nurses and thinking *go go go!* And he did! They had him pinned down and were about to haul him back onto the gurney, when he wrenched himself free and tore off down the hall, his blue, open-backed hospital gown flapping and revealing peeks of his hairy bum as he ran.

She couldn't help but laugh. Just a little. Funny things still happened even when you were surrounded by nothing but bad ones. Like flickers of light in the dark, she thought. Like good luck charms, only more effective.

Turning to Lias she said, "So what's the big deal with the arrowhead?"

"Elfshot." He kept his voice lowered, although the guard was more interested in the nurses than in them. "Might come in handy."

Nieve sighed. "Whatever you say." She studied him for a minute, "Why do you sound like a normal kid sometimes, and other times like a . . . I don't know what?"

"A freak?"

He *did* have only eight toes, hair that looked like the hair version of fire, and clothes that were several centuries out of date. "No. I mean that sometimes you sound old, really old. The way you say things."

He shrugged. "Old Country ways."

"Where Gran's from, you mean?"

"Listen, Nieve," he said, dodging the question. "Frances isn't coming back out. We've got to find her, *and* all your other friends, before we disappear ourselves. That's one of the things cunning folk do, find what's missing."

"Agreed, but I'm not one of them. And I'm not a hag, either, thanks. Or that other thing, what was it?"

"Megrim. Doesn't mean you've got warts and ride a broomstick. Only means you can do some things that other people can't. It's a *talent*. Like being good at music. So *do* them. You know, the way you sent that silver car spinning into the ditch, and the way you helped that man escape just now."

"Don't be silly. That had nothing to do with me."

He only smiled at her and shook his head.

"Look," she said, "you're the one who got the fire going at Gran's, and you're the one who can see in the dark, and *you're* the one who totally vanished in the car. Remember? *You* do something."

Lias gave her such a vexed look that she thought he was going to smack her (if he *dared*). Instead, he smacked his own knee, and said, "I've the brains of a nit. Here, hold out your hand." He reached into the pouch on his belt and fished out the silver cannister that Gran had given him. Turning his back to shield what he was doing, he twisted off the lid, and tipping it over, very gently tapped the bottom so that whatever was inside – fern seeds Gran had said – fell onto Nieve's palm. She had to assume that's what was going on because fern seeds – spores, aren't they? – are so tiny as to be almost invisible. "There!"

"What?" she said, a little grumpily.

"You've gone."

"Gone? What d'you mean?"

"Close your hand, hold it tight, and don't lose it. See, like this?" Lias tapped a fern seed onto his own palm, closed his fingers over it, and immediately vanished.

Nieve stared at the space where he'd been, then stared at herself, her arms, her legs. She wiggled the fingers on her other hand, the one that wasn't holding the seed. She didn't feel the least bit different, but she was definitely *gone*. The seat was visible, but she wasn't. So *that's* how Lias had done it in the car. She reached out and touched his sleeve to make sure he was still there. "Holy smokes," was all she could say.

"Aye," he whispered. "It's muckle *cool.*"

"Will you look at that," one of the nurses said. "Those two brats have taken off. Didn't see them leave, did you?"

"Sneaks," the other said. "Bad as the mother."

"They got that right," Nieve whispered back to Lias. "Let's go."

Another gurney had appeared, one wheel squeaking loudly as it rolled along, as if protesting its destination. This patient, however, was too sedated to cause any trouble. The orderly who was piloting the gurney grinned at the burly one guarding the OR doors as he passed through. Nieve didn't think he'd be quite so smug if he could see who was trailing behind him.

"Whatever happened to that yappy woman?" one of the nurses said.

"Who cares," the other answered. "She won't last long anyway. Not with her attitude."

If Nieve found this disturbing, there was worse to come. Much worse.

At first everything beyond the doors appeared as she imagined it might. Sterile, uncluttered, starkly lit, *busy*. Nurses and doctors – masked, gloved, and gowned – moved in and out of operating rooms with an air of brisk efficiency. It was cold, which she hadn't been expecting, although she supposed that wasn't unusual. What was unusual was the smell that tweaked her nostrils. Not the typical hospital odour (overcooked stew), nor the smell of antiseptic and bandages, but a sweet, flowery fragrance, cloying and somehow familiar. Was it anaesthetic? She shivered, not sure if she was ready for what she might see? People cut open . . . lots of blood?

They continued in the wake of the orderly, following directly behind him, so they wouldn't get in anyone's way. Even though Nieve was new to this invisible business, she knew enough not to become the unseen obstacle that tripped someone up. The orderly rattled past a couple of occupied rooms – doors closed, they couldn't peek in to see if Frances was inside – then he stopped abruptly before another, wider door. Too abruptly, for Lias trod on the orderly's heel.

"Hey! What the–?"

Lias backed off hastily, while Nieve clapped a hand to her mouth, stifling a nervous laugh.

The orderly was staring, puzzled, at the back of his shoe, which had gotten crunched, when the door of the operating room opened. A nurse stood in the doorway, grasping the handle of a shopping cart. Giving up on his shoe scrutiny, he said to her, "Done?"

"Done," she responded in an oddly flat tone.

When the nurse started off down the aisle, Nieve had to clap her hand against her mouth again, but not to smother a laugh. She was shocked to see that the cart contained *babies*, newborns, all wrinkly and red, but utterly silent and still. About nine of them were heaped in the cart carelessly, in the same way the corpses had been piled in that coffin at Ferrets. But surely these babies weren't . . . ? Her stomach clenched. During their tour of the hospital, the nursery in the natal unit had been unoccupied, all the bassinets empty and the room darkened. *What* was going on here?

Lias clutched her arm and pulled her forward as the orderly began to push the gurney into the operating room. Once inside, they saw that it was an operating theatre, with a bank of seats for observers located behind a glass partition. A full house of observers had filled those seats, too.

Nieve pressed herself against the wall closest to the door and gazed at them. Among the stone-faced medical staff in attendance, she located the ferrety features of Mortimer Twisden (handsome on a ferret, but not so fabulous on him). Seated beside him was his young, dark-haired fiancée. When he bent toward her to say something, she smiled with interest, but leaned ever so slightly away. Dunstan Warlock was present as well, jolly amid a gang of those putty-faced men with pointy teeth – *deilers* Gran had called them. Nieve was startled to see them here. The setting seemed too clinical and bright for figures so unreal. But she was even more startled when she noticed, seated off to one side, someone she definitely didn't want to see, not *here* with the rest of them. Her mother! Still wearing her finery from the wake, Sophie sat clutching her glittery evening bag and staring fixedly at the patient who had been wheeled into the room. Nieve didn't know whether to be worried or relieved that Sutton wasn't with her.

Following her mother's gaze, Nieve now turned her attention to the nurses, who were shifting the patient from the gurney onto the operating table and securing him in place with wide nylon straps. She felt jittery and anxious. If, watching, she got sick to her stomach would her sick be invisible, too? *Please* – she'd rather not find out.

More than anything, she felt anxious for the patient. If only there was some way to help him. He looked perfectly healthy . . . and terri-fied. His eyes were rolling in their sockets, but sedated and strapped in, he couldn't move. Whatever was going on here was unlawful and hideous – she couldn't understand why these doctors and nurses were involved. She couldn't understand, that is, until the head surgeon pulled his mask down onto his chin so that he could speak to the audience.

Holding a syringe aloft, a very large syringe with a very long needle, he said, "Child's play, anyone can do it, you all can do it."

He had a black tongue.

The barrel of the syringe was filled with a bright green liquid, some of which sprayed out as he jiggled the base of the plunger with his thumb. He was clumsy, and as zoned out as

134

Alicia had been when staring at that nasty black cake in Wishart's Bakery.

The peculiar flowery smell Nieve had noticed in the hallway filled the room, and she took short shallow breaths to avoid inhaling it too deeply. Still, it tingled in her throat and made her feel dizzy. She pushed herself more firmly against the wall for support.

"You simply find a vein, any old vein will do." The surgeon swivelled toward the patient and grabbed his arm. The man's eyes were bugging out of his head. With a flourish, the surgeon took a jab at a vein. "Whoops," he said. 'Missed!" He took another swipe at the man's arm and missed again. He gave the audience a goofy grin, then slurred, "Ah, what the heck, why not." He lunged at the patient once more, only this time aimed for a vein that was pulsing in the poor man's forehead. As the needle slid into his head, the man screamed. But only briefly – it was more a half-scream, followed by silence. His face was contorted and his mouth was opened wide as if he were screaming, but he was no longer conscious.

After the surgeon had emptied the contents of the syringe into his head, watching as the vein turned from a normal blue colour to a vivid green, he raised the man's arm and bent the hand, palm upward, like a waiter holding a platter. The arm remained upright and the surgeon dropped the empty syringe on the man's palm.

"As you can see," he addressed the audience again, while peeling off his gloves and depositing them on top of the syringe. "Not a drop of blood spilled and the body is completely ready for processing."

"Processing?" Nieve said aloud, outraged. She open her clenched hands wide, gesturing in dismay toward the unfortunate man.

No blood may have been spilled, but at that moment something else, much tinier than a drop of blood, drifted to the floor. The fern seed. She had forgotten about it completely.

The surgeon and nurses, the audience, everyone, began to shout and groan and gasp aloud, astonished to see a girl's face appear by the door. No body had appeared, and no head, only a face, but a furious one. One with intensely lit eyes that raked the whole room over with a scorching glare.

# –Nineteen–

# Murdeth

If looks could kill? Fierce-eye, Gran called it, this ability of Nieve's to stun with a look.

After witnessing that sick operation, Nieve certainly felt as fierce as she ever had. She didn't knock anyone dead – not that she wanted to – but she did stop them dead in their tracks. If only for as long as it took for them to get out of there.

They raced down the hall, heading straight for the OR doors. Lias was still invisible – she could hear his runners thumping along beside her – but more of her body was beginning to reappear, arms and legs first.

As they were about to scramble through the double doors, a couple of orderlies pushed through from the other direction, one after the other, wheeling in two more patients.

"Hey,"one shouted. "What's *that!*"

"Ech!" the other squealed. "Body parts! On the loose!"

Nieve stopped them dead in their tracks, too, and she didn't even have to bat an eye. Problem was they were blocking the way like two lumps of stone. The elbow technique wasn't going to work on them.

"Get her, you *fools*. Move it!"

Dunstan Warlock had stumbled out of the operating theatre, a pack of deilers gathering behind him.

One of the orderlies, the less squeamish one, lunged at her. She leapt aside, deftly evading him, and took off down a corridor to her right.

"Lias?" she panted.

"Here." He was directly behind. But so were the others, only a few lengths back. "I'll slow them down."

Something *snapped* like a cap gun, which started Warlock shouting again. Nieve glanced back and saw flames leaping up from a gold coin that was lying on the floor. The flames merged into a crackling curtain of fire that was drawn across the width of the corridor, separating them from their pursuers. The deilers were wrinkling their ugly faces and recoiling from it, while the orderlies stood dumbstruck. Warlock cursed, "A trick, it's nothing but a bleeding *trick*. Come on!"

"'Twas," whispered Lias.

"Good one."

"Won't last long. Which way?"

"Down here."

At the end of the corridor, instead of turning right and heading down another hallway, they veered left toward an alcove that housed a bank of elevators. One of the elevators was standing open and an orderly was hanging around outside, waiting for someone to arrive. He was staring at a clipboard and tapping it with a pen as he listened to music through a set of earbuds. Music leaked out of them, a screechy-scratchy sound, tiny but dire, like death metal for mice. He was bouncing his head up and down, keeping time with the beat, oblivious both to the commotion in the corridor and to Nieve, who snuck past. The elevator was crammed full of gurneys, with only enough room for one more, a space that she and Lias readily filled.

Nieve smacked the down button and the elevator door slid shut, slowly enough for the orderly to glance up in surprise from his clipboard, but too fast for him to do anything about it.

"Finally got an elevator," Nieve said, as they plunged downward.

"Grand. I've always wanted to be trapped in a runaway closet with a rickle of corpses."

"Oh!" Nieve whipped around and eyed the gurney she'd been leaning against, a pair of pale knobbly feet were sticking out the end of a black shroud. "Do they . . . that operation, is it . . . ?"

Lias had begun to reappear, head first. "Final? *Dinna ken*, but it's my guess this lot's off to the hospital morgue." The expression on his face was a mixture of apprehension and disgust.

"Lias, don't. I mean, stay out of sight."

"I put the fern seed back." His hand emerged, and in it was the silver cannister, which he offered to her. "You take it. They've seen you, not me. Be safer."

"Just give me another."

"There's only the one left. Used the last of the coins, too. Shame, that."

Lias didn't seem upset about the losses, but Nieve groaned, "I really blew it." She felt badly enough about dropping the fern seed in the first place, but worse now. "You keep it, Lias. Gran gave it to you." She glanced up at the panel that indicated what floor they were passing – second floor, first floor – then pressed the button for the lobby. And then she pressed it again, urgently, trying to get the elevator to stop, but it kept going down . . . lower level, lower lower level. "Is this thing never going to stop?"

"What will we do when it does?"

"Follow our noses, I guess. Remember? Or all of these noses." Nieve nodded toward their fellow-passengers, a few with noses sufficiently pointy to form little hillocks in the shrouds. "Maybe we'll find out what's going on."

Lias smiled gamely, or tried to. The presence of so many bodies gave him the jitters. She wasn't overly thrilled herself, but they were safe for the time being. Someone, or several someones, already alerted by Warlock, might be waiting to nab them when the elevator arrived at its underground destination.

Lower lower *lower* level . . . it finally bumped to a stop and the doors slid open.

They heard voices, but some distance away.

Nieve peeked out and saw two figures dressed in black, one tall and the other very short, walking briskly along a corridor, heading in their direction. The tall one was speaking curtly and at length to the other, neither paying much attention to what lay ahead.

"Quick," said Nieve.

About a dozen gurneys were assembled in the hall, empty ones with sheets tossed onto them in crumpled piles. They slipped out of the elevator and wedged themselves behind one at the very back. Nieve tugged at the corner of a sheet that was hanging down, pulling it over them for better cover. With any luck the men would pass them by or take the elevator up.

They did neither, coming instead to an abrupt stop in front of the empty gurneys.

Peeking out at them, Nieve saw that the short one was a deiler, the features on his murky face oddly twisted and mis-aligned, nose pulled one way, mouth and eyes the other. The other deilers she'd seen were by no means beauties, but their faces weren't contorted like this. It made him easily recognizable. He was the one who had stared at her, cold-eyed, from the back seat of the ambulance during Mayor Mary's abduction. The tall man, she recognized as well. It was that administrator, the man in the black suit who had been arguing with Julie in Malcolm's room. Seeing him again, it occurred to Nieve that she should have taken a look at the bodies while riding in the elevator. Mary herself might have been among them, or Frances, or Malcolm! A frightening thought, but still, she needed to know.

"Can't be done, Murdeth," the deiler was saying, his voice low and gravelly. "The factories aren't ready yet. Twisden's too distracted."

"I'll speak with that hag he's to marry. What's her name?"

"Sarah."

"Have her brought down. This can't go on, the warehouses are full to bursting. See here, Lirk, another batch *has* arrived, as I predicted." Murdeth indicated the gurneys in the open elevator, then frowned. "Where's the porter who's supposed to be managing this material?"

Lirk opened his twisted mouth to answer, but snapped it shut as a second elevator rattled to a stop. When the door slid open, Warlock jumped out. The deilers who were with him hung back, much less eager to leave the elevator once they saw who was standing outside.

"Ah, a dogsbody," said Murdeth. "Not as useful as a real dog and not half as smart, but you'll do in a pinch."

"That girl, did she–?" Warlock blurted.

"No idea. *Would* you like a pinch?" Murdeth rubbed his long forefinger and thumb together in a cooly menacing way that made Lirk wince.

"I'm looking for–"

"Trouble?"

"Yes, she's . . . I mean, *no*, I'm–"

"Enough dithering!" The nasty smile on Murdeth's thin lips vanished. "One more escaped patient isn't going to be the end of us. We'll catch her, we'll catch them all. What might be the end of us, end of *you* more specifically, is if we displease the Impress. We don't want to give her a headache, do we? I suggest you get this elevator unloaded and the cargo moved down to my office for sorting, *pronto.*" He turned on his heel and marched away. "Lirk, come with me."

Lirk gave a nod to the other deilers and moved away, although he took his time in catching up with Murdeth.

"You heard the sawbones," Warlock growled. "Get to work!" He sauntered casually back into the elevator, but his lips were tightly pursed and his face a blotchy red.

When the door closed, the deilers laughed, a seething snicker that sounded like someone shaking sand in a box.

While they were unloading the elevator and wheeling the gurneys away, Nieve nudged Lias and pointed in the opposite direction. With all the deilers headed toward Murdeth's office, they could make a break for it and find a better place to hide until things quieted down.

This plan might have worked if several deilers hadn't remained behind in order to push the empty gurneys back onto the elevator. Impossible to sneak away without getting caught. The thought of all those sharp little teeth made Nieve uneasy. Another blasting would help, but fierce-eye only worked sometimes, usually when she was furious. At the moment she was more nervous than anything. But she was also determined.

She nudged Lias again and pointed to the gurney itself. He returned an appalled look, but reluctantly nodded.

142

Waiting for a moment when the backs of the deilers were turned, both crept quietly up, each onto one of the gurneys, then quickly covered themselves with the sheets, while leaving them rumpled enough for the gurneys to appear unoccupied.

If *this* plan had worked, they soon might have found themselves back upstairs, possibly in an unguarded storeroom.

But . . . by the time the deilers got to the last two gurneys, one said, "Huh, bulky these." He gave one of the sheets a thump with his tough little hand. It was all Nieve could do not to grunt from the hit. "What's this? Some *glaik's* forgotten to dump the body. This one, too." Lias got a sharp rap on the head.

"Lirk?"

"'Spect so."

"Better take'em down," another rasped. "Don't want Lirk gettin' another *pinch*, eh."

As the gurneys rumbled along, Nieve lay absolutely still, playing dead, a game she really *really* didn't want to play.

# –Twenty–

## *Last Office*

*W*hen they wheeled Nieve into Murdeth's office, a chill slipped over her like an extra sheet, one that offered no comfort whatsoever. The room was super-cold, refrigerator cold, and she feared she might start shivering and give herself away. Unless the thought that she was entering a morgue didn't unnerve her first.

"Over here." The deiler who was pushing her gurney kept his voice low. "With this bunch."

"Good enough," said the other, docking Lias' gurney alongside hers. "Slabface won't know the difference."

"Hush, don't want to be wearin' *your* face back to front, eh."

The other gave a grunt, followed by one of those strange seething laughs, then they scuffled away.

Was she in a morgue? One quick look would settle the matter, but she didn't dare stir, not yet. For the moment, she concentrated on keeping absolutely still and warming herself up by imagining a blazing summer sun beating down. Whispering a word or two to Lias was also out. She'd have to play it by ear, figure out what to do once she had a better idea of what sort of fix they were in. In the meantime, *the sun, blazing . . .*

"Lirk, have you been fiddling with the temperature?" she heard Murdeth say. "It's gotten wretchedly hot in here."

"Nay."

A change in the temperature? It was freezing! The man was totally insensitive. She switched her attention to them. From the sound of their voices, Nieve judged that she was situated in the centre of a large room. It was a relief to discover that they weren't too near.

"Get these sorted then. Lumber at the far end, we'll have to stack them, no choice, and changelings by my desk, ready for realignment and shipping. Recognizable troublemakers off to Bone House, as usual. And Lirk, no funny business. I haven't lost my touch, you know."

Lirk said nothing, and presumably got straight to work.

What exactly that work *was*, Nieve couldn't guess. Nothing she'd heard made sense (outside of Murdeth's threat, which was clear enough). But . . . lumber? Changelings? *Bone* House? All she could hear were swishing and rattling noises. If she didn't look she'd never find out – or find out too late.

Tentatively, she raised the sheet and peeked out. What she saw were bodies, also on gurneys, row after row of them, a staggering number. The room itself was cavernous, but it wasn't a morgue, not a hospital morgue, because it was too cluttered and dirty . . . and far too weird. Amid drifts of hair on the floor, entangled with butcher's string and skeins of dust, were stained piles of hospital gowns, balled-up paper bags, toppled rubber boots, drifting feathers, and loose hanks of fur. Inching the sheet up, she took in more of it. Archaic instruments dangled from the ceiling – heavy iron tools, lead bodysuits encrusted with spikes, axes, scythes, shackles, thumbscrews. The shelves on one wall were filled with skulls in a range of sizes, small to extra-large, and on another, as neatly arranged as preserves in a pantry, were jars crammed full of ears and fingers and teeth. Thick rusted chains and fat coils of rope were piled on the floor, and in one corner stood a cluster of wide-mouthed buckets, all filled to the brim with a greasy unidentifiable substance out of which spiraled coils of smoke.

A skinny rat poked its nose out from between one of these buckets, then fled under the nearest gurney in a swift, skittering motion.

The rat was the least alarming thing she'd seen so far. A real morgue would have been far less terrifying.

Murdeth stood beside a massive stone block at the far end of the room, his desk presumably, for on it rested a tall stack of paper, a pile of musty old books, a black rotary-dial telephone, and a stuffed crocodile. Beside the desk, sat the shopping cart full of babies that they had seen earlier. Nieve watched as he reached in and yanked one out roughly, as if he were grabbing a sack of potatoes. Holding the baby in one long-fingered hand, he began poking at it with the other. He twisted its nose, pinched its cheeks, tugged at its ears. He was treating it as if it were a machine that needed adjusting, or a hunk of unmolded plasticine.

*Stop it!*

Murdeth paused, then dropped the baby, as if it had given him an electric shock. It bounced off the desk and tumbled to the floor, where it landed on a pillowy mound of oily rags. He looked at his hands in surprise, then glared at the baby. Nudging it with the toe of his shoe, he sneered, "A *born* troublemaker." He snapped his fingers at Lirk. "Get rid of it."

As Lirk hurried over, Murdeth turned his back and snatched up the phone. Lirk tucked the baby under his arm and carried it off through an archway to another part of the room obscured to Nieve. When he returned, he resumed his duties, which involved pulling sheets off the bodies, giving them a quick once-over, then hauling them off and dumping them onto piles of other bodies of similar shape and size.

The spectacle was appalling enough without realizing that Lirk was working his way steadily toward them.

"Nieve."

Lias, behind her, gave her gurney a tug. While she'd been surveying the room, he'd been silently – and invisibly – active.

"I'm using the fern seed again," he whispered. "When Lirk's not looking, I'll move you closer to the door. Tell you when we're near enough to make a break for it."

"A word with her, yes, and make it snappy, will you." Murdeth had the phone's receiver clamped fast against his ear. "The situation here is intolerable, absolute stacks of them. The sooner they're fully processed the better. Human resources, I ask you, more trouble than they're worth! Additionally, I require another order of that serum from Wormius and Ashe, most of the so-called doctors in this institution don't know what . . . what? *What* was that you said?"

"Now," said Lias.

Lirk was struggling with a tubby body four times his size, grunting as he wrestled it onto a pile of equally tubby ones.

Nieve let the sheet fall back over her face and lay rigid while Lias pulled the gurney toward the door, creeping along as he piloted them through the crowded room. She itched to make a run for it, although knew that the longer they remained undiscovered the better.

Murdeth slammed the receiver down and Lias immediately stopped.

"Lirk," Murdeth growled. "Apparently that filthy little megrim is on the loose. I'd better notify the Impress. I want every new arrival here checked at once. You hear me, *right now.*"

Murdeth snatched up the phone again, and Lias whispered, "Lirk's bolting the door, we'll have to–"

Then she heard nothing. She had no idea what was going on, until she realized that Lirk was standing beside her gurney, breathing close to her ear, his nose making a funny whistling sound. Slowly, he raised the sheet and stared at her with his cold eyes.

Nieve stared right back. Playing dead wasn't going to help now. Of course he recognized her.

"Thought something was fishy here," he said in his harsh scraping voice. "A hag always smells *off.*" He wrinkled his nose in disgust. "One way to fix that." He held up a small vial filled with an acid-green liquid, which, when he gave it a shake, began to bubble and hiss. "This'll clean you right up."

Nieve didn't respond, only continued to stare at him, his wrenched mouth, his squashed nose, his misaligned eyes. She thought of Murdeth tinkering with the baby's features, and wondered at the destructive sort of "touch" he was capable of. Lirk wasn't big – together, she and Lias could jump him – but he was tough, and wouldn't hesitate to douse her with whatever bone-dissolving stuff the vial contained.

"Let me go," she said quietly. "And you'll have your revenge on Murdeth. What he's done to you, it's vicious, undeserved."

He narrowed his eyes. "Don't trust a megrim."

"I can help. Ask my, um . . . my familiar. Familiar, answer!"

"Mistress?" Lias said, uncertainly.

Lirk eyed the empty space behind her head, unable to hide a glimmer of interest.

"Familiar my fanny," he said. "That's nowt but a thieving taran. Got his hands on a tricksy device, eh? Some charm."

Murdeth was murmuring into the phone, on the defensive this time, his bullying surliness reduced to a sycophant's cringing whine.

"A charm, yeah. I'll let you have it," Nieve said quickly. "Think what you could do."

Lirk stole a glance at Murdeth. "I'll have it anyway." He swished the vial in front of her eyes.

"No you won't," Nieve retorted. "You have no idea what *I* can do."

Neither did she, but the threat gave Lirk pause. He glanced at Murdeth once again, then gave a curt nod. "Off then!" his words sandpapered to a rough hiss. "And give it."

"Okay, Lias." Nieve rolled onto her side and slid off the gurney, then hunkered down, keeping close to the floor.

He sighed in exasperation, but his left hand appeared nonetheless, the silver canister held lightly between thumb and forefinger. Lirk snatched it away greedily.

Crouching low, dodging among the gurneys, Nieve skittered toward the door, as warily and anxiously as that rat she'd seen. Lias arrived at the same time, both hands now visible and easing back the bolt.

But fortunately not visible to Murdeth, who'd become too distracted to notice.

As they snuck out, Nieve heard him shouting, "Lirk, you hideous malformed freak, get over here! We've got to find her! D'you hear me? It's . . . she's . . . Lirk? Lirk! Where the deuce *are* you?!"

# Twenty-One

# Down Under

"Take the stairs." Nieve tore past the elevators, one of which was rapidly descending. The flashing lights on the panel above the door indicated its non-stop plunge past the second floor, first floor . . . .

"Whatever you say *mistress*."

She thought he was teasing, but casting a sidelong glance at him as she ran, saw that he was put-out. Really put-out.

"I wasn't serious, you know? About that familiar business."

"It's not that."

"The fern seed? I had to think of *something*. He was going to dump that acid stuff on me."

"Not that, either. But I can see why your gran entrusted them to me."

The elevator sounded a soft *ding* as it arrived. They had put some distance between themselves and the elevators, although not enough. No place to hide, the best they could do was press themselves up against the wall of the corridor. When the door slid open, Mortimer Twisden's fiancée, Sarah, stepped out, unaccompanied, and marched toward Murdeth's office. Luckily, she was intent on her errand and didn't glance their way. Her brisk walk, heels clacking on the tiled floor, reminded Nieve of her mother leaving the house to attend the wake. She felt a stab of anxiety, as if she'd been poked in the stomach with a sharp stick. Why was Sophie mixed up in all this? It was bewildering. She hadn't looked at all comfortable sitting in the operating theatre, but she *had* been there, in bad company, closely observing that odious operation. Was her mother going to start experimenting on people, too? Quickly, Nieve squelched the thought. It wouldn't help.

"So what's the problem?" she said to Lias. "How did I mess up?"

"You spoke my name. With all those dead to hear it. They'll *call* to me now, they'll come for me."

She gaped at him. "Dead people can't hear. Or speak."

"They can."

"News to me. Anyway, those people aren't dead."

"They are."

"Not."

"What are they then?"

"Don't know. Haven't figured that out yet."

"You're daft."

"Yeah? And you're a *taran*, whatever that is. Not the sharpest tool, would be my guess."

"'Tis a spirit." He spoke softly and in all seriousness.

She gave him a shrewd look, then stuck out a finger and prodded him in the ribs, sharply. "You feel pretty solid to me."

"Ow, get away! I'm a failed spirit."

"Oh, for heaven's sake, let's go. If we don't get out of here soon you might just have some success at it."

When they arrived at the stairwell, they found the entrance boarded-up. The thick sheet of plywood nailed over it was covered with graffiti, the usual crazy and rude slogans, among which, painted in puffy red and black lettering, was: **SEPTICLOPS RULE!!!**

"Septiclops are too goamless to rule," Lias said.

"No such thing. It'll be some soccer team with a dumb name."

"Aye, and they'll use a head for a ball."

As they hurried toward the only other exit, a door at the far end of the corridor, she said, "This has got to lead to the underground parking. There'll be more stairs, another elevator. Once we're back in the main part of the hospital we can go for help, tell them what's going on. Julie will back us up. Not all of the doctors and nurses have been . . . whatever's been done to them."

"Overtaken," said Lias softly, hanging back a little as they arrived at the door and Nieve pushed through.

She stepped out cautiously and scanned the area, mindful of any lurking dangers in the parking garage.

Except that there was no parking garage.

What she saw was a street, a long street with ancient-looking houses lining both sides, wonky houses, scrunched together and leaning into one another like a mouthful of crooked, snaggled teeth. The top floors of the houses leaned so far over the street that they touched the ones leaning over on the other side, creating an unusual, cloistered archway. In the moonlight, or rather with her moon-bright vision, dimmer but still in force, the houses seemed to waver as if they weren't quite solid enough.

"Every one of them haunted, too," said Lias, coming up beside her.

"You should feel right at home then." She tried to sound jokey, but the unexpected sight had unsettled her. "This must

be an old part of the city I've never heard about. So we're not underground after all."

"We are. That's where the Black City begins. Under, always under. And then it creeps out."

"Lias—" She was going to tell him to stop creeping *her* out, but he'd grabbed her arm and shook his head to silence her.

"Listen."

Something was moving along the street toward them, making a rumbling, creaking noise, faint at first, but growing louder as it neared.

"Over here." Still holding onto her arm, he tugged her toward the closest house.

Nieve balked, casting around for a better place to take cover. It's not that she believed him when he told her the houses were haunted; she just didn't like the look of them. Flimsy and jerry-built, they didn't appear safe – the slightest disturbance might make them collapse into a heap of rubble.

Lias' hand trembled as he clutched her arm, but he clutched it firmly enough to pull her up the front steps toward an entrance that was nothing more than a black gap, the door itself missing. He clearly didn't relish the idea of going in, either, but there was nowhere else to hide. No bushes, no fences, no outdoor ornaments. The area fronting the houses was barren, and their backyards, if they had them, inaccessible.

They paused briefly on the threshold as the rumbling grew louder and a bulky silhouette came into view at the end of the street. There was nothing for it – they plunged in.

A narrow, gloomy vestibule led into an old-fashioned sitting room, long-abandoned. The chairs and sofas, the rickety little tables, the gewgaws on the mantel, the rugs and paintings and mirrors, hadn't been cleaned in years. Stepping over to the front window, they broke through spider's silk as resistant as mesh and their feet sank into dust as deep as a layer of freshly fallen snow. But fresh it wasn't. The air in the place was cloying and damp, almost palpable, seeming to press in on them.

The window glass was cracked and covered in an oily grime. Nieve considered cleaning off a patch with her sleeve, but didn't in case the whole thing shattered at her touch. She had to settle for a muzzy and somewhat distorted view, which made what was to come even more unbelievable.

Crouching below the window and peering over the ledge, they watched as a wooden cart with huge wobbly wheels appeared. The cart was being pulled, not by horses or oxen, but by people, four in all, three men and one woman. All were barefoot, but otherwise dressed as they might be for a day at the office, the men in suits and ties and the woman in a pant-suit. But their clothing was in rough shape – rumpled, torn, filthy – and so were they. They were covered in cuts and bruises, struggling on, exhausted. They appeared to be in shock, too, and no wonder, Nieve thought ruefully. To go from pushing a pen in an office tower up among the clouds, to pulling a cart like peasants through some sort of grim, shadowy underworld. Not everyone ended up in Murdeth's nightmarish room, then? There were other kinds of nightmare to be had here as well.

Lumbering along beside the cart were a pair of thick-bodied guards, much taller than their captives, with overlarge heads covered in stiff bristles, like the ones on push-brooms. Their sullen, purplish faces were covered in boils and scars, and ranged across their brows, like marbles randomly scattered and embedded in mud, were eyes, lots of eyes. She counted them, astonished, then counted them again. Each guard had *seven* eyes . . . eyes that seemed to look here, there, every which way!

"Goamless," Lias murmured.

The office workers struggled ahead with the cart, dragging it up to the hospital door. As soon as they arrived, the door opened and two deilers emerged. Behind them stumbled a group of people, half-asleep, or drugged, and barely able to stand. The deilers herded this docile, unresisting group to the back of cart, where the guards seized each of them roughly by an arm or a leg, or by the seat of the pants, and tossed them on.

Three in the group were children not much older than Nieve. One child, the last in line, took a half-hearted swing at the guards. This earned him a clout on the head which sent him with a muted cry to his knees. A guard then grabbed him by the hair, yanked him to his feet, and flung him on top of the others.

It was Malcolm.

Nieve rubbed her eyes. It *was* Malcolm.

"My *friend*." She jumped up.

"Wait," said Lias. "Get down! Before they see you. That's the one thing they're good at."

Nieve slipped back into a crouch, fuming. They were pretty good at savagery, too. Noting that one had a whip slung like a coil of rope around his shoulder, and the other a bulbous club rammed into his belt, she more than ever regretted the loss of the fern seeds.

When the deilers returned to the hospital, the guards barked out some commands – along with a few kicks – to get the office workers moving again. They dragged the wagon around in a half-circle and started off down the street, groaning and struggling even more under the added weight. The

guard with the whip snapped it once in the air and the groaning stopped, if not the struggling.

As soon as they were gone, Lias was on his feet. "That's it." He bounded out of the room, cobwebs streaming behind and raising a flurry of dust. He couldn't get out of the creepy, airless house fast enough. Neither could Nieve – she had to save Malcolm! She might have even beat Lias to the open doorway if something hadn't caught her eye.

In one of the chairs, sitting pert on a cushion, was an object she hadn't noticed on the way in. A curiously familiar object. Stooping to retrieve it, she was surprised to see that it was indeed like one she used to own. A china cat, black, with green eyes, a pink nose, and gilded collar. She hadn't seen hers in years, and had in fact forgotten all about it until now. Rubbing the dust off this one, she was even more surprised to find that it had exactly the same chipped ear (she'd dropped hers once), and the same bare spot on the top of its head. (She'd rubbed the paint off hers, stroking it like a real cat, wishing she had one. Mr. Mustard Seed, a stray, had arrived at their door not long after.) Nieve turned the china cat over to examine its base. The back of her neck began to prickle as she ran her finger over the capital letter "N" etched there, raggedly scratched into the porcelain . . . with a penknife? . . . as she had done with hers?

"Mine!" someone said.

Startled, she looked up. A figure, slightly smaller than herself, stood at the other end of the room in an open archway. It was a girl, very pale, with dark hair like her own, and with features *very* like her own . . .

"That's mine," the girl repeated. "Mine, mine, *mine*. So are *you!* You're–"

With a shriek, Nieve dropped the cat and *ran* for her life.

—Twenty-Two—

# Lich-Way

"*W*hat *is* this place?"

Nieve stood, shivering, behind a dead tree. She had streaked past Lias with such speed that he'd despaired of catching up with her. But she herself had to stop short when she almost caught up with the cart, which the captives were dragging across a stark city square. The square had a lone, leafless tree in its centre, that Nieve – then Lias – had taken refuge behind. Not that it offered much in the way of protection from inquisitive eyes. A skeletal screech owl, all bone and feathers, was perched unnoticed on a branch high up, peering down at them.

"No place you'd visit less you had to," Lias answered, still out of breath. "What happened?"

"Saw something." She didn't want to describe it. She'd be describing herself.

"There'll be more."

"Not like that I hope." She inched away from him. "You *are* a spirit. You've been here before."

"Aye, I've been. But I'm no spirit. Failed, remember."

She gave him such a skeptical look, that he added, "This place, Nieve, think of it as a . . . a kind of net. A net that the present passes through as it flows into the past."

"What?"

"A net, and it catches things. The way memory does, how you remember some things, not others."

Nieve thought about this. "Are you caught?"

"I am."

"What about me?"

"Not yet."

"Okay, so the stuff caught in this make-believe net of yours, the people I mean, can they get back to where they came from?"

"Some can."

Nieve stared after the wagon, which had taken a turn down a narrow lane. "I'm glad Frances didn't see that guard hit Malcolm. What's happened to her, d'you think?"

"Might be she's still in the hospital looking for him."

"Yeah, maybe."

Nieve knew that neither of them thought this likely, since Frances would have attracted too much attention to herself not to get caught. But wherever she was, whatever had happened to her, she'd be counting on them to follow through if they could. Question was, *could* they? Whatever this place was, it was uncommonly . . . *heavy*. She could feel it like a weight pushing down on her, compressing her, sapping her energy. She would have liked nothing better than to make her escape – now.

The cart's noise had grown more distant.

"Do you know where they're taking them?" she said.

"Not sure. The city keeps changing, it's never the same for long."

"We'll lose them if we don't get going."

"We will." Lias made it sound like a good idea.

But they kept on nonetheless, entering the lane and moving cautiously along the dusty track between the looming houses. Outside of the cart, faintly creaking and rumbling ahead, the city was absolutely silent. No cars, no music or voices, no machinery humming or buzzing in the background. No white noise, only a black silence. It was unnerving. But even more so when something suddenly skimmed past with a keening cry. Above them a small, dark shape hurtled along, then vanished down the street.

"What was *that*?"

"Lich-owl," Lias shuddered. "They say it's cry portends a death."

"Good thing I never believe what 'they' say, then."

Brave words. Words Nieve hoped would quell her rising panic, or at least keep it in check as they continued down the lane. The houses on both sides pressed in on them, leaning even more steeply into the already tight passage, as if hungry for occupants. Not that they didn't already have plenty of those. Lias had warned her, but still she was unprepared for the hideous, ghostly faces that appeared in windows they passed. Faces that flickered in and out of visibility, that glared at them bug-eyed, or leered and laughed uproariously, if soundlessly.

"Don't look," Lias warned.

He didn't have to warn her twice about those ones, but there were others that compelled her to look. One kindly-featured old woman followed her from window to window, smiling sweetly, invitingly. She reminded Nieve of Gran. Drawn to her, unable to resist, she stepped closer. As she did so the old woman's grandmotherly face blossomed with delight and recognition. Perhaps she was a long-lost relative? How wonderful it would be to sink into her arms, to feel safe again, to forget all the frightening things that had happened.

Lias touched the pewter amulet on his cloak and muttered something under his breath. Instantly, the old woman's expression darkened and shifted. Her delight at observing Nieve turned into loathing, her adoring recognition into guile. Her soft features began to melt and contort into a face ghoulish and gloating. She bared her broken, bloody teeth and licked her purple lips . . . and then whirled back into the darkness, as though seized by an unseen hand.

Recoiling and sickened, Nieve stumbled back to Lias' side. "What did you say?" She couldn't help but think that while her brave words earlier were only that, he knew a language more useful, more powerful. The language of ghosts and dead things.

"Told her to flake off."

"Ah."

"Picked that one up in your schoolyard."

"Why don't I believe you?"

He shrugged. "Got me."

"You pick up a lot of things."

"I do. Am a scavenger, a scrounger. How I survive."

"*Who* are you Lias, really?"

"Later for that, Nieve. I promise. Haven't you noticed, the more we speak, the more they're attracted to us. They love the sound of it, our voices are like gold to them. Like . . . breath."

"Our voices *are* breath. You're just trying to shut me up."

"Exactly."

"Exactly? You got that one from *me*. You're not a scavenger, you're a thief, like Lirk said." Not the kindest accusation, she realized, seeing as he'd just saved her skin.

"There's only one thing I want to steal and you don't have it."

"Glad to hear it."

They walked along in silence for a few moments, but she couldn't *not* ask.

"Who does?"

"Will you *hush*."

He paused, listening closely. Before she could protest, he yanked her into another open doorway.

An eerie sound slit open the silence, a howling and baying that rapidly grew louder – and louder still – until finally a fearsome pack of wild dogs appeared at the bottom of the lane. In seconds, they were streaming past. Thirty, forty, frothing, red-eyed, black beasts running as one, like a many-headed river, turbulent and raucous. Nieve and Lias pressed back farther into the darkness of the house as the creatures coursed past, their feet never once touching the ground, a spectral horde. Not a single speck of dust trembled in the air after they had gone.

"Hell-hounds," Lias whispered, as their cries were swallowed up in the depths of the city. "Let's get out of here!" They hustled out of the house before the walls clapped shut on them, which they had been straining to do, bending and creaking. Once out and moving again, he added, "Old Shock, your doctor's dog, he's got some of that in him."

"Artichoke? Get lost."

"How do you think he was able to fight Gowl? How could he have led you through the dark so easily if he didn't have some of the dark in him?"

"I thought we weren't supposed to talk?" she challenged, irritated. Artichoke was a wonderful dog, but ordinary, nothing like those baying beasts. *She* was ordinary, her world was ordinary – not dull, not empty, but not like *this,* where everything was sinister and unreal and horrifying.

A coconut-sized clod of earth, stuck with shreds of dried grass and bone and buttons, was lying in the lane before her and in her annoyance she gave it a kick, a fiercer one than intended. The clod exploded into a cloud of dust and flying fragments, and in doing so released a small, furry, bat-faced man, who'd been tucked up inside. This little man jumped to his feet and began to hop around furiously, shaking his fist at her. Protesting still, he charged toward one of the buildings and wriggled through a crack in the steps.

Lias was about to comment, but before he could, she turned an angry eye on him. "I *don't* want to know."

They continued in silence, Nieve's a simmering one, which, if nothing else, stood her in good stead for what was to follow.

## –Twenty-Three–

# *Walleyes*

*O*n leaving the lane behind they entered a maze of streets, moving stealthily behind the cart, which had picked up its pace following a sharp volley of whip-snapping. In this part of the city the buildings they passed were more of a random clutter, a graveyard of old styles, crumbling and derelict, a number decorated with gargoyles – hideous, leering faces that appeared to leap out at them but were insensible, too dry-throated even to spew fetid water on them. Most of the buildings, the tenements and shops and taverns, were as empty as shells. All facade, no threat, as though someone had simply dreamt them up and hadn't bothered to fill in the details, including the ghosts.

When Nieve made the mistake of mentioning this to Lias, he responded that most of what haunted this part of the city – the wirricowes, the foliots, the rawheads – must have already infiltrated the upper one and would be spreading out into the countryside, and to her town, as Wormius and Ashe had done.

"Might still be a few leftover," he added. "I wouldn't count them out."

"Wonderful." She didn't enquire what a "rawhead" might be – she was in such a bad mood that she was beginning to feel like one herself. Might as well practice, she thought grimly, because if they got lost, which they'd almost done a couple of times in miscalculating the turn the cart had taken, they too might end up as nothing more than phantoms drifting endlessly through the streets of this nothing city. Her, a distinctly evil-tempered one, bumping blindly into things. What she hadn't mentioned to Lias was that the eyedrops Gran had given her were losing their power and her vision was fading. She could still see well enough at present, but had no idea how fast her sight would go. Hours from now? Minutes?

In her uncertainty, as if trying to outrun it, she put on a burst of speed.

"Hey." Lias scrambled to catch up.

As they progressed, the houses grew larger and grander, the streets wider and laid with slate. Since it was more open here, they had to keep themselves far enough behind so as not to be noticed, while at the same time Nieve longed to rush ahead. Added to the problem of her diminishing night-sight was her growing conviction that they were being followed. Not that she'd heard any steps dogging theirs, any rustlings or patterings, however faint. It was more a feeling, a tingling alertness, a strong sense of something at her back.

She spun around and surveyed the street behind. Nothing there. Or nothing her weakening eyesight could detect.

"What is it?" whispered Lias.

"Don't know. Something."

They kept on – what choice was there? – if more warily.

Walls rose up on either side of them covered with dead ivy, branches crawling over the stone like thick, black veins. Inside the walls were decayed mansions of the sort Nieve sometimes read about in novels, safe in the company of fearless fictional children. She'd found the brooding menace of those houses thrilling and fun, while the very real menace of the ones that lay behind these walls was not thrilling at all – and as for fun? How she wished she could take the Black City in her hands like a book and snap it shut, never to be opened again.

Lias motioned to her, pressing a finger to his lips as he moved nearer to the wall on his left.

The cart had finally come to a stop and the guards appeared to be fiddling with the latch on a gate. After rattling it and cursing at it and giving it a boot, the gate swung open and they herded their business slaves in, which involved more cursing and boots all round for them as well. Squinting after them as the wagon disappeared through the gate, Nieve wondered how it was that the captives had been able to see in this solid darkness, and realized that they probably couldn't. Same for their human cargo, same for Malcolm. All might as well have been muffled in black hoods, prisoners of a lightless nightmare.

Once the others were inside, they moved ahead, staying close to the wall. With her ear practically grazing it, Nieve heard a tiny, raspy sound that she took to be an insect of some sort – a welcome sign of life, no matter how small. But then, pausing to look at the wall more closely, she was startled to see a face staring out at her through a network of ivy branches. Gargoyle, she thought, although this face wasn't anything like the grotesques she'd seen earlier, the grinning monsters and glaring devils. This face was pretty, the face of a young child. Curious, she was about to reach out and touch its cheek – it seemed so lifelike – when Lias waved her on impatiently – this was no time to dawdle.

But it wasn't long before he stopped, too. When Nieve caught up with him, he was staring at the wall, transfixed. It had evidently crumbled at some point and been repaired, although not with stone. A much softer material had been used. Bodies. Human bodies of all sizes, all ages, male and female, were woven together, arms and legs twisted and linked and wound, in places awkwardly bent or cruelly contorted, whatever was required to tighten the weave. Some were upside down. Some faced out and others in. Some had their eyes closed, but most not. All were expressionless, faces blanched of emotion, and all, Nieve was sure, were alive.

"Can they feel anything?" She kept her voice low, and tried to keep it steady.

"Probably not," said Lias, his own voice a bit shaky. After a moment, after they'd both absorbed the worst of the shock, he added, "We're obviously in the right place."

"What do you mean?"

"Bone House, remember? Where the troublemakers end up. Are you sure you want to go in? The odds aren't much in our favour."

"Are you?"

He nodded. "Have to."

"Me, too." She thought of Malcolm, in *there*, behind this living wall. She couldn't help everyone, couldn't free everyone, but one person, maybe *one*. . . . "We can sneak in, check it out first. Like I did at Ferrets."

"Gate's still unlatched, I think."

They edged closer to it, both keeping their own eyes averted from those that stared out, wide-eyed, from the wall. The gate itself consisted of two tall, skinny men, their feet and shins badly bruised. The hand of one, stiff as iron, reached out to clasp hands with the other, who did likewise. Nieve shivered to see it, the hands of these unfortunate brothers, twins, serving as latches. She shivered again . . . and then *froze* as a hand, much smaller, but as cold as metal, seized her arm.

A girl who had been wedged in beside the gate, stuck in like mortar to fill a hole, had swiftly – and improbably – reached out and clutched her. Nieve barely stopped herself from screaming. She tried to yank her arm away, but the girl held fast. Struggling to free herself, Nieve looked quickly at her, then more closely, shocked at what she saw. *Who* she saw.

It was Alicia Overbury, cold as death and as immobile, except for the one hand that grasped Nieve so firmly, fingers digging into her arm. Alicia's eyes, too, seemed overlarge with anguish. An awareness flickered in them.

"*Alicia,*" Nieve whispered. "How did . . . ?" Useless question. Alicia was incapable of speech. It was that night school, Nieve thought, that vile teacher. She had never liked Alicia, but felt sorry and sick to see her trapped here. Maybe she'd stopped eating those poisonous treats, as Nieve had advised, and had woken up enough to cause some trouble. But how had she overcome her numbness, unlike the others here, to reach out? And to what end? Nieve didn't know if Alicia was trying to stop her from entering Bone House and suffering the same fate, or if she was imploring her for help.

"I'll do what I can, Alicia, " she promised. "I'll do everything I possibly can."

Feeling her grip loosen, Nieve touched her hand lightly – how cold it felt! – and pulled away.

Alicia's arm fell by her side, heavy as a plank.

Nieve turned back to the "gate," expecting Lias to be waiting anxiously. Odd that he hadn't tried to intervene when Alicia seized her.

But Lias wasn't there; he hadn't waited for her. She decided that he must have gone in before Alicia grabbed her, assuming that she was following right behind. In that case, he wouldn't have gone far. Nieve took one last look at Alicia, nodded, and then slipped into the grounds of Bone House.

"Lias?" She spoke as softly as possible. "Can't see you." Her eyes were worse. It was getting harder to make things out.

Something swished by overhead, crying sharply. The lich-owl again. That harbinger of . . . Nieve shuddered. And then it struck her, as though the owl itself had told her: Lias was gone. Something had happened to him. *Lias was gone!*

She cast around desperately, dearly hoping she was wrong, knowing she wasn't. No idea what to do – she had to *think*, she mustn't panic – she ran behind what she took to be a bush that was branching massively and palely in the dark.

The second she crouched behind it, the bush shot out a spray of wiry branches, several of which snaked around her neck, cinching her as inescapably as a rabbit caught in a snare. She clutched at them, fighting and struggling to free herself, but this only caused the coiled branches to tighten.

A figure, appearing out of the air like a twist of smoke, began to take shape as it advanced slowly toward her.

He was barely visible to her, but she knew exactly who it was. Not someone she had *ever* wanted to see again.

"My, how *stupid* of you," observed the Weed Inspector, closing in. "As I predicted. Eh, *Nieve?*"

# Twenty-Four

# Our Mutual Fiend

Once he spoke her name, he didn't stop. He uttered it quietly enough, creepily enough, but as he marched her through the long halls of Bone House, taunting her, the walls themselves picked up her name and bounced it along between them until it got louder and louder: Nieve . . . . **Nieve** . . . . NIEVE! Her name preceded her like an announcement, echoing along corridors bleached and brittle-looking, as if the place really were made of bone.

Nieve reached up to touch her neck, trying to assess how badly she was hurt. The coiling branches that the Weed Inspector had roughly unwound and torn off, had left painful, throbbing welts on her skin.

"Hands at your sides." The Weed Inspector walked behind close as a shadow, breathing dank air on her head. "*Nieve.*"

Nieve . . . **Nieve** . . . NIEVE!!

"Why?" she challenged. "Are you afraid I'll hurt you?" She'd been caught so easily that she *did* feel stupid. And if, under the circumstances, belligerence was stupid, too, then fine, she didn't care. She delicately probed the welts.

The odious man (if he *was* a man) chuckled. "You don't really believe all that megrim nonsense, do you, Nieve?"

*No, I don't*, she thought. But said, "You'll see. You'll see what I can do." A threat that sounded as empty as her own name did echoing down the hall.

He chuckled again, mirthlessly, and breathed more dank air on her head, but didn't say anything more until they arrived at a huge set of double doors at the end of the hall. "You are to have the great honour of meeting Elixibyss." This name sank with a tremor into the walls and was not repeated. "The Impress, Elixibyss. Behave. I highly recommend it."

The Weed Inspector opened the doors and shoved her in, then hastily closed them again. She heard the lock turn.

As she had surmised, the woman before her was the one who had pursued her at Ferrets. She still wore the hat with the veil covering her face, although she was now dressed in a shimmering purple gown with long batwing sleeves. She sat in a blocky regal chair at one end of a long, limestone dining room table, drumming her long fingers on its dull surface, raising little puffs of dust as she did so.

The room wasn't well-lit by any means, but was bright enough for Nieve to see. Besides the flickering butt-ends of candles stuck in old bottles arrayed on the table and set in sconces on the wall, there were curious bluish-white lights that roved independently around the room. About the size of ping-pong balls, they wove in and around the chairs at the table and floated past the adjacent fireplace, pausing to hover over a large, covered object in the corner, a trunk possibly. Nieve watched them, fascinated. She hadn't expected to see anything here quite so . . . .

"Enchanting?" said Elixibyss, her voice surprisingly soft, even pleasant. None of the harshness she'd heard at Ferrets. "Don't stare at them, my dear. Naughty spherals, they'll

173

mesmerize you and then the next thing you know you'll be walking off the roof. Wouldn't want that now, would we?"

Nieve turned to observe her, this Impress. Which was supposed to mean what? Queen of the imps? The thick veil shrouded her face entirely, which suggested that she was a fright, a gorgon with features too alarming to expose. Still, Nieve knew she had to prepare herself for the shock of seeing her unveiled. The woman (if she *was* a woman) was about to dine, after all. The table was set for two, with plates and glasses and silverware, and she had a sinking feeling that one place setting was intended for her.

She was right.

"Take a seat, please. You are late, but as this is your first night here, I have forgiven you. There will be many nights, dear, many *many* nights. Do sit down."

Nieve took the seat indicated at the other end of the table, relieved to be situated some distance away from her. She'd been eyeing the peculiar ropey thing – some sort of bizarre jewelry? – that was slung around Elixibyss' neck. Red as a sinew, it seemed to be alive, a skinned "thing" that twisted and writhed.

Repulsion overcame her alarm, and she blurted, "Why do you have that wall in front of your house? With those people . . . it's *horrible!*"

"Why, thank you. It *is* horrible, isn't it. I'm so glad you like it. I do so enjoy being surrounded by people."

Nieve stared at her dinner plate. She couldn't believe this was happening to her.

"Bone china," commented Elixibyss.

Nieve examined the plate and sucked in her breath. The *bone*-handled cutlery, the freckled, skin-soft napkins, the *finger* bowl containing what looked like . . .

175

"Marinated fingernails. A little something to nibble on if you're nervous. I can understand how excited you must be to finally meet me . . . *Nieve.*"

That voice.

"*You're* the one," Nieve said, looking up at her quickly. The haunting and insinuating voice that had followed her when she'd been walking to Ferrets. Likewise the one that had burrowed into her head during that fog attack.

"I am the one, yes. Absolutely the *One*. I've been calling and calling you, Nieve. Because you're mine."

"I am *not* yours." Trying not to be too obvious about it, she glanced aside, sizing-up the room. The double doors were the only way out, and the Weed Inspector had locked them.

"You can't run. Not this time, not from *me*."

Nieve glared at her. If only she could penetrate that veil, she'd knock her out of her chair with a good blasting.

"You have spunk," Elixibyss observed. "I like that."

She continued to glare. "Did you follow us here? That was *you*, wasn't it?"

"Follow you?" Elixibyss laughed. "Life's too short. Well, it *is* for some people. Perhaps it was the boogeyman. Not a very solid citizen, I'm afraid."

Joke all you want, thought Nieve, undeterred. "But you have Lias, you took him, I know it."

"Ahh, the boy. Would you like to see him?"

"Yes," she said, indignant. "Of course. You better not have hurt him, either."

"Ha, you are so delicious, my dear. So feisty, eh?" She got up and walked over to the large object in the corner near the fireplace that was covered with a black felt cloth. "On the contrary, I'm keeping him safe." Elixibyss whipped off the cloth. "Violà! Here you see a rebellious young heart where it belongs. In a rib cage!"

"Lias!"

Nieve jumped up, but the Impress stopped her with a pointed finger and a command, "Sit! Did I give you permission to leave the table? I did not."

She sat back down, glowering.

Lias was imprisoned in what indeed was a cage made of ribs. Ribs and all kinds of other bones. A dismantled skeleton, minus the skull, had been assembled and wired together with more of that sinewy red stuff, forming a cage about the size of a medium dog kennel. No room to stand, Lias was curled up inside, face tucked into his knees, his fiery hair flat and lifeless on his head.

Elixibyss reached up and plucked a small gold box with a hinged lid off the mantel. She gave this a rough shake, an action which also seemed to make Lias shake. The contents, whatever they were, rattled around inside like dice.

"This little piggy . . . "she said, amused, watching Lias tremble. She rattled the box once more and tormented him a moment longer before replacing it on the mantel and tossing the cloth back over the cage. "A harmless little game," she explained to Nieve, as she strode back to the table and resumed her seat. "The boy and I, we understand one another."

"Doesn't look harmless to me," Nieve said. "Looks vicious and cruel."

"No more vicious and cruel than turning someone into a glob of jam."

"What?"

"I understand that my head administrator at the hospital, Murdeth, has been discovered in a sticky situation, shall we say, on the floor of his office. Completely boiled down – nothing left but jam with eyebrows! A bore, if you must know, he'll have to be replaced. But still, wickedly funny of you, my dear. I'm so glad to see you have a sense of humour."

Lirk, Nieve thought, remembering the vial of acidic stuff he almost poured on her. "I didn't have anything to do with . . . with *that*."

"Now, now, don't fib to your darling mother."

"You're not my mother!" The woman was clearly insane. Nieve realized she shouldn't have said anything. Better to go along with her, not get her too worked up. She'd have to bide her time (assuming she had some) until she could rescue Lias . . . then together, Malcolm.

"Oh, but I *am*," Elixibyss said quietly.

Nieve tried to hold her tongue, but failed. "*My* mother doesn't trap anyone in cages, or offer fingernails to her guests to nibble on, or . . . or have *moss* growing on her arm. Or mould, whatever it is." When the Impress had pointed at her earlier, the sleeve of her gown had fallen away, revealing a patch on her forearm that was greenish and weirdly furred.

"Ah, but does she look like this?" Elixibyss promptly raised her hands and flipped the veil back to show her face.

And Nieve, astonished, saw that it was true. It *was . . . she did* resemble her mother, shockingly so. The same eyes, the same nose, the same everything, including her smile.

No, the smile wasn't quite right. It had a wryness, a twist of cruelty in it that Sophie's never had.

"Let's eat then, shall we!" Elixibyss rubbed her dead-white hands together in anticipation. "Weazen will bring our dinner presently, now that we've had our cozy little reunion. I'll be dining on snake tonight, keeps one young, that's the thing. And you, my love, will be having Gowl. You remember him, don't you? Poor creature never quite got over that nasty turn you gave him, and I thought, well, what a shame to let him go to waste."

Nieve said nothing, only stared and stared. If she were the fainting type, she might have done that and gotten some relief, a respite from this horror, from *her*, however brief. But she wasn't, and she didn't.

# —Twenty-Five—

# *Leftovers*

Nieve did not dine on the charred, gristly, stinking, and still-smoking lumps of Gowl that the elderly deiler servant, Weazen, dumped onto her plate from a platter that was almost as big as Weazen herself. She refused to touch anything on the table, including the water (was it water?) and sat motionless, watching Elixibyss dig into a fresh, raw python with gusto.

"Not hungry?" Elixibyss enquired, fork aloft and waving a bloody chunk of snake in the air. "You'll have to finish every crumb on your plate before you leave the table, you know." She smiled. "That's what mothers always say."

"Not my mother," Nieve said, watching her closely.

"Naturally." The smile faltered a little. "I'm different."

Nieve couldn't agree more. How had she done it, this impersonation? Some impish trick? She supposed it could be an illusion of some sort. Or theft, an identity theft that was actually physical. But what did it mean for Sophie herself? If this . . . this creature, had taken her form – and it was so very much like her, disturbingly accurate – then where and in what form was she?

"My mother wouldn't hurt a fly," Nieve said.

"Oh, flies!" Elixibyss waved a hand, the one holding the knife. "Overrated. No flavour. You're right, I definitely

180

wouldn't do that." She wound a strand of snake innards around her fork like a piece of spaghetti.

"You have blood on your chin," Nieve said.

She looked up sharply at Nieve, nettled, but then cleared her throat and said, with a little laugh, "Dear me, how gauche." Snatching up her napkin, she gave her chin a vigorous wipe. "Daughters can be so critical."

She wants me to *believe* her, Nieve thought, incredulous. They really do think I'm stupid.

"If you're my mother," she said, trying to sound genuinely inquisitive, "where's Dad, and why are we here, why aren't we at home?"

Elixibyss gripped her cutlery. "Questions, questions! Children ask so many questions, don't they? Well, figure it out, Nieve. That fool Sutton isn't your father . . . and Sophie *isn't* your mother. She's my sister. You're not blind are you? You can see how perfectly I resemble her! The truth is you're *my* child. Mine!" She paused to let this revelation sink it. "They were minding you for me."

"For *twelve* years?"

"Time flies. I've been busy." She slammed her cutlery down on the table. The knife blade quivered like a tuning fork and the fork itself spread out its tines like a hand fending off a blow. "If you must know, that meddlesome old granny of yours kept trying to stop me from fetching you."

Good old Gran!

"So you're saying Gran is your *mother*?" This was getting to be more incredible by the minute.

Elixibyss made a face. "One doesn't always get the mother one deserves."

Nieve made no response, only thought that somewhere, buried in this foul heap of lies, was a glimmer of truth. But what was it? Before she was born, there *had* been an Aunt Liz, an older sister of her mother's, who had died, but surely not . . . .

"The boy has been very useful in that regard. Bringing you here to me . . . oh yes, I hope you didn't think he was actually helping you." Elixibyss cast a sly look at the covered cage. "He'll do anything to get at that little treasure in the gold box. *Anything.*"

"I don't believe you." Nieve followed her look. Not a whimper out of Lias, not a sound.

"Plenty of time for that, if belief is your thing. You'll see how trustworthy he is." She turned back to Nieve, her dark eyes – Sophie's eyes – intent. "Oh, we'll have such fun . . . fun and games, I can promise you that. Now that everything is progressing so nicely, we'll be free to live where we prefer. Our ancestral home here, or abroad. Yes . . . the darker it grows, the freer we'll be."

"What does darkness have to do with it?"

"Because I can't tolerate light!" She pinched her brow with her long pale fingers. "It gives me migraines. I'm highly sensitive, as I'm sure you can tell. Sunlight hurts my eyes. And it makes everything too hot! On top of that it also makes things grow, and my dear, you simply wouldn't believe the racket things make while they're *growing*. Noise, noise, noise! Dead things are much more agreeable . . . so soothing." The Impress reached for the candy dish that Weazen had set out before her. The dish was heaped high with what Nieve had thought were mints, but now realized were pills, a lot like the kind Sophie herself took whenever she had headaches, which, now that she thought of it, had been often.

As Elixibyss stuffed a handful of headache pills into her mouth, Nieve slumped in her chair, all at once felled by exhaustion, hunger, dismay. And fear. That too, it twisted and coiled within her, as if she'd been the one to eat a snake. But she wasn't going to let it show, wasn't going to give this, *whatever* she was, the satisfaction.

"My dear child, you're tired! Time for beddy-bye. I was so looking forward to playing some games. Checkers. Crokinole! I'm a marvel at that, a champion! Much better than you. No question, I'd slay you, blast your markers clean off the board, obliterate them, pulverize them to . . . *ahem* . . . but I tell you what, I'm such a softie that I'm going to let you finish Gowl tomorrow. We'll have leftovers! *You* will, anyway. Weazen will show you to your room. But before you go, I have something for you. Something that will let me keep a watch over my darling girl and keep her safe. Now that I have you here, I simply can't keep my eyes off you."

*

As Nieve mounted the wide, dusty stairs, following behind Weazen, the ring that Elixibyss had slipped onto her forefinger blinked in the dark. When she raised her right hand to look at it, she saw it radiating a sickly sulfur-infused light. Presumably the kind of light the Impress *could* tolerate, being a "nightborn thing," as Lias had called her. Even shadows need some light to exist, don't they?

The instant she'd passed through the doors of the dining room, Nieve had tried to pull the ring off, but the band resisted, tightening as she tugged at it. The more she tugged, the more it tightened, squeezing her finger painfully until she gave up. It looked like the rings Sophie and Dunstan Warlock had been wearing, only this stone was even more lifelike, a moist eye with a dark, gold-flecked iris roving in its setting like a real eye in a socket. She was keenly aware of it as she climbed the stairs, cold and heavy on her finger.

Although Weazen carried a candle, and some spherals from the dining room had tagged along, she still found it difficult to make out what this part of Bone House was like. It smelled fusty and slightly rotten, like a damp and mouldering basement, and she guessed from the hollow, echoing sounds their footsteps made on the stairs that the place was empty, not much in the way of furniture or carpets. There were some portraits on the wall at least, for she saw some elaborate, gilded frames as the floating spherals crisscrossed above her head. But when she stopped to look at one in passing, holding the ring up for light, she saw that the frame contained a mirror, not a painting. The ring winked coyly at its own reflection, and gave Nieve's finger a painful pinch when she dropped her hand.

They progressed slowly upward, Weazen huffing as she mounted the steps. Observing her creaking around during dinner, Nieve wondered at her age, and thought she had to be ancient. So old that her wrinkles had wrinkles. But not so old that her wits had deserted her. She served Elixibyss, true, but Nieve got the impression that she was in no way subservient. Like Lirk, it wouldn't do to cross her. A glob of jam? Nice fate! Well, she wasn't going to shed any tears over what had happened to Murdeth.

Up to this point, Weazen hadn't uttered a word, so Nieve was surprised to hear her say, in her raspy deiler voice, "Remember, miss, she can see you, but she can't hear you."

They had reached the landing of the second floor. Keeping her head averted from Nieve, Weazen continued, "Times she sleeps, too, while she claims not to. This way, miss." She turned left and advanced down a narrow hallway, while the spherals, unable to tempt Nieve to take a headfirst plunge over the banisters, whirled off in the opposite direction.

Nieve, following, whispered, "Can she see everything?"

"Most everything, depends."

"Depends on the ring?"

"Aye, take care with that. She's not to see us talking."

They passed several closed doors before Weazen stopped at one, and, clutching the doorknob awkwardly with her bumpy, arthritic hand, gave it a twist. She entered the room ahead of Nieve, hobbling over to a nightstand, where she set the candle. Then, with what seemed like sleight-of-hand, she produced a small jar from out of her apron pocket, along with a waxed paper package, and slipped them into the nightstand's drawer.

"Salve for your neck." She addressed this to the wall. "And summat to eat."

Nieve continued to hover on the threshold of the room, gaping at it. She had expected to be lead into an empty cell, sterile and cheerless, without any comforts whatsoever. What she saw before her almost made her weep.

The illumination was dim, but she had no doubt that what she was seeing was *her* room, her room from home! It had been copied down to the last detail – the desk with its peeling decals, the birds' nest and fossils perched on the book-shelf, the tattered dictionary, the hooked rug on the hardwood floor (flooring complete with scorch mark), even the baseball bat leaning against the nightstand. Copied or stolen? The only thing that was different was an oddly-shaped rocking chair that had been shoved into one corner. And the window. Her window at home didn't have steel bars on it.

"I . . . thanks so much." The deiler's offerings had been as unexpected as the room. She moved cautiously toward the

185

bed, observing it more closely, running a hand over the comforter, her old blue dinosaur-patterned comforter from when she was little. It *shouldn't* be here, even though she was desperate to dive under it and hide.

"You're very kind, Weazen." Unless the salve and food were poison, but she didn't think so. "I'm starving. I promise I won't let her see."

"Don't worry, miss, this room, it's mirror-made. Except the chair, that's real enough. Good night."

"Is it night?" Nieve sank down onto the bed, spirits, already low, sinking with her.

"Always," Weazen responded, face still averted as she left the room and quietly closed the door behind her.

# Twenty-Six

# A Few Words from the Chairman

Mirror-made? While pretending to settle, Nieve surveyed her room, trying to see it as best she could in the scant light cast by the wavering flame of the candle. Even in the weak light there was something cockeyed about it. Her desk was the wrong way around for one thing, with the drawer on the left side, not the right. And, although it was hard to tell from her vantage on the bed, the titles of the books heaped on it appeared to be in the same kind of mirror writing she'd used in her school report on the World's Backward Walking Champion, Plennie Wingo (!TNELLECXE, Mrs. Crawford had written in the margin).

The dinosaur comforter felt oddly insubstantial, too. Hers had grown somewhat thin and worn over the years, but was still comfy and warming, while this one, when she pulled it up over her, felt as light as the meringue on a pie. Same with her sapphire blue pajamas, which she'd found folded and tucked under the pillow as they always were at home. These ones, though, weren't made of flannel, but of a lighter, silkier material. No way was she going to put them on, even though the ring repeatedly dragged her hand toward them.

She detested the thing. When she slid her hand under the covers, burying it, in order to check out unobserved what Weazen had left in the drawer, the band grew fiery hot and burned her finger, which was now as sore and puffy as the welts on her neck. She would have loved to poke the ring in its eye, but instead made a big show of yawning. She yawned and yawned until – yawning being contagious – it worked! The ring stopped bugging her, began to blink with fatigue, and even slackened its grip.

Weazen had claimed that Elixibyss would fall asleep, and the ring's glow did gradually begin to fade, like a nightlight that was losing power. Nieve stretched out and lay motionless staring up at the ceiling (the billowing cobwebs above didn't look real, either), waiting for the spying eye to glaze over completely and for its heavy golden lid to close. The trouble was, before the ring stopped watching, Nieve did too. Utterly exhausted, she closed her own eyes for the merest moment to give them a rest . . . and spiraled into sleep.

*

A voice woke her, a very strange voice that had drifted into the crowded darkness of her dreams in search of her. "Nieeeeve," it creaked. "Nie-e-e-e-v-e."

She jerked awake and sat up straight. The Impress! But no, it hadn't been her voice she'd heard. This one had been too scratchy and slight. She checked the ring. Luckily, it hadn't been roused and the eyelid remained closed.

"Weazen?" She spoke barely above a whisper, even knowing that the ring couldn't transmit sound.

No one responded.

She slowly reached for the candlestick with her free hand – the candle had burned down to a nub, how *long* had she been asleep? – and held it up to scan the room. No one. Only a dream, then? She sometimes did dream noises – a phone ringing, distant laughter, a balloon popping – noises that sounded genuine, and usually woke her up, but weren't. What if the room was haunted, she thought with a shiver? This was not something she would have believed possible a day ago, but a day ago she hadn't been imprisoned in the unbelievable, either.

Still, all was quiet. Nothing leapt out at her. Nothing was there.

Nieve cursed herself for falling asleep, yet she felt better for it, not so downhearted. She was no less famished, though. Replacing the candlestick on the nightstand, she opened the drawer and retrieved the wax paper package, which she unwrapped one-handed. It was a cheese sandwich with wilted lettuce and a bite taken out of it. The teeth marks left in it were kind of pointy. Too hungry to be squeamish about finishing what somebody else, maybe Weazen, had started, she devoured it.

When it came to the salve, that was trickier, but she managed well enough after first unscrewing the lid with her teeth. She dabbed the greasy stuff carefully on her neck and rubbed it in, breathing in its familiar, healing fragrance. What was it?

"Aloha," the voice, squeaked. "Ve-r-r-aaaa," Squeak, *squeak.*

Nieve dropped the jar and made a grab for the baseball bat that was leaning up against the nightstand. To her amazement, the moment she seized it the bat shattered in her grip. It flew apart like some impossibly fragile Christmas ornament, its thin shards tinkling as they tumbled to the floor.

"Che-e-e-ap." Squeak, squeak, *creak.* "Po-o-o-r quali-t-y-y merchandiiiise."

It was the chair. The *chair* in the corner was talking!

They've rigged up this room to make me think I'm crazy, Nieve thought indignantly, or to drive me there.

"Meee? Rememmmber me? Nieeeve."

"Oh my gosh!"

Nieve slid off the bed and again reached for the candlestick. Holding her other hand stiffly so as not to disturb the ring, she hastened to the dark corner where the chair was quietly rocking on its own. She hadn't paid it any attention before, but now, holding the candle up, she saw that it wasn't really a chair, but a man whose body had been twisted and wrenched and bent into the shape of one. If that weren't shocking enough, it was a man she knew. It was Mr. Exley, the pharmacist who had without warning sold his business and left town. Except, obviously, he hadn't. He'd been abducted, like Mayor Mary, and Alicia, and Malcolm . . . and turned into a piece of *furniture.*

"Mr. Exley." She wanted to touch his hand, but didn't dare move the ring too much. "Does it hurt badly? I mean–" She didn't know what to say!

He was cunningly made. His arms formed the arms of the chair, his lap the seat, his torso and shoulders the back, and his long legs were bent at the knee for rockers. His face was squashed almost flat, rising above the back like a headrest. Despite this, he could move his lips to speak, if at times more creakily chair-like than was easy to understand.

"My de-e-e-a-r, ohh myyy . . . don't-t-t-t waaant to compla-a-a-i—n. Cooould use a dustiiiing, mind, a bit-t-t of pol-i-s-h-h-h."

Mr. Exley had always been fastidious in his personal upkeep.

"How did they do this to you?" She could feel herself

getting angry, as though the candle she was holding was burning inside her. "Was it that serum they inject into people?"

"Thaat's it-t-t, Nieeve. You alllways we-e-e-re a smart one. Faaactories. They ha-a-v-e faactori-e-e-e-s. Twisssden does-s-s."

Nieve hesitated. She could hardly bear to say it. "He makes things out of people? All the people who've gone missing?"

"Yes-s-s, oh yees, Nieeve, buut not all. She-e-e keeeps some herr-ss-s-e-l-f-f. A chairrrr heeears thiiings. There's a-a-a r-o-o-o-o-m."

A room? Where the troublemakers end up. "*Where*, do you know?"

"Sorry, Nieeeve, thaat I–"

Mr. Exley stopped rocking and his face stiffened into what could have easily passed for a wooden mask, a peculiar decoration on a most peculiar chair.

Puzzled, Nieve glanced down at her hand. The ring's eye had begun to glow. It blinked blearily a few times, but seemed unfocused, unseeing, as one often is when woken in the middle of the night. She pivoted on her heel, quickly pointing it away from Mr. Exley and toward the darker side of the room, until the eyelid, still heavy, fell shut, its watcher succumbing once more to sleep.

Nieve turned back to Mr. Exley, who'd resumed his rocking and squeaking. "She doesn't know you can talk, does she?"

"Nooo! I'dd be on-n-n th-h-h-e scrap heeeap. Kindling, I'd-d-d b-e-e-e."

"But Weazen does? And she put you here?"

Mr. Exley rocked faster, which she took to be a nod of agreement. Then he creaked, "The s-a-a-a-lv-e, Nieeve. Use-e-e it."

191

"The salve?" She thought for a moment. Advice from the pharmacist, or . . . ? "*Yes*, of course. Wait a sec, Mr. Exley."

Not that he was going anywhere, but Nieve thought she just might be.

She hurried back to the bed, and, placing the candle once again on the nightstand, picked up the jar of salve. Dipping a finger in, she scooped up a gob slick as butter, which she rubbed onto the finger that wore the ring. It soothed the burn and almost immediately reduced the swelling, which was a help. It must have helped, too, that Elixibyss, the eye behind the eye, remained asleep and the ring itself was more relaxed. Nieve wriggled and worked it gradually, carefully, along her slippery finger until she was able to pull it off.

Delighted to have rid herself of the odious spying thing, she raised it up for Mr. Exley to see.

"I'm going to find that room," she announced. "And I'm going to get us all out of here. You too, Mr. Exley."

Talking big, as Gran would say, but that was better than talking like a chair, which is surely what would happen if she didn't do *something*. She eyed the ring, now held between her thumb and forefinger, and couldn't resist: She plunged it into the jar of salve. After shoving it as far into the guck as it would go, she twisted the lid back on, secured it tightly, and tossed it onto the bed.

Not the wisest thing to do, but *very* gratifying.

Mr. Exely let out a loud *creak* of alarm, but Nieve was already out the door and halfway down the hall.

# Twenty-Seven

# Troublemaker

Nieve had been warned about the spherals, but followed a trio of them down the stairs regardless. Seeing as Elixibyss had been the one to issue the warning, she didn't know how seriously to take it. They seemed harmless enough and helped to light the way, three softly glowing beacons that floated above and before and around her. So far so good anyway.

Once on the main floor again, she made her way back to the dining room and stood with an ear pressed against one of the doors. It was utterly silent within. Slowly, she tried the handle. The room was locked. She bit her lip, wondering what to do. If only she could whisper some words of encouragement to Lias through the door, let him know that she hadn't forgotten him. But that would be stupid. A guard might be stationed in the dining room. She'd passed by one earlier roving the hall – his seven eyes roving, too – before following Weazen up the stairs. Elixibyss herself could still be in there, having nodded off at the table. If so, she might wake up at any moment, check the spy ring and find herself staring at the bottom of a jar of salve.

The spherals were hovering in an archway nearby, waiting for her. Waiting to lead her astray? Could she be more astray than she already was? She pictured herself stepping through an open trap door and plummeting down a shaft into a pitch black, rat-infested dungeon. Then she pictured Malcolm being clobbered by that huge mud-faced septaclops. She decided to follow the spherals, trust her instincts.

As soon as she moved toward them, they wafted away, leading her down yet another hall. Trailing after them, she reflected how this whole long night was like an extended, frustrating dream of hurrying down hallways, never reaching the end.

This one, however, came to an end shortly.

The spherals arrived at another set of double doors and briefly wavered in front of it, illuminating patches of ornate gold embossing on the panels. A special room, then. One after the other, they then poured through the crack between the doors, leaving her behind in the dark hallway.

Nieve hesitated, queasy with nerves. She sensed that they were taking her exactly where she wanted to go, but wasn't at all sure she was prepared for what she might see.

Prepared or not, she pushed ahead through the darkness, arms stretched out before her like a sleepwalker in a cartoon. When she reached for the doors, she ran her hands along the panels' fancywork in search of the knob. Fat as an orange, she found it easily, and it turned just as easily in her hand.

Stepping inside, Nieve found herself in a shadowy ballroom, vast as a gymnasium. The massive crystal chandelier that hung from the ceiling in the centre of the room was unlit, but, as in the dining room, there were lit candles in sconces on the walls. Visibility wasn't great, but she immediately saw enough to make her want to turn around and run.

The spherals were gliding around the room, moving along the rows of chairs that lined the walls. The chairs were normal enough, if fussy – spindly legs and gilded woodwork – but what filled them wasn't. Every single chair was occupied by a person who sat unmoving and staring straight ahead, like wallflowers at a dance. No one spoke or made a sound of any kind. Everyone sat in exactly the same position, very straight, with hands in their laps and feet flat on the floor – no crossed legs or waggling feet, no slumping or restless twitching. They very strongly and eerily resembled wax figures, but of course they weren't that.

Steeling herself, Nieve moved closer to examine them, and began walking along the nearest row, following one of the spherals. It was drifting and circling slowly, casting a bluish glow on each face as it passed. She recognized the man who had escaped from the orderlies at the hospital, and felt her heart sink, sorry that he hadn't made it after all.

And then she stopped moving. Stopped and stared. The next person in line was her teacher, Mrs. Crawford. She was seated beside an older boy Nieve also recognized from school. Most of the faces she'd seen so far had been drained of emotion – the boy's was, but Mrs. Crawford's certainly wasn't. Her frowning expression had been caught and frozen while she'd been speaking, and speaking her mind by the looks of it.

A troublemaker.

As was Mayor Mary. Nieve knew she'd find her here, and she did, not much farther along. The spiders' silk still clung to her in thick strands, although her head was mostly uncovered. She looked furious. Her face was locked in an angry snarl that was startling it was so unlike her.

"Now, see? See what happens when you make faces, dear? Your face gets stuck. She looks ridiculous, doesn't she?"

The Impress. She had risen, unnoticed, from the last chair in the row. As she approached Nieve, she mused, "An experiment, the cobwebs. Interesting results, but not particularly useful."

Nieve glared at her, this creature with the borrowed face, her *mother's* face. Was that an experiment, too? She was glad to see that Elixibyss' right eye was smeared-looking and watery.

"Go ahead, glare all you want, dear. Your fierce-eye isn't going to work on *me*. You *have* been naughty, haven't you? A very bad girl!" Elixibyss squinched her one bleary eye. "Not only throwing away my beautiful gift and sneaking out of bed, but take a look at *this*." She raised a sleeve, exposing her mossy arm and a tiny black patch of skin. "A disfiguring bruise! I wasn't going to mention it, but *someone* forced my car off the road earlier this evening and we had a little accident."

Nieve looked at the arm, then looked again, trying to take in what she was seeing. She was sure it hadn't been there before.

"That's not a bruise," she said slowly. "It's a . . . puncture." A puncture beneath which there was *nothing*. No layers of skin, no muscle, sinew, or bone, only emptiness. "You have a hole in your arm."

Elixibyss dropped her sleeve instantly. "Don't be absurd! It's a *bruise*. Your eyes haven't adjusted to the light here yet."

Nieve knew what she'd seen.

Elixibyss flinched, pain evidently streaking across her brow. She flicked a hand and a teeming pile of headache pills appeared on her palm. These she crammed into her mouth, crunching and grinding them, while saying, "Yes, you've been a most disagreeable daughter. Punishments are called for, spoil the rod, etcetera, I *do* want to be a good parent." She swallowed the pills down in one acrid lump. "However, I am willing to overlook your insolence and disobedience and *bad* attitude this one time. *If* you cooperate." She sniffed loudly. "I have a little chore for you to perform."

"What kind of chore?"

"You'll see."

"What I want to see is Malcolm."

"A *what* not a *who*, eh? Now you've got the right idea, darling. Your tutor will be able to skip the grammar and get down to the real lessons. Genevieve Crawley, didn't I tell you? I believe you've met. I must say she's done some fabulous work at your old school. Absolutely everyone has graduated and become most . . . *useful*. But come, this way."

As Elixibyss marched toward another line of chairs, Nieve, following behind, caught a flicker of movement out of the corner of her eye. She stopped and surveyed the other side of the room, unable to see anything, only more seated, comatose bodies lining the wall. But she had the distinct impression that someone had waved at her.

"Dawdle, dawdle, dawdle!" Elixibyss called back. "Come, before I lose my patience."

Nieve hurried toward the spot where the Impress was waiting, tapping her foot noisily, as if cracking beetles with the toe of her shoe. In the chair before her sat Malcolm.

Nieve crouched down in front of him and placed a hand on his ice-cold one.

He looked terrible, gaunt and worn, his forehead marked with a ugly bruise (a real bruise). He stared straight ahead, but not with resignation, Nieve thought. She knew Malcolm could be a scrapper if it came to that. Another troublemaker. But how much trouble can you make with only an ounce of life left in you?

Elixibyss smiled down at him.

"*Why* are you doing this?" Nieve clenched her jaw.

"That's obvious, isn't it, dear? I'm doing it for you."

"*Me?*"

"Really now, there's no need to play the ignoramus, is there? Mothers make sacrifices, that's simply what we do. Your dreary old granny has told you, surely, that you have a few minor abilities, nothing to boast about. But they haven't anything to do with *healing*. That's sentimental nonsense. Quite the opposite, in fact. Why, you could quench this boy's light with a snap of your fingers." Elixibyss raised her hand, as though she were about to do exactly that, but paused and dropped it again. "It's fantastic luck to touch the dead, you must know that. Everyone's lined up here, ready and waiting. Think, a whole roomful of luck to harvest! Yes, you're going to be a busy girl indeed once the wedding is over."

Nieve was so astonished by this, all she could think to say was, "What wedding?"

"Twisden's, of course. To that Sarah person, hand-picked for the job. Finalizes a few matters for me, but honestly, wedding, divorce, funeral . . . humans have the most pointless rituals. Which reminds me, I have preparations to make, and *you,* my dear girl, have a job to do. Remember, no more naughty behaviour. We wouldn't want your little friend here to perish before his time, would we?"

With that, Elixibyss gathered up the hem of her gown and walked briskly toward the double doors. "Get a move on!" she ordered, without once glancing back.

Nieve herself rose, heartsick, giving her friend's hand a squeeze, passing along some warmth, some hope, even though there seemed precious little of that to go around. On rising, however, she saw that flicker of movement again. Then, from across the room, someone – a short familiar someone – jumped up from one of the chairs, dashed over to Elixibyss, and began making faces behind her back.

Lirk!

He hopped around and cavorted behind the unwitting Impress, imitating her regal walk, jeering and thumbing his nose at her. After which he simply . . . vanished. He *mostly* vanished, that is, for the stubby fingers that waggled on the tip of his snub nose were visible for a few seconds longer before they too winked out.

# –Twenty-Eight–

# *Nayword*

When it became evident that Elixibyss was leading her back to the dining room, Nieve gave up wondering about Lirk. One thing, he had *nerve*. She figured that he was probably the one who had followed them to Bone House, but with what intention she couldn't guess. (More jam!?) Instead, she tried to prepare herself for another confrontation over Gowl. If the chore she had to perform was to finish him off, then no thanks. Let the Impress make her. Let her try! It was the threat to Malcolm that worried her more, much more. How best to respond so that he wouldn't come to further harm?

Entering the dining room behind Elixibyss, she glanced quickly at Lias' cage and at Weazen, who was busying herself near it, then at the stone table. What she saw arrayed on it made her cry out. Not a gross serving of leftover Gowl . . . but Dr. Morys! He lay flat out, wearing his blue hospital gown, his white legs and knobbly feet sticking out, his arms at his sides, his kindly face composed, although showing no signs of consciousness.

Nieve rushed over to him and touched his arm, running her fingers down to his wrist, where she felt a faint, distant pulse. His hand was clenched into a fist, which she thought odd, until she remembered what Rob Cooper had said. That before Dr. Morys collapsed, he had reached out with one hand as if grasping at something.

"My, aren't we the little doctor," sneered Elixibyss, standing by, arms folded.

"That's what he *needs*." Nieve ignored the sneer. "We have to get him to the hospital, right *now*."

"That could be arranged, I suppose. Depending."

"On what?"

"Your chore, my dear. How quickly you forget. Nothing to it, really. No pain involved for the old geezer here. I simply want you to unclench that fist of his. Open his hand."

Nieve scrutinized the Impress, searching her cool face for a clue as to what this was about. It had to be a trick of some kind, but she had no idea what.

"Why don't you do it?" she said.

"Not my sort of thing." Elixibyss folded her arms and smiled. "Go ahead."

Keeping an eye on the Impress, Nieve put her hand on Dr. Morys' fist, which, curiously, felt much warmer than his arm had. Reaching for the tips of his fingers that were pressed tightly into his palm, she tried to prise his hand open, but gently. It was too firmly clenched, though, and she couldn't budge it.

"You'll have to do better than that," said Elixibyss. "Elbow grease, my dear."

Nieve didn't want to consider what, in this house, elbow grease might truly be. Before she was offered any, she tried again, putting more effort into it, but his fist was squeezed tight, closed up like a clam.

"Break his fingers," Elixibyss suggested. "Or, I don't know . . . *use* your imagination. Saw them off."

"Yeah, right." The woman was disgusting.

"That's my girl!" Elixibyss surveyed the table as if searching for the appropriate tool with which to do the deed. Fortunately the cutlery had all been cleared away.

Nieve cast a helpless look at Weazen. The old deiler, standing by the cold fireplace, had been silently watching, and now stepped in front of the poker that was leaning up against the hearth, hiding it from view.

"Hmmn," pondered Elixibyss. "We want to crack open the fingers, but not lose the . . . wait, I have just the thing." This said with an evil little chuckle. "Weazen, keep the girl out of mischief. I'll be right back."

But mischief happened, and Weazen had no intention of stopping it.

The moment Elixibyss was gone, Nieve did something unusual and very surprising. She certainly surprised herself. Out of frustration and fear for Dr. Morys, and contempt for the Impress, she opened her mouth, ready with a good strong curse, a tough schoolyard oath . . . and instead spat out, *"Flaught."*

This wasn't what she meant to say, but for some reason she *had* to say it, had to get it out of her mouth, as if it were a stone or a piece of glass. It had felt that hard on her tongue. She didn't even know what it meant – *flaught* was just another Old Country word of Gran's, and not one spoken in anger – but it clearly meant *something*, because the moment it was out in the air a series of startling things happened.

First, a loud flapping noise filled the room. It sounded like a flock of birds flying through, huge, invisible birds. This was followed by a brisk wind that swept in, stirring everything that could be stirred, including the ashes in the hearth and the flames on the candles, which bent and swayed crazily. The black cloth that covered Lias' cage fluttered, as did Dr. Morys' hospital gown. The wind picked up the ends of Nieve's hair, swirled them around and around, tied a few strands in knots, and then, as suddenly as it had arrived, it was gone.

But the best was yet to come, for once the room was still again, Dr. Morys' clenched fist began to relax. His fingers slowly unfurled, like the petals on a flower (although not *that* slowly), and soon his hand lay open on the table. In his palm Nieve saw what appeared to be a small bright patch of . . . what? She bent down closer to inspect it . . . not a jewel, because it was transparent, and it floated on Dr. Morys' palm like . . . .

*"Daylicht,"* said Lias, crawling out of the cage. "What happened? Where are my shoes?" He looked around the room, bemused. "Oh, hello Weazen."

"Master Lias," Weazen said with a tight smile. "Caught again."

"But still kicking. Ah, *Nieve*, it was you, wasn't it? You discovered the nayword! I knew you could do it, what did I tell you."

"Lias! How did . . . what's a . . . you two *know* each other?"

"Aye," Weazen said, staring anxiously at the door. "She won't be long away."

"Better take it now, Nieve," said Lias. "Hurry."

"Take what?"

"The *lux*. You know, the daylight."

"That?" She pointed at the patch of light, about the size of a quarter, that continued to float on Dr. Morys' palm. "How? I can't pick up light! Besides . . . ." She couldn't help but think of what the Impress had said in the ballroom, how she'd be able to put out Malcolm's light with the snap of her fingers. "What if it's the only thing keeping him alive?"

"Accept it, miss," said Weazen. "He wants you to have it."

Footsteps sounded in the hall outside, heels hammering into the floorboards.

"Blast!" Lias scanned the room, then scrambled into a corner and crouched in the shadow of the sideboard. This furniture had no human attributes at least, outside of a burly, imposing presence, which made it a handy place to hide.

Nieve, panicked, didn't know what to do. *What was right?* What if she hurt Dr. Morys? Fatally? But there was no time to consider. She held her hand out, palm upward, and slid it quickly toward him until the tips of her fingers touched his. The second she did this, the little light skimmed onto her hand, hovered briefly on her palm, then disappeared up her sleeve like a timorous mouse making a dash for safety. It didn't tickle, as a mouse would scurrying up her arm, but she did feel a slight trace of warmth as it settled in the hollow of her shoulder.

She dropped her hand hastily by her side as the Impress burst into the room, holding a drill. She took one look at Dr. Morys' open hand and screamed. "You little minx! What have you done?!"

"I did what you told me to," Nieve said simply.

"Where is it, then? What have you done with it?"

"Done with what?"

"The . . . *thing*. The secret *thing* in his hand."

"Don't know what you're talking about. He didn't have anything in his hand. Was he supposed to be holding something?"

Elixibyss narrowed her eyes. She raised the drill and pointed it at Nieve, then pressed the switch. It made an excruciatingly shrill noise, like a dentist's drill. "You're lying."

Nieve shook her head, trying her best to stand her ground

as she watched the drill bit, aimed at her own head, whizzing at high-speed.

"She's not, ma'am," Weazen spoke up. "Was nothing in the old man's hand. Could be you was misinformed."

"Shut up," she snapped. "Think I'd trust a deiler to tell the truth?"

Elixibyss seemed to take this in nonetheless, and, turning off the drill, stood fuming and glowering at Nieve until interrupted by a knock at the door. Weazen creaked over to open it, taking her time, and admitted someone Nieve never thought she'd be glad to see: Dunstan Warlock.

He stepped into the dining room, huffing and red-faced, cowboy hat in hand, nervously rolling and unrolling its rim into a tight tube.

The Impress turned on him with a snarl. "What is it, Toad?"

Warlock was about to speak, until he saw Nieve. He gave her a slightly bug-eyed look, then glancing back at Elixibyss, jerked his head toward the door.

"Oh, *all right*," she sighed. "Nieve, I'll deal with you shortly. Be prepared to *suffer*."

Once she and Warlock were through the doors and murmuring together in the hall, Lias leapt out of his hiding place and began to search the room. As he searched, he said, "Don't worry, Nieve, your 'mother' isn't going to hurt you. She wouldn't dare, she *needs* you. Where is it, Weazen, where's the box?"

"Mantel," Weazen answered, at the same time that Nieve said, testily, "She's *not* my mother."

"I know," he said, moving like a cat toward the fireplace and toward the gold box that was resting on the mantel. "She's mine."

# –Twenty-Nine–

# *Inoculation*

Surely Lias meant that the gold box was his, and not the mother, *not* Elixibyss? But as it turned out, the box wasn't his, either. Just as he was about to grab it, the Impress returned. She angrily pushed through the dining room doors, slamming them against the wall. They vibrated as they bounced back and were left hanging halfway open. Luckily, she was so intently focused on Nieve that she didn't see Lias slinking back into his hiding place in the shadow of the sideboard.

Whatever Warlock had told her hadn't been welcome news. Striding over to Nieve, she smiled at her in an effortful, fake-motherly fashion, which was scarier than some of her more grim expressions.

"Darling," she said, white-lipped. "We're going on a little jaunt."

"A jaunt?"

"Indeed. We need a vacation, don't you think? Let's do some shopping! We could pick up some . . . *Danish* furniture, modernize our digs here, Danish people do make the niftiest furniture. Yes, we'll have some quality time together, time to bond, eh, and make up for all those years we've been kept apart."

"Sounds, um . . ." Revolting? Like a nightmare? "Nice." Escape might be possible once she was out of this place. That and finding help.

"I've never been a big fan of 'nice,' but I can see you're finally coming around." Elixibyss reached out to pat Nieve on the head, then hastily pulled back her hand. "Good. We'll leave right away. One quick stop at the hospital, then we'll be off."

"We can take Dr. Morys. Like you said."

Elixibyss laughed, which was even more ghastly than her fake maternal beaming. "I'm afraid you've already fixed him, my dear. He's done like a dinner."

"No!" But turning to him, Nieve saw that Dr. Morys did look paler, and somehow sadder than he had before she had taken the daylight from him. His mouth was turned down slightly, and he seemed to be less present, less *there* in himself.

"Let's go, we're wasting time. Oh, and mustn't forget this." Elixibyss swept over to the fireplace and snatched the gold box off the mantel. "Weazen, clean up the mess on the table. And be sure to keep my baby tucked up safe in his crib. His snug rib crib!" she laughed again, clutching the box as she swept out. "Come, Nieve, *right now!*"

Nieve reached out to touch Dr. Morys. What had she done?

As soon as she touched him, though, grasping his open hand, she could have sworn that she saw his lips twitch ever so slightly. As if, even in death, he had found something that amused him.

She glanced up, bewildered, looking first at Weazen, who gave her an encouraging nod, then at Lias, who, pressed up against the wall, was miming for her to go, *go!*

Nieve reluctantly relinquished Dr. Morys' hand and moved toward the open doors.

Unable to resist one last look before leaving, she glanced back over her shoulder just in time to see Weazen snatch at something in the air. A fly, she thought at first, but no, it looked more like an *ear* than a fly. A pointy, putty-coloured ear suspended in mid-air, scarcely higher than Weazen herself.

*

Riding to the hospital in the silver car wasn't exactly a barrel of laughs. Dunstan Warlock was at the wheel, and his driving skills were minimal to non-existent. But that wasn't the main problem. The car itself was a menace. Bent out of shape after its tumble into the ditch, with a crumpled fender and a wonky tire, it wobbled along through the desolate streets of the Black City in what, for a car, was a foul mood. (Nor did it help that its vanity licence plate – **ME!ME!ME!!!** – was also dangling from its rear and about to fall off.)

The upholstery in the back where Nieve was seated kept buckling up and pinching her, until she gave it a good hard punch. The car groaned and stopped pinching, but then the seat started bouncing her up and down trampoline-style, and tossing her back and forth, from one door to the other, until she hissed, "I get carsick, you know. How would you like *that* all over you?" It stopped promptly.

Next, the radio came on, full blast. The dial was set on a news channel, an extremely weird news channel, that recounted gruesome current events:

*Tonight a boy named Jimmy ran away from school and was eaten by a troll. Serves him right, stupid kid! MWAA-HA-HA! Earlier this evening, a girl named Priscilla was dragged under her*

*bed by a giant worm, you should have heard her scream!*
*MWAA-HA-HA!! A girl named NIEVE, I repeat NIEVE, is*
*going to the hospital to get a—*

Elixibyss, who was seated in the front beside Warlock,
flicked the radio off.

*Mmnnph!!* it went, but there was no more harassing news.
Nieve had certainly heard enough.

"What am I getting at the hospital?" she asked quietly.

"Nothing much," said Elixibyss, gazing with interest out
the window at a rat the size of a spaniel that had begun chasing
the car. "An inoculation. A teeny-tiny shot, you won't feel a
thing." She smiled as the car blew the rat away with a blast of
exhaust the smelled like rotten eggs. "Nothing but a precaution, my dear. So many creatures that *bite* out in the big world,
so many diseases. You wouldn't want to catch the plague,
would you?"

Nieve didn't respond. She knew precisely what kind of
shot she was going to get: the same "inoculation" that everyone got before they were turned into a piece of furniture.
Although Lias had said that Elixibyss needed her. (Poor Lias!
*This* was his mother?) Needed her for what, though? Something to stand on, to wipe her feet on?

She stared down at her hands, which were cupped in her
lap. The spot of daylight slid out of her sleeve and nestled
comfortingly in the palm of her right hand. Experimentally,
she tipped her hand and let the light drift onto the seat. After
the radio had been silenced, the car seat had been growing
colder and colder, and she was beginning to feel numb, as if
she were sitting on a block of ice. She wondered if the little
light might just warm things up. It did more than that. It concentrated itself into an intensely hot beam, like a ray of sunlight refracted through a magnifying glass . . . and burned a

hole in the seat! The car gave a *yelp*, and Warlock gave a shout, losing control of the wheel. The car swerved, and barely missed hitting a man, formally dressed in top hat and tails (several), who was sauntering along the street.

Once Warlock got the car back under control and it continued along, albeit more timidly, the Impress jerked her head around and glared at Nieve. By that time, the daylight had slipped back up her sleeve, where it generated a more gentle heat that warmed her up.

"This car's useless," said Nieve, in answer to the glare. "It almost hit that man."

"Yes," observed Elixibyss, still eyeing her with suspicion. "Nothing worse than vampire splattered on the windshield."

Nieve assumed she was kidding, but knew better than to ask.

The rest of the trip was uneventful, if one doesn't count crashing through the entrance doors of the hospital, careering wildly down hallways, bouncing up stairs like a ball, and sending people running and shouting in a panic at every twist and turn of the way. By the time they came to a stop and parked in the OR waiting room, the silver car itself was not only a wreck, but a nervous wreck. It sat idling and shaking, with steam pouring out of its hood, as two orderlies approached, pushing a gurney.

Although the orderlies were gowned and masked, they obviously weren't the ones Nieve had encountered earlier.

They were both women, possibly nurses. Not that this made her feel any better. Since when did one get carted off to the OR for an inoculation?

"Don't be alarmed, dear," said Elixibyss, rolling down the window to speak with the orderlies. "You're getting special treatment."

"I bet."

"I'll be waiting here," Elixibyss instructed them. "Have someone send me some headache tablets *on* a silver platter, a hundred or so will suffice, plus a Band-Aid and a cup of espresso. Otherwise, you know what to do. And make it snappy!"

The orderlies both nodded and moved around to Nieve's side of the car. Without saying a word, one yanked open the door (*Ow, ow!*), while the other latched a hand onto Nieve's arm. While they pulled her out of the car and hoisted her onto the gurney, she considered her options. Make a run for it as soon as the gurney started to roll away? Or wait a bit longer, try to summon up a blasting, stun them both, and take off?

They must have anticipated trouble, or possibly it was routine practice, because once she was on the gurney they pushed her down flat and began to secure her with straps. She wouldn't be running anywhere. Nieve began to struggle and kick. "Don't!" she shouted. "Leave me alone! Get your grubby hands off me!!" If they thought they were going to haul her off and turn her into a piece of lumber, they were crazy. She'd kick and bite and scratch . . . .

One of the orderlies put a hand on her chest and pushed her back down, firmly, but not unkindly. She gave Nieve a keen look, her eyes above the mask crinkling with an amused appraisal. *Familiar* eyes. The very same flecked hazel ones that

211

Nieve had seen observing her much earlier that night in a rear-view mirror.

It was Frances.

–Thirty–

# Container Gardening

As they wheeled her through the doors that led to the operating rooms, Nieve continued to put up a struggle, but only for show. What she really wanted to do was laugh. Or cry. Well, she wasn't going to start *that*. She was so happy to see Frances that a surge of renewed determination and hope took hold of her.

Her only moment of alarm came when they veered down the hallway that led away from the operating rooms and wheeled her into a room that was more like an office, with crammed bookshelves and stacks of files and paper piled everywhere, including the floor. Frances locked the door and the other orderly began undoing the straps. While doing so, the mask slipped down over her chin and Nieve saw that it was Sarah, Twisden's intended. With a stab of fright, it now occurred to her that Frances herself may have been overtaken, that things weren't as great as she thought.

But her alarm lasted only as long as it took for Frances, pulling down her own mask, to say, "Nope, they haven't brainwashed me, Nievy. Same old unwashed brain." She hurried over and helped to unfasten the straps. "My *gosh* it's good to see you! We thought we'd lost you, too."

As Nieve sat up, Frances enfolded her in her arms. She *knew* she was safe.

Sarah, standing to one side, gazed at her approvingly. "You know, you really do look like your mother."

This was the sort of thing adults loved to say, whether there was the merest trace of resemblance or not. Nieve returned the gaze less approvingly. "I'm not the only one who looks like my mother."

"The Impress, yes, that must have been terrible. Look, Nieve, it's not what you might think, believe me. I'm *not* marrying that creep Twisden. I'm . . . well, you'll see. We don't have the time now, it's not going to take her long to catch on."

"Things are tight," agreed Frances. "We'll have to save the chinwag for later, but where's Lias? And did you, I mean . . . ?" She braced herself for the answer. "Malcolm?"

"I've seen him!" Nieve filled them in quickly, if sketchily, about Bone House and Lias and Dr. Morys and what she'd witnessed in the ballroom. She couldn't bring herself to tell them that Elixibyss was preserving people, Malcolm included, only to kill them off later. Nieve's job, no less!

"Right," Frances said, sounding both relieved *and* worried. "We know about that process, everyone zonked out. It's a sort of hypnosis they've discovered that sends you into a deep sleep. Must be how they caught Dr. Morys. Not like that other thing they do . . . the serum, the shots." She shuddered. "At least Malcolm's not a footstool."

"Is that what she planned to do to me?"

"You were slated to receive a lighter hit of the serum, same stuff they sneak into the food here, just enough to dumb you down some. We intercepted the order. You're trouble, Nieve. She needs you, but she also needs to control you."

"But why? I don't get it."

"Because you can do things she can't." Frances paused and gave her a quizzical look. "I don't think you realize how . . . *interesting* you are Nievy. Take those plants you're growing in your back pockets, for example."

"What!" Nieve glanced down and spied a green shoot, a vine with a tiny leaf, twisting around her waist. She hopped down off the gurney and craned her neck around to look at her backside. "Crumb! What is it?"

"Runners!" said Sarah.

"Beans?"

"No, no. *Shoes*, buskins really, but very special ones. This is *perfect*." Sarah clasped her hands together, delighted.

"I don't–" Nieve started to say, mystified, until she remembered the useless, tattered shoes Gran had given her. She hadn't given them a thought since stuffing them into her back pockets. But . . . they'd sprouted?

"Okay, Sarah." Frances was equally mystified. "You've got ten seconds to fill us in."

"In a word, Nieve, they'll make you run *very* fast. That's what I understand; I've never seen a real pair before, only illustrations. They're extremely old."

"I already run fast."

"These will help you run faster."

"Faster than a horse?"

215

"Faster than . . . anything. Let's have a look at them. And then we'll tell you what you have to do. This makes it so much easier."

Nieve doubted that, nothing had been easy so far, but overwhelmed with curiosity, she tugged the forgotten shoes out of her back pockets. It was amazing how they had changed. The brown crackly-dry leaves that had been tumbling apart, now adhered together, overlapping like pliant scales, soft as the softest leather and a brilliant green. They even smelled new, like a morning in early spring, verdant and fresh. As she held them up, surely the wildest pair of shoes she'd ever seen ("Rad!"said Frances), she couldn't help but wonder if her bright stowaway, the daylight, was somehow involved in this transformation.

"Put'em on," urged Frances. "If you can figure out how."

No problem there. Nieve pulled off her old runners, then eased the new ones on as one would a pair of socks. They extended to mid-calf and fit beautifully. Once they were on, vines thin as laces wound up and around of their own accord, fastening the shoes securely and comfortably.

"You shouldn't have any difficulty now," Sarah said. "As long as you steer clear of wafts and the like."

"Wafts?" Nieve was admiring the shoes. They were extremely cool ("*Très* dash," said Frances) and would be fantastic with her new green shirt. (*Not* that she was into that sort of thing.)

"They take the form of ordinary people, but they're definitely not that."

This got her attention. "They're here in the hospital?"

"Listen, Nieve," said Frances, suddenly more serious. "We need your help, that must be pretty obvious. I wouldn't ask if there was any other way, and I sure hope your Gran'll forgive me. There's a group of people here, medical people mostly, who're fighting this craziness that's taking over. I stumbled into a couple of them, lucked out when I went running off like a maniac, or I might *be* a gurney myself right now. And I'm so sorry for abandoning you like that . . . but, I know you understand."

"Of course," Nieve nodded. "You were looking for Malcolm. Me too."

Frances gestured toward the stacks of paper on the floor and spilling off the shelves. "We've discovered something. There's an antidote. Dr. Manning, remember him, he used to live in town, he invented the serum that those sickos Wormius and Ashe have been producing and distributing from their nasty little drugstore. But he also invented an antidote. Or anyway a formula for one."

"Which we think is hidden at Ferrets," added Sarah.

"You could find him and ask him for it, couldn't you?" Nieve could see all too clearly where this was going.

"No one knows what happened to him. He disappeared when Ferrets, or rather Woodlands, was sold to Mortimer Twisden. Some say he disappeared *before* it was sold."

Both Frances and Sarah were staring at her intently. She knew there was no point in asking *why me?* because they'd only tell her that she was *different* . . . and *interesting* . . . and that she had *abilities.* All she had was a pair of leafy shoes with an untested reputation for speed. Plus a tiny light that was presently illuminating her armpit.

"What happens when I don't show up in the waiting room?"

"Originally, we were going to wheel you back to Elixibyss, with you pretending to be drugged and compliant. We have word that she's headed to Ferrets to deal with Twisden, something's come up, but we're not sure what. If you were to go with her, you'd be able to search for the antidote. She'd think you too doped-up to need watching. Mind, it's pretty risky. She might just decide to vanish and take you with her."

Nieve made a face. She wanted to ride in the silver car again about as much as she wanted to continue chumming around with the Impress. "I don't think it's at Ferrets, this formula or whatever. Someone's already searched the place. Don't you remember the furniture and stuff scattered around outside?"

"You're right," Sarah said. "Twisden turned the place upside-down and still didn't find it. He told me he was looking for a diamond brooch to give me that had belonged to his wife. Poor Molly." She shook her head sadly. "He never found the formula, but I'm pretty sure it's still in that house, somewhere."

"I'd drive you there myself," said Frances. "But some jerk stripped the car, picked it clean. No cars anywhere, the streets are deserted because everyone's freaking out, huddled in their closets at home biting their nails. Taxis won't even answer calls anymore."

"Let me get this straight," Nieve sighed heavily, more exasperated than anything. So much for feeling safe! "You want me to *run* through the city and back to town, which is what, fifty miles away, all by myself, in the dark, with . . . who know's *what* roaming around out there?"

"You'll be moving too fast for whatever's out there, Nieve." Sarah touched her shoulder. "Believe me."

Nieve wanted to believe her, but Sarah hadn't exactly earned her trust yet. Poor Molly indeed!

"We'll distract her," said Frances. "One of our doctors will go out with a complementary bucket of headache pills and tell her there've been some unexpected complications with your treatment. We'll make sure you have enough time one way or another, don't worry. I'll keep an eye out for Lias, too. He'll be looking for you."

Nieve gazed down at her shoes, thinking it over. Was this scheme as crackbrained as it sounded? Ferrets was close to her home, after all, and there wasn't a place she'd rather be right now. She ached to see her parents, and Gran, and Mr. Mustard Seed, and Artichoke. What if they needed her help, too?

While considering this, she watched, intrigued, as a ripple of motion passed through the leaves on her shoes, making them flutter and tremble. Clothed in these living shoes, her feet felt wonderfully light, really, and tingly, restless, itching to move it. Yes, *yes*, she wanted to go home more than anything. In fact, she couldn't wait to go. She began to bounce up and down like a sprinter preparing to take off.

"All right," she said. "I'm out of here."

# –Thirty-One–

## *Fast Forward*

Streaking down the deserted streets of the city, Nieve couldn't believe how fantastic she felt. Normally, she'd be unnerved – and perhaps she *should* be unnerved – to be running all alone at night in a place that was scary enough at the best of times for a kid. Anything might jump out of an alley and grab her, and desperate humans weren't the worst of it. The denizens of the Black City had migrated to the upper world and were at large, as both Lias and Sarah had said. They were like nocturnal predators that no longer had to keep themselves hidden in burrows and under rocks and deep in shadowy woods. Predators that were after much larger quarry than nervous rabbits or fearful, scampering mice.

But . . . no scampering for Nieve. She ran *so fast* that the buildings she passed were almost a blur, doors and windows and signs flowing one into the other like run-on architecture, like one endless building. Sarah had been right about that.

Despite this, at the last minute Frances had been reluctant to let her go.

"Maybe this isn't such a hot idea," she'd said. They had crept down to a side door of the hospital and both stood gazing at the darkened and looming buildings that lined the street. "Let's skip it, Nieve. We'll hide you here and send someone else."

"No, it's okay. I want to go, have to. These runners, I don't know, I feel protected wearing them."

"How reliable is that? This is Cinderella territory, if you ask me."

"Well, *I'm* not planning on losing my shoes."

"Look, we couldn't even scare up a flashlight for you, how are you going to see where you're going?"

"With this, I guess." Nieve had held out her hand and the daylight zipped onto her palm and hovered there, glowing even more brightly than before. She still felt so conflicted about taking the light from Dr. Morys that she hadn't mentioned it when she told Frances and Sarah about finding him at Bone House.

"Way out," Frances had grinned, somewhat reassured. "Like I said, Nievy, you're interesting."

Nieve could only hope that she'd be too interesting, flavour-wise, for anything roving around that had an appetite for children and could move faster than her.

*Could* anything move faster? So far, no. She passed a lone car that had been scooting along, almost causing the driver to plow into a store window. He gawked at her, incredulous, as she scorched past, and must have thought her yet another uncanny night creature on the loose.

Not long after, one of those uncanny creatures picked up her trail and scuttled after her, snuffling and clattering along like a pig wearing armour. She had no idea what it was, and never found out, because it couldn't keep up and eventually collapsed in a gasping heap. That these fantastical night creatures themselves had limitations gave her courage. (Although, maybe it *had* been a pig wearing armour and not much of a threat.)

Nieve flew along past shops and apartments, and it did feel like flying, she was so light-footed. It was like running a magical marathon – no pain or exhaustion involved. *Like the wind I go . . . ha, something she used to say as a joke.*

Did the wind ever get lost, though? Some of the streets were vaguely familiar from earlier trips into the city, and she did pass that grim art gallery and candy store again, so had to trust that on some level – street-level, down with her shoes – she knew where she was going.

The daylight helped. If she hesitated at all or slowed to a stop, it flowed down from her shoulder where it was perched like a tiny headlight (sometimes it even rode on her crown like an actual *head*light), and skittered up the appropriate street, leading the way.

Once the landmarks became more familiar, Nieve was able to locate the road that led out of the city and back to town. Finding it was like meeting up with an old friend, yet she knew she had to keep a sharp lookout. The fields and ditches on either side of the road were overgrown with vicious weeds, clacking their leaves like knives, their meaty flowers reeking. She kept well away from them, running along the centre of the road while the whole time they snapped and hissed and lunged at her. A herd of horses in one field had not been so lucky. Nothing was left of them but skeletons, still standing and swaying slightly as if about to bolt. Unless the skeletal horses were themselves phantoms.

At one point, she caught sight of a group of children with white hair and pale, translucent skin, playing in one of the fields. She tried not to look at them, but they were having so much fun, laughing and skipping around, and they were

222

so . . . attractive. She'd never seen such beautiful children before, and they spoke so sweetly, their voices musical and endearing. They waved at her and called out . . . *come play, Nieve, join us, come on! Forget those ugly old people. Forget what they asked you to do. They don't care if you're alone and afraid, they don't care if you get hurt. Come with us, we'll take you to a secret place, the most wonderful place in the world, Nieve, forever safe* . . . . Nieve gave herself a shake and pulled her eyes away from them. She began humming loudly to drown them out, and determinedly kept going, while they continued to spin an enticing, melodic web around her. She felt herself slowing, struggling, as though running in a dream and not getting anywhere. Although she knew she had to be because she soon passed a dilapidated barn on the side of the road out of which issued a rending, hair-raising screech. For some reason, this stopped the voices. It cut them dead, but not her.

Like the wind, she thought, a *blistering* wind . . . and she stormed on.

Nieve was running so fast that she didn't see the figure that rose up directly before her until it was too late. It pulled itself up out of the dusty road, a huge, ragged apparition with a cloaked hoary head and fingers as long and sharp as ice picks. She ran straight into it, gasping with shock, as if she'd just taken a plunge into arctic waters. Once enveloped in it, she couldn't see a thing, only a kind of cloudy nothingness. *She* was a cloudy nothingness. But no, she thought, *that's not true!*

223

With every cell in her body straining to go forward, she pushed and kicked and punched, until finally she tore through the thing, ripping it apart. As she burst through, its body exploded into a freezing shower of ghostly hail that poured down around her, while its cloaked head spun off shrieking into the dark.

After *that*, Nieve thought, meeting a waft or two would be nothing.

She should be so lucky.

She had been running hard, going flat out and still curiously untaxed by the effort, when she realized that something else was following her. It, too, seemed to run without effort, moving swiftly and silently. And while it made no sound, she could *feel* it at her back, her skin prickling as it closed in. Was it the same shadowy creature that had followed her on her night run to Gran's? Or was it like that winged terror that Gran had once told her about, the Wild Beast of Barriesdale? The creature had only three legs, yet bounded easily, half-flying, over hills and houses and rivers in pursuit of its prey.

Nieve poured it on, running even faster. The daylight quivered on the knuckle of her fisted hand, as if it were straining to pull her forward. But, no matter how fast she ran, the thing behind stuck with her, it was at her very back, its breath hot on her neck.

Concentrating all her effort on her feet – what would happen if she stumbled and fell? – and trying with all her might not to think of anything else, struggling to stay utterly focused, something Gran had said nevertheless flickered across her mind. *If things start to go amiss, get word to me. Lias knows how.*

What word? How? *Lias knows . . . what!? Lias!!*

224

She heard the roar of a car. It was barreling down the road behind her making an unholy racket – no muffler, radio wailing, horn blaring. The car was travelling so fast that Nieve was sure it was going to hit her. She scrambled to get out of the way, diving into the ditch, with no thought of the thing at her back or the clacking, carnivorous weeds.

The driver of the car hit the breaks and she heard an ear-splitting squeal of tires, followed by a tremendous *BANG!* and a *CRACK!*

Then silence.

Nieve peeked out cautiously. She could only guess – and hope! – that her beastly pursuer had paused in confusion for a split-second as the car bore down. A split-second too long.

Pulling herself out of the ditch, with a weed seedling gnawing on her sleeve, she checked to see if the creature was dead, expecting to see roadkill of the most revolting kind. But all that was left of it was a greasy smear on the road.

Then she looked at the car, knowing it couldn't possibly be the silver one, which was too wimpy to flatten a monster. What she saw was more like a car skeleton. It had no body, no windows, no doors, and *no driver*. But it did have an engine, a chassis, seats, headlights, and a radio that was playing an obnoxious popular song full blast.

And . . . it had Lias!

He hopped out of the passenger side and ran over to Nieve, sidestepping the greasy smear.

"Didn't I say you could run? Never thought we'd catch up with you. Hey, *swank*," he eyed her shoes. Then he took in the smear. "Second one of those we hit. Nothing left for the crows, eh?"

Nieve was so happy to see him, all she could say, with a laugh of relief, was, "We?"

Lias nodded at the car. "A wild man on the road, even worse than Frances, but a mechanical genius."

"Lirk!" Nieve saw two small hands appear on the steering wheel, one of which now saluted her. "How did you ever . . . say, isn't that Frances' car, what's left of it?"

"Aye. We got to the hospital just after you left, got the lowdown, and here we are, your humble servants." Lias gave a mock bow.

"Uh-huh," Nieve smiled. "But I thought Lirk was . . . you know."

"On their side? Turns out he's Weazen's nephew, and Weazen's my old nursemaid, which you've probably figured out by now." (She hadn't.) "None of us have any reason to side with *them*, believe me." He paused, looking sheepish. "Had to bribe Lirk with your friend's elfshot, mind. But don't worry, I'll get it back. Say, we're not the only ones who did some damage here."

Lias walked over to the ditch where Nieve had taken refuge. There was a wide circular scorch mark where she'd been crouching, and strong smell of barbequed yuck permeated the air.

Joining him, she stared at it, puzzled. "What happened? It wasn't burnt when I jumped in. Ick." She wrinkled her nose. "Stinks."

"It was that *lux* of yours," said Lias. "'Tis a wonderful thing."

Nieve raised her hand up to appraise the little daylight anew, but it had disappeared from sight (she could feel it hovering at the back of her neck). She did now notice the weed seedling, its tiny teeth clamped on her sleeve. Carefully, she tugged it off and looked at it, wriggling like a worm between her fingers. She was about to drop it into the charred ditch, but then changed her mind and stuck it in her pocket instead. Might be helpful to study it (also, it was kind of cute). She decided that if it chewed a hole in her shirt, she'd get rid of it.

"Might as well hitch a ride with us," said Lias. "We're almost there anyway."

"Yeah?" Nieve gave the car's carcass a dubious once-over.

Lirk, who had fully reappeared, crooked grin and all, motioned impatiently to her, urging her to hop to it and hop on.

Funny that she was the reluctant passenger now, and Lias not. "They'll hear us coming that's for sure."

"Aye, and quake in their boots! Let's go."

## –Thirty-Two–

# Molly

The trip to town *was* noisy. For one thing, they couldn't convince Lirk to turn off the radio, his newfound passion. Worse he'd taken to shouting along with the songs, his voice gravelly and raspy. He wasn't half-bad, either, a little tin-toned man singing the blues, but Nieve knew that if they drew the wrong kind of attention to themselves they'd all have something to moan about. If there was any other kind of attention left but the wrong kind.

They cruised into town past her house up on the rise, usually well-lit and inviting at night, but now sunk in darkness. All the buildings downtown were dark, too, including Wormius and Ashe's apothecary, and farther on, more alarming still, Gran's cottage. In Nieve's absence, every single light in the town had been squelched, snuffed out, extinguished.

When they passed the lane that led up to the cottage, she had to restrain herself. How much time would it take to dash up there in her swift new runners to check on Gran? But then, who knows how much time they had to find the antidote before Elixibyss came after her, as Nieve knew she would. Not much, she suspected, not much at all.

How they were going to search Ferrets with Twisden at home was also a good question, although it was better to be forewarned of his presence.

They left the car at the gates hidden among some bushes. Seeing as there were no brakes, this proved crashingly easy to do. After brushing themselves off and shaking the twigs out of their hair, they sprinted down the long driveway. Nieve tried not to outdistance her companions, but she couldn't help it, and had already been scouting around outside the house for several minutes before they caught up with her.

"Doors are all locked," she said. "There's only one light on. It's coming from that same room I looked in before."

"He's there?" asked Lias.

"I was just going to check. Lirk, can you find a way in, maybe an unlatched window?"

"Aye," Lirk grunted, and scuttled off.

Nieve moved around to the side of the house, stopping beneath the drawing-room window. Lias, following behind, kept going toward the back. "I've a way with locks," he said. "*Some* locks."

Handily, the wooden crate she'd used before was still in place. She clambered up, then stretched to her full height, standing on tiptoe to peer into the large drawing-room. It looked much as it had before, although the coffin was gone. The bodies, however, weren't! They were propped up, leaning this way and that, in chairs and on sofas in front of the fireplace, which now had a fire roaring in the grate. She saw Theo Bax among them, and Mrs. Welty from the Post Office, and . . . she saw her father! He was off to one side seated in a red velvet wing back chair, stiff as a mannequin and staring blankly. Hypnotized, Nieve thought. They all were. Not total goners as she had earlier believed.

Twisden was wandering around the room, dressed in a yellow silk housecoat trimmed with skunk fur, overtop a pair of black and white check pajamas. He also had on a pair of novelty slippers, bright orange, with Pekinese dog heads sticking up at the toes. Holding a glass of champagne in one hand, while gesticulating with the other, he was making some sort of speech. Or practicing a speech, Nieve decided, as she strained to listen. He stopped and started, repeating some of the same phrases in a different order: " . . . the passing of my dear wife Molly . . . my darling wife, dear Molly, passing to her reward so unexpectedly . . . my loving wife Molly . . . I've been so fortunate to meet a lovely young woman, Molly I know would approve . . . ."

Yeah, right, thought Nieve, as Twisden took a swig of champagne then went on to tell an anecdote about firing one of his employees. This he addressed to those seated around the fireplace, as if they were regular guests. He apparently found the story highly entertaining, guffawing and snorting as he recounted it, while his audience sat in stony silence. Eventually, their stunned reception began to bother him and, frowning, he stopped speaking and marched over to them. Moving from person to person, he poked at their mouths and rearranged their lips until everyone was wearing big smiles, Sutton included. That done, he took up a position before the fireplace and continued his tale (". . . and then I said to her . . ."), basking in everyone's fixed and weirdly amused expressions.

Until he noticed Sutton, whose mouth had drooped, which gave him an expression of both sadness and censure. Annoyed, Twisden strode over to him and prodded his mouth into a smile again. But it wouldn't stick. Twisden jabbed at his lips repeatedly and with increasing roughness, but always with the same result. Sutton simply could not be made to smile.

"Listen up, dummy!" Twisden spat. He was getting very angry, and *so* was Nieve.

Before she could stop herself, she pounded hard on the glass. Twisden looked up in surprise. Catching sight of her face hovering in the window, glaring furiously at him, his mouth dropped open . . . and stuck. Without intending to, she'd given him a blasting. An über-blasting. He was thoroughly immobilized.

Lirk, who had found a way in and was hanging around the shadowy entrance, bolted into the drawing-room. He gave her a thumbs-up, then pointed toward the front of the house. She jumped down off the crate and ran around to the front, where Lirk met her at the open door. He'd also switched on a light, which flickered dimly in the foyer. This seemed to tickle him almost as much as Nieve blasting Twisden. "She don't allow this!"

Nodding her thanks to him, Nieve said, "Why are you helping us anyway, Lirk?" He now had the fern seed *and* the elfshot, for what it was worth. What more did he want?

"Didn't Auntie tell me to? When Weazen's got a job for you, girl, you *do* it. Besides, you're one of us, eh."

One of *them?* Got that wrong. "Pardon?"

Lirk only cackled in response, making a noise like a maraca filled with thumbtacks, and said, "Got to get to work before old ratface snaps out of it."

Nieve glanced around uncertainly, the enormity of the task confronting her. She didn't even know what, precisely, they were looking for, let alone where to look for it in this huge, messy house. Peeking into the sitting room on her left, she saw chairs were flipped over, legs in the air, sofa cushions ripped open, drawers spilling their contents, piles of books and knick-knacks strewn on the floor. She had to wonder if the antidote hadn't already been found, possibly by Twisden himself, given his cheery, champagne-swilling mood. Well, he wasn't so cheery now.

"Psssst!"

Lias, on the second floor and leaning over the banister, was holding a flashlight and playing its beam over them.

"You're in!" Nieve gazed up at him. "Is that mine?"

"'Tis," he nodded. "Come up. Found something. Besides your torch, that is."

Nieve and Lirk raced up the stairs, then followed Lias up another flight to the third floor and along the hall to a room at the end that overlooked the front drive. Pushing open the door, he said, "This one was locked, so I reckoned there had to be something interesting in it. Or some*one*, as happens. No lights in here, bulb's missing." He directed the flashlight's beam along the wall to the right. "You know him, Nieve?"

Amid all the junk piled in the room – antique dressers and hat boxes and twig brooms and cauldrons and stuffed owls – sat a middle-aged man on a steamer trunk, obviously in the same submerged state as the people downstairs. He was swathed in cobwebs and felted with dust, but Nieve recognized him at once. "Professor Manning!"

Rushing over to him, she started to brush away the cobwebs. A spider the size of a date scrambled behind his ear. "Gosh, he's been here all along. Twisden *stole* the house from him." Gently, Nieve stroked some of the dust off his face, which wore a kindly if baffled expression. He stared at

232

her dumbly, vacantly. "If this *is* a kind of hypnosis, there's got to be some way . . . ." She raised her hand, hoping the patch of daylight would put in an appearance so that she could see the professor more clearly. It didn't, so she gave her hand a shake.

"Snap your fingers," suggested Lias.

"Not one of my talents." Besides, she thought finger-snapping might seem kind of bossy.

She gave her hand another shake, but it still didn't appear, so figured she'd better try snapping her fingers anyway. After a couple of tries, she produced a snap that wasn't very snappy . . . but it worked. The daylight zipped out of her sleeve, as if newly woken, perched for the merest moment on the end of her fingers, then hopped onto the end of Professor Manning's fleshy nose, illuminating it.

"Hey!" said Nieve.

Professor Manning's nose twitched.

"Ha!" said Lirk.

The daylight then swirled up onto his wide forehead and skated around, taking a few twirls in the inlets where his hair was receding. The Professor began to frown. Next, it dropped down and flickered across his eyelids, which themselves began to flicker, and then it zipped across his lips, unzipping them.

Facial tour complete, it flitted back up Nieve's shirt sleeve.

Professor Manning began blinking rapidly and scrunching up his mouth. He twitched his nose a couple of more times before starting to come around. When he did finally, he registered considerable surprise at seeing two children and a peculiar, wry-faced little person staring intently at him.

"My word!" he said, flustered. "Has . . . has . . . anyone seen my pipe?" He began patting the pockets of his corduroy jacket, raising clouds of dust that made Lirk sneeze. "I seem to have mislaid it."

"Professor," Nieve said, delighted. "You've mislaid much more than that. We'll fill you in as soon as we can, but right now, it's urgent, I have to ask you something."

"Ah, well then . . . certainly. Fire away, young lady."

"You invented a serum that turns people into, um, usable material, right? Doesn't kill them, but . . . ." Might as well, she didn't add.

"Oh dear," he said, abashed. "Yes, yes, an accident that was. Discovered it when I was working on a new formaldehyde formula. Got the idea from some old diaries that belonged to my great-great-grandmother. Alchemy, you know. Exciting result, I have to say, wrote a paper on it. No one in the scientific community believed it!" His face clouded. "But then this industrialist fellow got wind of it, wanted to put money into its development."

"And you didn't?"

"Heavens, no. Sent him packing. Invention of that sort, dangerous really if you think about it."

Too bad he hadn't! "So you invented an antidote just in case."

"That's right. When the serum went missing. Funny that, can't imagine what happened to it, really."

Nieve sighed. Everything she'd read about unworldly

professors, including the leather elbow patches on their baggy corduroy jackets, appeared to be true. "Where is it, Professor Manning? The antidote, is it hidden somewhere in the house?"

"Yes, indeedy. In a highly safe place."

"Where? We've *got* to know."

He gave her a crafty little smile, and tapped his broad forehead. "In here!"

"Ah, I see. Okay, great, in that case could you–"

"All I have to do is *try* to recall it. Hmmm, now, let me think . . . ."

"Nieve, look at this." While listening to the professor, Lias had been shining the flashlight beam on all the unusual odds and ends in the room, items, including a jar of powdered newts and a dried scorpion, that wouldn't have been out of place at a witch's garage sale. Standing in the farthest corner, stiff as a pole, was a woman practically buried in coats and jackets, several looped on the fingers of her upraised hands. A straw boater was hooked on one ear and a plaid scarf draped over the sharp tip of her nose.

"My, *my,* what a handsome coat rack," said Professor Manning. "Don't recall seeing it in the lumber room before."

"That's because she's not a coat rack." Nieve walked over and tugged the scarf off her nose. "It's Mrs. Twisden. Molly Twisden."

"Most handsome," murmured the professor dreamily of the tall, stick-thin and not particularly comely Molly. So lost in admiration was he, that he was completely unaware that the others were regarding one another in alarm.

Nieve clutched the plaid scarf in her hand, listening to the sound of a car whining as it crunched down the gravel drive *(ouch, ouch)*. This was followed almost immediately by the sound of a door slamming *(whaaaa!)*, someone pounding up the front steps, then crashing explosively through the front door of the house, bellowing as they stormed through it.

"Guess who's here?" said Lirk.

# –Thirty-Three–

# *Toehold*

"*I* have a bone to pick with you, Twisden!" Elixibyss was bellowing. "Wake up, you idiot!!"

Bone-picking, a specialty of the Impress.

Hearing her icy voice raised to a murderous pitch sent a shudder of apprehension through them all. It's a wonder they didn't run off and hide. Instead, Lias said, "Right. This time it's *mine*." With his hair standing straight up on his head, practically crackling, he darted out the door and down the stairs.

"Lias, be careful!" Nieve called, and took off after him, still clutching the plaid scarf. "Kids," Lirk grumbled, shaking his head as he reached into his pocket. In a moment he was still shaking his head, the only part of him still visible.

A disturbing enough sight in itself, but not one to bother Professor Manning, who was lost in thought. "Molly," he muttered to himself. "Now, wasn't . . . Molly . . . ."

When Nieve ran into the drawing-room on Lias' heels, Elixibyss was busy throttling Twisden. She had him by the neck and was giving him a bone-rattling shake, while the unconscious audience that was gathered around the fireplace looked on and smiled happily (except Sutton).

"She betrayed us!" she screamed. *"You* chose her, I should have known you couldn't do anything right. Nitwit! Tell me that you've found that formula. Come *on*, tell me!"

"No, he hasn't," said Nieve.

Elixibyss dropped her hands from Twisden's neck and spun around. She was wearing large bone-rimmed sunglasses, which sat askew on her nose.

"Erk," Twisden croaked.

Elixibyss adjusted her sunglasses and hissed, "You! You little ingrate! Running away after all I've done for you! I knew you'd be here. Simpleton! You cannot, I repeat, you *cannot* get away from me."

"What have you done for me?" Nieve stuck out her chin, hoping she wouldn't get it knocked off.

"I let you *live*. I could have extinguished you in a trice." Elixibyss passed a hand before the leaping flames in the fireplace and they vanished instantly, some few left flickered abjectly on the logs.

"You let me live so you could *use* me."

"Naturally." Elixibyss pinched her brow with her long fingers. As the sleeve of her gown fell away from her scaley arm, Nieve saw that she'd patched-up the hole in it with a Band-Aid. "Get with it, dear. That's the name of the game. People have their *uses*, that's how the world works. If you believe otherwise then you really are a simpleton."

"And *you*," Elixibyss now turned her attention to Lias, who was slowly advancing on her, flashlight raised. "You *are* utterly useless. Think you can hurt me with that feeble little light? Ha! Think again, for once! Honestly, I've no idea why I've kept you around for so long."

"But he's your son!" protested Nieve.

"Stolen," she said. "And a pain from day one, no matter how much I punished him." She reached into the folds of her gown and produced the gold box. "But a pain for which there *is* a cure."

"Give it to me," he said, his voice so low it was almost inaudible.

"Oh, sure." She gave the box a shake, rattling the contents noisily, then raised it high above his head. "Jump, Spot. C'mon boy! Grrrrrr," she taunted.

Nieve winced to see Lias humiliate himself. He dropped the flashlight and made a jump for it, which of course Elixibyss snatched away with a laugh. Whatever was in that box, he wanted it badly. "Give it to him," she demanded, moving toward her.

"Don't touch me!" Elixibyss stepped back quickly.

"Why not?" asked a woman who suddenly walked into the room. "You're her mother, aren't you? Don't you want a loving hug?"

The woman looked terribly pale and exhausted, but intent, and *fierce*. A fierceness Nieve recognized, because she so often felt it herself.

"Mum," Nieve whispered.

"Go ahead, sweetheart," Sophie said. "Give her a hug."

"Don't you *dare*," Elixibyss warned, backing up to the fireplace. She swept her hand over the grate and the flames leapt up again with a hungry roar. "You touch me and this box goes straight into the fire. And with it, my dear, goes your cousin's life."

"Cousin? I don't have a cousin."

"You do, Nieve," Sophie said, regarding Lias sadly.

"Spare me the sob story–" Elixibyss began, then stopped.

Something caught her eye. In fact it almost plunged into her eye. "No!" she cried.

Nieve heard it before she saw it. A curious kind of home-made spear whizzed by overhead and struck the Impress. It was made of a brass curtain rod, snapped in half, and was decorated with owl feathers. Malcolm's arrowhead – the elfshot – was lashed onto its tip with a brown shoelace.

"*Get it out,*" Elixibyss snarled, bent over and clutching at the spear, which had sunk into her forehead and was stuck fast. Her sunglasses tumbled to the floor.

"Bit gimcrack," Nieve heard Lirk mumble, although he was nowhere to be seen. "Fixed the headache, heh."

As the Impress struggled to pluck the spear out of her brow, black smoke began to leak out from around the edges of the elfshot, as well as from around the loosened Band-Aid on her arm.

Seizing his chance, Lias lunged toward her and made a grab for the gold box.

"No you don't, *dog!*" She whirled around and pitched the box into the flames.

Lias dropped to his knees, shocked, and everyone began to shout and . . . bark?

Artichoke, baying loudly, bounded into the room. Both he and Nieve dove toward the hearth at the same time. But, as she shoved past Mortimer Twisden, who was now fully alert, he caught hold of the tartan scarf still clutched in her

240

hand and yanked her toward him. "You rotten interfering hoyden–"

"Get your hands off my daughter!" Sophie sprang to her defense, but the weed seedling Nieve had picked up in the ditch, sprang even faster. It shot out of her pocket like a jack-in-the-box and sank its tiny, razor-sharp teeth into Twisden's ear. He wailed so loudly that Sophie snatched up the fallen scarf and stuffed it in his mouth, saying, "*Now* Nieve, only you can do it. Embrace her."

"Mum, the *box*."

"Artichoke has it."

Nieve cast around desperately, and saw that Artichoke, standing shakily by the fire, his fur singed and smoking, did indeed have the box clamped in his teeth.

Smoke, deep black and toxic, was also pouring out of the puncture in Elixibyss' forehead. She had the spear gripped firmly in hand and was crawling toward Lias, who was staring at her, as if mesmerized.

Embrace her? Elixibyss? What a repulsive, sickening, bizarre idea. Why on earth–?

"Please," Sophie implored. "Do it!"

Nieve glanced quickly at her mother, nodded, took a deep breath, and ran toward the Impress, arms extended.

Elixibyss dropped the spear and scuttled backward. "Don't touch," she pleaded, " . . . your mother."

It was the most difficult thing Nieve had ever done – and the easiest. Elixibyss could have been her mother's twin, so closely and disturbingly did she resemble her. The iciness gone from her voice, she even sounded like her again, so much so that the softened and beseeching tone tore at Nieve's heart. But the eyes, when Nieve looked at them, had changed. The whites and irises had melded into a smooth silvery metal, cold and frightening. Gazing into them for the merest moment, she caught her own reflection gazing back – a Nieve she never knew existed, didn't *want* to know – before jerking her head away.

Without hesitating, she reached out and grasped the Impress' arms . . . and where she touched . . . she marked her. She left glowing handprints on Elixibyss' arms, prints that stretched and spread rapidly engulfing them in light. Nieve gasped. The floor beneath was visible through them. The long-fingered light spread over her shoulder, down her back, and along her side. Elixibyss spoke a few faint words in that strange tongue Nieve had heard her use in the garden, and then she sighed once before the light consumed her body entirely, leaving behind a column of black smoke that wavered and dissipated until nothing was left of it but single hair-thin strand, twisting and writhing in the air.

"Catch it!" someone shouted.

Nieve turned quickly, thrilled, to see Gran. She was hurrying toward what was left of the Impress.

Artichoke barked, dropping the gold box, and Lias grabbed it. It was his! But instead of clutching it protectively, as one might expect him to do, he immediately flipped open the lid and dumped the contents on the floor, as if they mattered not at all. Then he went after the wiry wisp of smoke. It twisted away from him, then shot back, twining around and around his wrist. He shook his hand free of it, and pursued it again, leaping after it, snapping the box's lid, trying to trap the smoke inside. Once, twice, he almost caught it . . . but no, no luck, not this time. It swirled into the fireplace, plaited itself into the rising plume, a night-black strand among the lighter grey, and vanished up the flue.

"No!" he cried, as Elixibyss herself had done only moments before.

"Never mind, Lias. She'll do you no more harm." Gran had her arms around him. "Och, better mind *me*, though. Stepped on your toes." She bent down and scooped up two small bones from the floor, which she then placed delicately on his palm. "Hang onto these, lad. Seeing as you've no shoes now. I suppose she stole those, too."

Lias nodded, speechless, staring at his long-lost treasure.

"*Gran.*" Nieve was the next to feel Gran's arms around her. "But, those bones are . . . *toes?*"

"Aye. I'm sure he'll tell you about it when he can. Good work, Nievy!"

She shook her head. "Dr. Morys. Oh Gran, I didn't mean to–"

"Hush, pet. I've had word. Frances got a team to Bone House before it vanished altogether. He's poorly, but he's alive. Thanks to you."

Nieve wasn't sure she deserved any thanks, but felt a tremendous surge of relief. And a rising excitement. "Gran, d'you know what? I can wake Dad up. And Malcolm, and everybody. I know how!"

"That's because you're a cunning girl, love. Ah, here comes your mother. Looks like I'm going to have to share you."

Sophie was moving toward her, face alight, but didn't quite make it. Someone else had come charging into the room. It was Professor Manning, red-faced and flustered, with one shoe missing. A rigid Molly Twisden was tucked under his arm and sticking out like a battering ram. Sophie had to leap aside as the professor hurtled her way, enthusing, "Eureka! I have it, the formula! There's only one ingredient missing!"

Mortimer Twisden, weed seedling still dangling from his earlobe like a kitschy earring, had just yanked the scarf out of his mouth and was about to start bawling again, when Professor Manning spotted Nieve. He turned sharply toward her, which caused Molly Twisden to whack her husband on the head with one of her sensible penny loafers. Much to her satisfaction when Molly later heard about it, she gave him such a sound crack that it not only knocked him off his feet, but knocked him out cold.

"Young lady," the professor exclaimed, bustling over to her.

Nieve ducked, while Gran and Lias scurried out of his way. Artichoke *yipped* and danced away, too, then trotted over to Twisden to give his Pomeranian slippers a sniff.

Professor Manning set Molly down, propping her up against the mantel. Then, getting down on all fours, he gave Nieve's shoes a close study. "Hmm, aah, I thought so. Amazing, truly amazing."

"What?" Nieve laughed. The shoes *were* amazing, true. But at the moment they looked like nothing more than a bunch of tattered and wilted leaves clapped around her feet. That marathon run had been hard on them.

Professor Manning stretched a trembling hand out and lifted up one of the leaves. Beneath it was a delicate white flower, freshly blossomed, which he plucked off and held up to the firelight.

"Moly," he said, quietly, reverently.

"Awesome," said Lirk, less quietly and a lot less reverently. "By the way, old fella," he added, finally putting in an appearance, head first, with a twist of a grin on his twisted face, "here's your shoelace. Came in nice and handy it did."

No one – not even Nieve – noticed as Sutton's lips began to twitch and lift into a tentative, and genuine, smile.

# Thirty-Four

# Punchline

*N*ieve was staying at Gran's while her parents were in the city buying supplies for their new business venture. Both of them were sick of weeping for a living. Nieve hadn't wanted to go with them in case someone recognized her – being famous had gotten to be really boring, really fast. After she'd awakened all those who'd been hypnotized, her picture had appeared in the city newspaper above the headline, **FINGER-SNAPPING GIRL GENERATES LIGHT!** Incredible, seeing as she'd dreamed that one up herself not that long ago, while never in a zillion years thinking it might actually happen.

Professor Manning had credited her with discovering the antidote as well – a bit craftily, she thought, seeing as he didn't want anyone to find out that he'd been responsible for the original body-numbing serum. While everyone who'd received the serum was being treated in the hospital, including the babies, he explained to the press that the affliction was a rare kind of virus, *hinges immobilus*, that, when it struck, twisted people into the shapes of armoires and tables and such. (Nieve was sure he'd made that up on the spot, while the unquestioning reporters eagerly wrote it down in their spiral notebooks. *She'd* do a little fact-checking if it were her.)

Frances and Mayor Mary and Mr. Exley were singing her praises, too, although Mr. Exley was doing more squeaking than singing. Gran told her not to worry, that everyone would forget soon enough. Nieve hoped so. Alicia Overbury certainly seemed to have forgotten. After being liberated from the living wall and treated, she was back home and back to being her irritating old self.

"Let's see this famous finger-snapping trick of yours," she'd demanded.

Nieve only laughed and walked away.

"Can't *do* it, can you? Showoff. Smart Alec."

True, she couldn't. After she had snapped and snapped and *snapped* until she thought her fingers were going to snap off (one thing, she'd become an expert at finger-snapping) and everyone had been wakened, the little daylight, the *lux*, itself dropped off her finger. It had floated in front of her for a few minutes, zipping around as if searching for something, then began to unfold before her eyes, stretching and expanding, growing bigger and bigger, until there was more daylight than darkness and gloom. Nieve reasoned that she couldn't miss it, because it was everywhere.

The days were getting colder, but there had been weeks of sunlight and beautiful, clear, starlit nights. She sometimes thought she couldn't get enough of the sun, like Mr. Mustard Seed, who'd followed her to Gran's. Waiting for the kettle to boil, she watched him through the kitchen window lolling in a bright patch at the base of the sundial, one contented cat. He seemed a lot bolder these days, and Nieve had to wonder if he'd gotten up to some mischief himself when that truant officer had broken into the house. Maybe the monster had a terror of cats, she'd never know. Just as she'd never know what exactly had happened to the *others*.

"Gone," Gran had said, lips tightened. "But *not* forgotten." Then she smiled just a little, and Nieve knew she was remembering Dunstan Warlock's comeuppance. The silver car, driven to distraction by Warlock (he *was* a terrible driver) and honking like mad (*bleep bleeping bleep!!*), had chased him around and around Ferrets' driveway and finally chased him right out of town. He might be running still for all they knew. Nieve figured he could use the exercise.

She poured the boiling water over the tea leaves in the Brown Betty, then arranged it on a tray with the cups and saucers, spoons, milk pitcher and sugar bowl, and a heaping plate of oatmeal cookies crammed with raisins and nuts, Dr. Morys' favourite. Tray-laden and dishes clinking, she carried it carefully into the living room. Dr. Morys started to get up from his chair by the hearth to help, but Gran beat him to it.

"Jim," she warned. "Rest! Doctor's orders." She took the tray from Nieve and set it on the coffee table. "Lovely, Nievy." Artichoke, dozing at Dr. Morys' feet, was immediately alert, tail thumping, and eyeing the cookies with interest.

"Megrims, eh Nieve." He gave her a quick wink. "Cunning *and* bossy."

"I'll say," Nieve grinned. "But guess what, I looked that word up, megrim. It means 'headache'."

"Makes sense," he nodded. "Given the ones I know."

"'*Whisht*'," scolded Gran.

"Ow!" he pinched his brow theatrically.

Artichoke, meanwhile, delicately snitched a cookie from the tray.

"You know the stuff on Elixibyss' arm that I thought was moss?" Nieve had been doing some research for her own newspaper, now called simply *Lux*. "It's called grave scab, you get it from walking over the graves of unchristened babies, which also makes sense, because of what you told me about Elixibyss stealing Aunt Liz's form after she died."

"Aye," said Gran, grimly. "She was a fetch of sorts. They steal people's appearances, but I've never known one to steal a child. In a way, awful as it sounds, she saved Lias. Stillborn, or thought to be, he was buried with his mother . . . and yet, 'tis unco, he had a tetch of breath left in him."

Nieve shuddered at the thought. No wonder Lias had such a fear of those bodies in the hospital. And it didn't help that Elixibyss had always kept him teetering on the edge of death itself. Even though Nieve had been told the story a few times now, she understood why Gran had to repeat it. Saddened and appalled by her daughter's fate, and her grandson's, she was still trying to come to terms with it. "I'd no idea that our Liz was expecting when she ran away from home, blind fool that I was. Nor any idea of what became of her. Your mother never got over it, either, Nieve, losing her older sister."

"Then all this time later," Dr. Morys added, "Sarah, Nora Mullein's daughter, comes along with news of Liz. Or what she suspected had happened to her, and her imposter's involvement with Twisden."

As Sophie had explained it, Sarah was a law enforcer in the area of unnatural law-breakers, a kind of paranormal police officer. Nieve found this incredibly interesting and wanted to do a piece on it for her paper, but Sophie had said it all had to be kept hush-hush. Which is why she herself had been so secretive, not even telling Gran when Sarah had approached her for help. That, and the fact that she was skeptical of the whole investigation, until she realized the danger Nieve herself was in. The eye-ring had allowed Sophie to infiltrate *them*, but she hadn't fully understood its spying function. When she did, down the toilet it went. Let them spy *that*.

"I never seriously bought any of this superstition business before," Sophie had confessed to Nieve only days ago. "Gran's hocus-pocus."

Nieve knew that she was buying it now, seriously, because that's what her parents were doing in the city – stocking up on crystals and 'magic' wands and pointy witch hats for their new store downtown.

"Junk," Gran had grumbled when she heard about it, which Nieve had thought pretty funny, considering.

Too bad they couldn't locate any moly to sell, the plant that had provided the miraculous cure, not to mention the miraculous leafy shoes (which were no longer leafy, but back to being brown and dry and tucked into the crevice of Gran's mantel). Professor Manning had explained, however, that moly was extremely rare and only to be found in ancient Greece. Well, no one was going *there* to pick some, that's for sure.

Sipping her tea, Nieve glanced up at the clacking mantel clock, which was now keeping ordinary time – the best time there was, in her view. Soon, she'd join Malcolm and Lias, who were helping to clean up the store, getting it ready for the grand opening on Friday. Then on Saturday was the wedding at the newly rechristened Woodlands. Professor Manning and Molly Twisden were getting married! Everyone was invited, including Sarah, who was thrilled *not* to be getting married. Lirk was invited, too – he'd been asked to spin some discs – although Nieve wasn't sure if he'd show. After plastering on a special wrinkle cream that Professor Manning had invented, his face had turned bright blue. Malcolm told him that he looked like a Smurf, and Lirk had been so annoyed that he'd vanished on the spot. No one had seen him since.

"Always thought that Twisden guy was a shady character," said Dr. Morys, as Artichoke nabbed yet another cookie. "But, my golly, house theft, tax evasion, polluting, cruelty to animals (including the human kind), not to mention turning his wife into a coat rack. Not murder, but as good as. Or as *bad* as, I should say. He'll be in the clink for life."

"Helps that Molly's brother is a judge," agreed Gran. "And a former *chaise lounge*."

"Didn't take it lying down?" offered Dr. Morys.

"Tsk, Jimmy," Gran admonished, but chuckled nonetheless. "Nieve, more cookies, pet? Tea?"

"Have to go help, Gran. Thanks, though. Be back for dinner."

"Bring Lias."

"If he'll come. He's getting . . . more and more restless. Can't sit still."

Lias had been living at Nieve's place, trying to get the hang of family life. Her parents wanted to adopt him officially, and Nieve loved having a 'brother,' despite all the bad things she'd heard about the species from female friends. Lias himself wasn't exactly overjoyed with the idea. He liked everyone a lot, especially Sutton, who had been teaching him how to play baseball, but claimed they were spoiling him with all the good food, and comforts, and attention . . . and kindness, especially that. Something that only Weazen had shown him before.

"So?" Nieve had asked. This was a problem?

He shrugged. "It's too nice, I'm not used to it. I'd rather be out roaming, free, *ye ken*. Not trapped, in school an' all."

Nieve could understand that, the school part, although it was great to have Mrs. Crawford back in the classroom. "You just want to hunt for *her*, in whatever form she takes." She knew he had terrible nightmares, she'd heard him crying out at night. But he never told her about them.

"Maybe."

"Not maybe. You *do*. And you don't have to, Lias. You're not tied to her anymore. She has no power over you."

"Ah, *phalanges*." Lias rubbed his hands together. "Splendid samples."

Nieve laughed. This is what Prosfessor Manning had said when he noticed the toe bones in Lias' hand, all that remained of the toes that Elixibyss had sliced off his feet when he was a baby – not a laughing matter. She had used them to concoct some sort of binding – or bonding – spell. Her hold on him. She'd convinced *him* of it, anyway. Convinced him that there was no escape, no matter how many times he ran away.

"Did the professor ever find his pipe?" Lias asked.

"Doesn't smoke. He only remembered later."

And at this they had both laughed.

"Want me to read your teacup before you go, hen?"

Nieve peered into her cup, blackened tea leaves clumped together ominously on the bottom. "Um, no, I don't think so. Thanks just the same, Gran."

"How about a little joke then?" said Dr. Morys.

"Okay." He'd tell her anyway, no matter what she said. "Shoot."

He cleared his throat, and asked, "Now, why is it, do you think, that ducks fly south to Florida every year?"

She smiled. How many times had she heard this one before? Ten? Twenty? But he had to tell it, he had to finish the joke he'd started so many weeks ago. "Gosh, don't know, I give up."

"You do, eh? Well, because . . . it's too far to walk!"

251

He cracked up and Nieve's smile widened. It was the best she could do, but she meant it.

"I'll tell you something else, Nieve," he said, more seriously. "That's what happened to me. When I was in that coma, the way ahead was like a long dark tunnel. I trudged on and on, thought I'd never get to the end. Then all at once I felt your hand touch mine. I turned and saw a light moving in the other direction, the direction from which I'd come, and that's when I decided, *what the heck*, I'm going to follow it, I'm going back. That other way is just too darn far to walk!" He reached out and patted her hand. "Some other time for that journey, eh Nieve, some other time."

"Not soon, Dr. Morys. Please." She glanced once more, worriedly, at the leaves in her teacup, and at the alarming pattern they were forming. "What would we do without you? What would Artichoke do?"

"Artichoke?" He smiled at the brave and true friend resting at his feet, then reached down to scrub his head. "Why, he'd eat *all* the cookies."

# Thirty-Five

# Amulet

*N*ieve ran down the hill to town, fast. She knew she had to hurry, a bad feeling was crawling around in her stomach. As always, though, she loved the running itself. It felt great to be wearing her old runners, too, and booting along on her own steam. Feet pounding the ground, hair slapping against her back (Gran had picked out the knots), wind whistling past her ears. The leafy shoes had been an adventure, and she would never again run with such astonishing speed and ease – but she much preferred this. Besides, she was no slouch, and was on Main Street in no time.

She waved at Mr. Exley as she peeled past his renovated store. He'd cleared out all the jars and boxes full of creepy stuff left behind by Wormius & Ashe (gone before Sarah could deal with them), and had opened an antiques business, claiming that he'd developed a real feeling for old furniture. As he returned her wave from behind the counter, Nieve noticed that he was wearing his "Rock On!" T-shirt. She wondered if his legs still creaked when he walked.

Her parents' store was next door. They'd taken over Dunstan Warlock's bookstore when he hadn't returned to town. His landlord, Professor Manning as it turned out, discovered to his surprise (and no one else's) that Warlock hadn't paid any rent in years. Good thing the professor didn't pay much attention to mundane matters like money, Nieve thought. Her parents' screwy business would need all the help it could get. As for grunt work, she and Lias and Malcolm had been packing boxes full of dusty old dog-eared books for days, cleaning the shelves, painting the walls, and getting ready for the first delivery of stock, which had been delayed. The opening was only a few days away and the store was still bare. It didn't even have a name – nothing but a blank sign swinging above the door! (Gran had suggested they call it "Bats.")

She skidded to a stop and was about to go in, when Frances and Mayor Mary stepped out, laughing together about the upcoming wedding.

"Nieve!" said Frances. "My compliments. You guys have done great work. The store looks fantastic."

"Thanks. I keep telling Malcolm to take it easy, though."

"Nah, he's so happy, it's been good for him."

"Think it'll be ready in time?" asked Mary. "I must say, it's a dandy new addition to the downtown. It's bound to bring in some tourist trade. I was going to get rid of those quaint old street lamps, you know, but I've changed my mind."

Spoken like a mayor. "Oh yeah, one way or another, we'll be ready." She glanced through the window at Malcolm, who was polishing the antique brass cash register, a donation from Mr. Exley. "Even if we have to conjure stuff up with one of those magic wands my folks are getting."

"Ha! I'd like to see that," said Frances, although she *had* seen more incredible things, especially during her rescue mission to Bone House. "Say, Nievy, I heard you were going to be the flower girl at the wedding."

Nieve made a face. "Molly decided to give the job to her revived Pomeranians. I don't care, honestly."

"Cripes, I can just picture it," Frances groaned. "Pure mayhem. If those yappy little mutts were mine, I'd be tempted to go the slippers route myself."

Mayor Mary started to edge away. "C'mon Fran, we're late. Getting our hair done, Nieve."

"Yeah, Mary's still trying to comb the cobwebs out of her hair, and I'm gonna get myself a beehive. Lotsa wildlife, eh?"

"Good luck with the opening," Mary said. "We'll be there!"

"Looking gorgeous," Frances added, catching up with the mayor. "What's the store going to be called, anyway?"

"Can't tell, it's a surprise. See you Friday!"

A surprise for everyone, including me, Nieve thought, pushing through the door and scanning the empty store. Empty except for Malcolm, who was playing with the cash register, pressing down the keys, pulling the crank on the side, and making the cash drawer zing open with a loud *briiiiiiing*, then slamming it shut.

It was true, what Nieve had feared.

"Hey, Nieve!" said Malcolm. "This old machine is so cool."

"Mal, hi." She was delighted to see him, as always, home safe and sound, but . . . "Where's Lias?"

"He went out. Said . . . um, said there was something he needed to do, he wasn't sure how long he'd be."

"Right," she grimaced.

Malcolm gave her an apologetic look, and clutched at the arrowhead that Lias had returned to him. It was attached to a leather cord that he now wore around his neck – always.

Although he had recovered amazingly well from his illness and from the abuse he'd endured, it had left him with more than a residue of anxiety. "Should I have tried to stop him?"

She shook her head. "No point. I wish he'd waited to say goodbye."

"Maybe he thought you'd give him a blasting to keep him here."

"I *might* have," Nieve couldn't help but smile.

"Look, though, he left you this." Malcolm pulled down the crank on the cash register and the drawer sprang open again. He picked a small object out of an otherwise empty change compartment. "He said you didn't need it, but he wanted you to have it anyway."

When Malcolm handed it to her, Nieve saw that it was Lias' pewter amulet. She also saw, observing it more closely for the first time, that it wasn't an abstract design as she had thought, but was roughly molded in the shape of a sun. When she folded her fingers over it, enclosing it in her fist, it felt as if something was scrabbling in her palm, as if she had captured a tiny creature. A spider, say.

"Mal," she said suddenly. "I know what to call the store."

"Yeah? Really?"

"Amulet," she smiled. "That's it. *Amulet.*"

He considered it, but only for a moment. "*Yeah,* really. Your parents are going to love it. It's perfect."

"Why don't we paint the sign?" she said. "Surprise them, everything else is ready."

"Let's! Good idea. We'll make a real humdinger, with loads of colour, it'll be *psychedelic*." Malcolm hustled off to the back room, where they kept a supply of paints and brushes and rags. "I'll bring the ladder, too."

"Excellent." Nieve intended to follow, but moved instead toward the front door. Stepping out into the sunny street, her favourite street in the world, she gazed down it's length, and far into the distance along the road that led out of town, the fields alongside still blackened with sun-scorched weeds. In the spring those fields would be furred with fresh green shoots.

As for Lias?

Well, because she was a wait-and-see person, and not someone who jumps to conclusions, she decided that she'd just have to wait and see.

But on the other hand . . . Nieve clenched her fist once again and the amulet dug into her palm, warm and spiky and *maybe* even lucky. She had a feeling he'd be back.

# Glossary

A rickle of words drawn mainly from the Scots language, including some names for supernatural beings taken from British folklore. Many of these words have other meanings as well, but I've concentrated on the ones pertinent to *Nieve*. *The New Shorter Oxford English Dictionary* is the source for most, while my not so short Glaswegian mother is the source for others.

**auld Shock:** A Suffolk name for a phantom black dog.

**bawheid:** Fool, idiot.

**Bloody Bones:** A Cornish spirit who haunts holes and crevices.

**brag:** A shape-shifting goblin. A headless, naked man.

**cunning folk:** White witches, wise women or men, who practice beneficent magic. They are often consulted for a variety of services, such as finding missing persons or lost objects, herbalism, curing illness, making amulets, casting or breaking spells, and identifying those who practice malevolent magic.

**daft:** Silly, stupid, reckless, wild, crazy.

**daylicht:** Daylight.

**deil:** The devil, an imp.

**dinna ken:** Don't know. (Which is to say, I *do* know that this means 'don't know.')

**elf-shot or bolt:** A flint arrowhead, regarded as an elf's weapon.

**fetch:** A phantom who takes on the appearance of the person who sees it. It is said to be a death portent.

**flaught:** A flying or flight, a flock of birds, fluttering or flapping, bustle, great hurry, shake, tremble, vibrate, a sudden gust of wind.

**forfare:** Pass away, perish, decay. As *forfared*: Worn out with travel, age, etc.

**foliot:** A kind of goblin or demon.

**freets:** Superstitions.

**glaik:** A foolish person.

**goamless:** Stupid.

**gowk:** A fool. A half-witted or awkward person. (*Verb*) Stare foolishly.

**gowl:** A howl, yell, or cry.

**gyre carline:** A supernatural being, an ogress, a witch.

**latchets:** Shoe laces.

**lias:** Light.

**lich-way:** A path along which a corpse has been carried to burial, in some districts establishing a right of way.

**lich-owl:** A screech owl, its cry supposedly portending a death.

**lirk:** A fold in the skin, a wrinkle.

*lux* (Latin): Light.

**megrim:** Migraine. Vertigo. A whim, a fancy. And, for the purposes of *Nieve*, someone invested with unusual powers. (Plural) Low spirits, depression.

**mizzle:** Disappear suddenly, decamp, vanish, take oneself off.

**moly:** A mythical plant with black roots and white flowers. In Homer's *Odyssey,* Hermes gives it to Ulysses to protect him from enchantment by Circe.

**muckle:** Great, large. Considerable in size and importance.

**nayword:** A password, a catchword.

**nieve:** A clenched hand, a fist.

**rawhead:** An evil spirit, a bogey or bugbear, devourer of naughty children.

**rickle:** A loose heap, a skeleton.

**rouk** (also **roke**): Smoke, steam, mist, fog, drizzle.

**swank:** Agile, active, nimble. Stylish, posh.

**taran:** The ghost of an unbaptized infant.

**thrawn:** Perverse, contrary, cross-grained, ill-tempered. Twisted, crooked, misshapen, distorted.

**unco:** Unknown, strange, unusual. Weird, uncanny.

**waft:** A Yorkshire term for a gliding spectre, a stealer of souls that appears in the guise of the person it has come to destroy.

**weazen:** Shrink, shrivel, wizen.

**whisht:** Become or keep silent, hush.

**wirricowe:** A hobgoblin, demon, mischievous person.

**ye ken:** You know.

# Acknowledgments

I wish to extend my gratitude to: The Ontario Arts Council for their support, The University of Windsor's English Department for a most welcome and welcoming residency, Dennis Priebe for his technical expertise, and Daniel Wells, for his publishing savvy and devotion to literary endeavour. A very special thanks to my son Sandy for his artwork, amazing *and* hair-raising.

# About the Author

**Terry Griggs** is the author of *Quickening*, which was shortlisted for the Governor General's Award, *The Lusty Man*, and *Rogues' Wedding*, shortlisted for the Rogers Writer's Trust Fiction Prize. Her children's books *Cat's Eye Corner*, *The Silver Door*, and *Invisible Ink* have been nominated for multiple children's writing awards. In 2003, Terry Griggs was awarded the Marian Engel Award in recognition of a distinguished body of work. Here latest book, *Thought You Were Dead*, was published by Biblioasis in 2009. She lives in Stratford, Ontario.

# About the Illustrator

**Alexander Griggs-Burr**, a student at the University of Guelph, is currently finishing a degree in philosophy and visual arts. He lives in Guelph and Stratford, Ontario.

Recycled
Supporting responsible use
of forest resources
www.fsc.org  Cert no. SGS-COC-003153
© 1996 Forest Stewardship Council

FSC

100%

Marquis Book Printing Inc.

Québec, Canada
2010

Printed on Silva Enviro which contains 100% recycled post-consumer fibre,
is EcoLogo, Processed Chlorine Free and manufactured using biogas energy.

YOUNG ADULT